Praise for Charles B. Neff's Novels

"It's all here in this story: love, decency and old, bone-crunching evil. Neff weaves them together brilliantly in a memorable page turner." Roger Wilkins, Pulitzer Prize winner

"... an intriguing and entertaining read, highly recommended." Midwest Book Review

Neff used his substantial depth of knowledge and experience well to draw the reader into a vivid image about life and just how easy it is for the power of evil to enter at any time." *The Cuckleburr Times*

"I admire writing that doesn't resort to frills and flowers to fill space. Just build the characters and tell the story. The author does that very well." Patricia Stoltey

"Keeps the reader fascinated and supremely entertained. Neff knows his business. This is a terrific read!" Grady Harp, 2012

"Charlie Neff gets better each time." C. Harald Hille

"Readers of Neff's delicious book will garner an exciting view of other lives." Ernst Schoen-René

"... another gripping page-turner by Charles Neff." Shannon Farley

"A swift timeline and memorable characters ... genuinely fascinating, intriguing and exciting." Sheila Deeth

"Don't start this book after noon – you won't be able to get to bed." Julius H. Anderson

Also by Charles B. Neff

Dire Salvation, 2012

Hard Cache, 2010

Peace Corpse, 2008

Patriot Schemes, 2006

Hidden Impact, 2004

FRACTURED LEGACY

by
Charles B. Neff

B&H Bennett &
Hastings Publishing

Edited by Adam Finley
Cover photo of a mountain lake: Robin Lorenzi
Cover graphics: Sid Santiano

ISBN: 978-1-934733-86-8, paperback

Library of Congress Control #: 2014937159

For my brothers
John and Sam, and "third twin" Ben Jones

FRACTURED LEGACY

For Bob
From
Charlie

Charles B. Neff

On the following pages you will meet:

Bebe Sorensen, Director of History House in Swiftwater, Washington

Bill McHugh, a police officer in Swiftwater and Portal

Jeff and Sara Winter, owners of the company Cascade Adventures

Greg Takarchuk, a police officer in Swiftwater and Portal

Grant Tomson, a Seattle-based entrepreneur

Aaron Elkhorn, an assistant to Grant Tomson

Tom Cisek, Chief of Police, Swiftwater and Portal

Philip "Mac" Champlin, a Washington State legislator

Roper Martin, a Native American rodeo champion

MARCH 15, MONDAY

Bebe Sorensen's foot had just landed on the first step of the exterior stairs when she heard a strange sound around the corner of the building. She stood stock still, then, hearing it again, shrank back, seeking protection that wasn't there.

A figure emerged in the hazy morning light: dark clothes, a mask covering the lower part of his face. In front of himself he held a long tubular object, pointing at her. Her pulse spiked.

Abruptly, the intruder stopped, pulled the mask down around his neck, and lowered the tube.

"It's okay, Ms. Sorensen. It's just me, Herb, getting a start on the knapweeds. They're getting worse each year, what with the warming, and the County wants us to hit 'em extra hard and early. Sorry to have startled you. Didn't think there'd be anyone here yet."

Bebe's lungs demanded air as she tried to calm herself enough for a shaky reply.

"I'm all right. That's the first time anyone's been around here before me."

Herb was already screwing down the pump handle on his tank and shouldering his equipment.

"No reason I can't finish later."

He seemed embarrassed and gave her a funny look as he left. They knew each other only from Herb's infrequent visits, and chances were pretty good he'd figured out, along with a lot of others in the community, that she was a bit odd.

She watched Herb's back recede into the gradually lightening background and waited even a little longer before resuming her climb up the steps to the broad porch of the three-story brick and wood History House. Once there, she took another look around to make sure she was actually alone.

The air was still chilly, maybe forty degrees. The season she called "sprinter": the beginning of spring and the end of winter, grass still brown and trees leafing. One day it was one season, the next day the other. Substantial snow still topped the Cascade Mountains behind her but was mostly gone here at the two-thousand foot level.

11

If town residents were lucky, the afternoon would be rimmed with warmth. But it would take more than the thermometer to erase the chill inside her.

The solid oak front door pivoted inwards with an ease that might surprise some people, but not Bebe. She made sure that its hand-forged hinges stayed oiled. Through its stained-glass inlaid panel she caught a glimpse of the kaleidoscope of familiar objects on the other side. Once in, she locked the door behind her until opening hours.

Then, as usual each morning, she carefully inspected her surroundings.

A hanging fixture with a Tiffany shade washed variegated colored streaks over the wallpaper of the entry hall. To her left, a generous opening in the wall revealed a formal parlor, small and unremarkable by today's standards, but quite the talk of the town in the 1920s when Swiftwater's then-largest home was built. The Swiftwater *Conductor*, the town weekly, had published a small piece commenting on the parlor, calling it "perhaps the grandest space in our fair community".

Bebe knew those kinds of things because they formed part of her job: collecting and cataloguing documents and artifacts linked to the town's past. Officially she was Executive Director of the Swiftwater and Portal Historical Society; unofficially she was also chief janitor and fixit specialist for the old building. Mostly her knowledge went unused, though she basked in carefully masked pride when a visitor expressed surprise that she knew some obscure fact about Swiftwater's history.

Not that Swiftwater and History House were so very obscure. The town of five thousand was just off Interstate 90, over the summit of the Central Cascades and an hour and a half east of Seattle. Its main street served as a bypass connecting two of the Interstate exits, and History House was a scant three blocks from the business center of town.

It would have increased her satisfaction if more people came through the door she had just locked behind her. Both Portal and Swiftwater occupied major places in the archives: Portal with its glory days in the early twentieth century as a thriving mining town where Bing Crosby once lived, and Swiftwater with its role as an important switching yard for the railroads during...

She stopped herself, suddenly realizing what was happening. The confrontation with Herb had unnerved her to the point where she was reciting local history as a substitute mantra. And doing so was keying her up more than providing relief.

She mounted the broad main staircase to the second floor, where she glanced into three bedrooms—one toward the front with a commanding view of the street below, considerably larger than the other two. A bathroom, grand at the time it was installed and now needing upgrading, opened onto the central hallway. Everything seemed in order.

Except… What was that paper near the foot of another set of stairs leading higher? She was sure it hadn't been there the night before when she locked up. Today was the Ides of March, she remembered automatically. A bad day for Caesar in Rome; but here, on a Swiftwater Monday, not necessarily bad for her. A scrap of paper is just a scrap of paper.

The bottom of the fragment was straight, and the top a ragged tear. She guessed it might have been torn from a computer print-out. The only typed words were "Tomson family records". That name she knew: the Tomsons had donated this very building to the city seven years ago.

She shoved the paper into a pocket and breathed deeply. She knew it shouldn't bother her so much to find such a tiny detail out of place. But, well, it did.

The third floor consisted almost completely of a single room with a high dormer ceiling and one small window on each wall. Two newer tables and eight chairs filled its center. No attempt was made to present this room as anything other than what it now was: the working space for an historical archive. Three file boxes sat at the center of one of the tables, part of an ongoing study assisting the Chamber of Commerce in writing a long-term economic development plan for Swiftwater. She decided to move those files to a storage area under the eaves.

She opened the door to the storage area and realized immediately that her careful ordering system had been disturbed. Papers were scattered between two rows of filing cabinets. She knew she should call the police, although that would mean interacting with a stranger. But Board members would consider her derelict if she didn't. She picked up the phone.

An hour later, she hadn't been able to concentrate enough to get anything else done, and still no one had arrived. Maybe she'd been too tentative in reporting what could be a break-in here at History House. When you spend a lot of time alone, a friend had once told her, you can end up sounding tentative.

She called again and, in reply, was told that an Officer Bill McHugh would be over as soon as he was available. She unlocked the front door and, while she waited, used the Internet to find out what she could about

Officer McHugh. There was a detailed bio on the Swiftwater police department website, and some news articles about him. He had a reputation for being able to handle volatile situations. One article noted that McHugh was half Native American, had spent several of his early years on a reservation, and had transferred only recently from the Sheriff's office in Esterhill to the Swiftwater police department.

She heard a knock at the door. Anticipation turned to nervousness, and Bebe rose to stretch hamstrings that were beginning to feel tight. She waited an additional few seconds to calm her rising heartbeat, then circled her desk and walked to the front door.

The man before her filled most of the door frame. First impression: tall, well over six feet, and wide at the same time, especially across his shoulders. Black, close-cropped hair topped a broad face with dark brown, almost black eyes locked into an officially neutral expression. Lips were slightly down-turned, projecting serious attention. One more click down and they could look cruel. Those lips might be able to smile, she thought, but they probably didn't very often.

He wore police khaki. Open shirt, no tie or hat, and short sleeves revealing arms that were thick and well-muscled. His left hand held a notebook, a thumb securing a white card and a cheap blue ballpoint pen, cap on, diagonally across the notebook's cover. On his opposite hip hung a holstered gun.

Before Bebe could open her mouth, the policeman reached across his waist, pulled the white card out from under the pen and held it out to her.

"Good morning, ma'am. Officer Bill McHugh, Swiftwater police, here in response to your call about a possible break-in."

Bebe nodded and took a step back to encourage the officer to enter, all the while letting first impressions sink in. She always made judgments about how much people were likely to make her anxious—a condition that could be caused by anything from standing too close to staying around too long.

McHugh was a contradiction—a man who exuded action but also gave off a feeling of stillness. There was strength there, a lot of it, ready to be used in an instant. Maybe the short sleeves were part of the readiness and not just for show this time of year.

She made up her mind. There was no immediate danger. She'd give him five minutes max. She'd be all right as long as her office door remained open. She motioned McHugh toward a chair in front of the desk, moving to her own place so that the desk formed a barrier between them.

Quickly she told him about her discovery of the disturbed records. McHugh asked two brief questions to determine time of entry and the sequence of her actions. He jotted in his notebook as she replied.

The notebook snapped shut and he stood. Bebe tensed, her hands gripping the lip of the desk. He didn't seem to notice, and his tone was so neutral that it could have passed for indifference.

"I may have more questions when I see the records you've mentioned."

The wall clock above his head showed that only four minutes and forty seconds had passed. That was a good sign, and she could feel tension flowing out of her arm as she raised it to indicate they should go to the records area.

Even so, she wondered what she had gotten herself into—and how quickly she could rid herself of this nuisance and get back to normal.

Once out of the office, Bill McHugh stood aside, giving Ms. Sorenson space to lead. She moved past him and he turned to follow.

They walked past furniture and older objects arranged for display rather than daily use, their appearance suggesting an aging era. Yet the odors around him were clean and dust-free, with no trace of superimposed chemical fresheners.

It was likely that the lady striding in front of him was in charge of both order and cleanliness. For one thing, the clothes she wore reminded him of some bygone time more than of the present. Two other ladies they passed—volunteers, he guessed—dressed like all the other people in town: a northwest casual that was big on jeans, shirts that were colored but not too colorful, and sturdy shoes.

Sorensen's ankle-length brown skirt emphasized her tall frame. The long-sleeved blouse above it could have been handed down from a frontierswoman. But any thought that she was purposely copying the past stopped at her feet: dark gray running shoes with maroon borders.

She moved fast and he didn't try to keep up, absorbing details of the place as he followed. On the second floor, up a broad staircase, she was waiting for him, arms crossed. A door to a bathroom stood ajar while three others off the landing, presumably doors leading to bedrooms, remained shut.

Sorensen freed one arm to indicate the stairs.

"We need to go up there to see the area that was disturbed. But I have to ask you to stay where you are and wait until I'm all the way up before you get on the stairs."

He looked at the staircase, hung from the wall but with support posts descending on the outside. They seemed strong enough to hold both of them without any trouble. She must have seen him making that assessment.

"Nothing dangerous about the stairs. It's just me. I have some trouble with heights and, though I've gotten used to these stairs, I still get nervous when anyone else is on them with me. Sorry about that, but that's just the way it is."

Bill had met people with acrophobia before. It was pretty common. But people affected by it often tried to cover it up. Not so with this woman. Her tone was matter-of-fact, and she added no nervous laughter to disguise embarrassment.

"No problem. I'll wait."

She went up the flight with a calm rhythm, her gaze forward and steady. When she reached the top, Bill mounted the stairs.

The ceiling of the large room he entered was lower than its counterparts on the floors below. It was ample, made to feel larger by a broad slanted ceiling that ended in a peak about ten feet up. Side walls, seven or so feet high, ran down from the slant. Dormer windows at each end of the side walls looked at the eaves extending over them.

Sorensen stood beside one of the two tables that took up much of the floor space. One of her hands rested on the table's surface. She stood still but gave the impression of leaning toward him, as if for a closer look.

He could still feel her eyes searching *him*, not just his face, as he did some looking of his own. Downstairs she had been mostly sitting; now he noted her full-length details. Five-ten or five-eleven. Large-boned, solid, not thin. Maybe 140-145. Hazel eyes and brown hair with auburn overtones, cut in what he thought was called a "pageboy" or something like that; bangs almost to her eyebrows cut straight across,; the rest of her hair hanging down smoothly to the mid-point of her neck. Face still young, just starting to show faint lines. Forty, plus or minus three, for a guess. Large hands, maybe from farm stock, but too smooth to be doing much grunt labor now.

Attitude: intense. I'm in charge. Don't get too close. Don't call me; I'll call you, maybe, and when *I* choose.

She lowered her eyes and turned to the side.

"Not much to see out here. What you want is in the storage space."

She took two long strides toward one of the side walls, grasped a metal ring in a recessed space and pulled. A wallpapered door, perfectly matching the pattern around it, opened with a slight squeal. She continued to grip the ring as she reached around the door frame to flick a light switch and motioned for him to enter.

He had to duck, but found he could rise to full height if he stayed in the area closest to the door. A five-foot-wide floor lay under a flat ceiling about seven feet high. The rest of the ceiling slanted downward, following the eaves. Four-drawer file cabinets filled most of the space on either side of him, one of the arrays under the slanting ceiling. A small table with a reading light occupied one end of the oblong space, lit by two long neon fixtures on the ceiling.

His instinctive survey of the space was faster than usual because his attention was drawn to a clutter of documents, some on top of the file cabinets on the entry side, a few more on the small work table, and most on the floor.

He could feel Sorensen behind him. As he turned toward her, she took a quick step backward, increasing the distance between them. He sensed her discomfort and gave her as much room as he could in the cramped space. Then he hurried into questions—no need to prolong her obvious uneasiness.

"Has anything like this happened before?"

"Never. At least not as long as I've been at History House, which is about five years. Before that, everything was such a mess that you couldn't have told."

The nervous look in her eyes dimmed slightly.

"Any initial ideas about who might have done this and when?"

She answered immediately.

"When is definite. Sometime between six last evening, when I left, and eight-fifteen this morning, when I arrived."

She lowered her gaze, thought, and spoke again, with her head still down.

"I work with the two volunteers you saw downstairs. Both are married and have families with teenagers. They leave earlier than I do to go home and fix dinner. I stay for a while after they leave. They have never asked to come back in the evening. But in case you're wondering, they do have keys to the house."

Defensiveness was gone, though some awkwardness remained. He'd seen all he needed to, in here.

"Let's continue in the big room."

He glimpsed a flashing look that combined relief with surprise. They exited the file room, turning out the lights, and sat down across from each other at one of the work tables in the main room. Five feet of hardwood separated them. Sorenson now sat back calmly, waiting for the next question.

"Is this place alarmed?"

"No."

He'd seen no alarm panel near the front door, and had assumed as much.

"Care to explain why? You must have some valuable objects in here."

A fleeting smile almost reached her eyes and quickly vanished.

"Your assumption was shared by some of our board members. I think a lot of people assume that old means valuable. So we hired an appraiser. Turns out that, with the exception of one painting, the sum total of everything else comes close to zero in the estate auctions market. We're not a wealthy organization, and a good security system costs money. Besides, this has been a no-locks community for most of its existence. Even as that changes, our old place would be less of a target for thieves than the McMansions not far from here."

That was a longer answer than he needed, but it did reinforce his impression that here was a person who collected and valued details. Your average witness was weak on both points.

"So what you're telling me is that your volunteers would not likely have made the mess back there, and that thieves would have little interest in the contents of this house. I saw no obvious evidence of a break-in."

She nodded. He waited for more, then prodded her along.

"Any other ideas?"

"I think the only possibility is that it was one of the Tomsons."

"The Tomsons?"

"They gave this place to the city, and members of the Tomson family were granted unlimited access to their family home."

"Specifically, who would that be?"

"The parents are dead, but the twin Tomson boys are still around. Will lives up beyond Portal. He's a woodworker and makes high-end furniture and musical instruments. Grant's a developer and lives in Seattle."

Bill was about to ask more when his cell rang. He excused himself, stood, and walked a few paces away. His move was only out of courtesy, since Sorensen would be able to hear him anywhere in the room.

His boss's voice filled his ear. Chief Tom Cisek always sounded official, but Bill could hear extra weight in these words. He listened, and less than a minute later ended the call.

"I'll go over there right now."

Sorensen was looking out one of the windows at the end of the room. He cleared his throat to bring her gaze back to him.

"We'll need to continue this discussion later. The police have identified a man who died in a motorcycle crash. I'm pretty sure the victim's name couldn't be a coincidence. Will Tomson? Is that the man who might have been in here last night?"

The shock on Sorensen's face looked real.

Bebe closed the door to her office. She was glad to be alone again. What a morning: Herb's sudden appearance, then Officer McHugh's. Her red alert had settled to pink, then to steady yellow. She was never wholly comfortable—or fully functional—when other people were present.

Think!

If she was going to be of any help to Officer McHugh, she needed to dredge up all she could remember about the Tomson family, and why one of them would find it necessary to come in alone and late at night. Will Tomson was the most likely possibility. A lot of people in and around Portal knew Will's name, but few had laid eyes on him. Will kept his work private and his doors closed.

When she first took this job five years ago, she already knew the fundamentals. Some years ago, after old Mr. Tomson died, this house had been bequeathed to the Historical Society, with surviving family members having unlimited visitation rights. That meant mostly the twins Will and Grant, since their mother had moved back east. Bebe had considered it her duty to contact the twin brothers.

She got a written response right away from Grant's assistant—a terse, formal acknowledgment and nothing else. Her other letter, to a Portal address, remained unanswered for over two months. Out of curiosity, she set out one Sunday afternoon to check on the location. Portal itself contained a surprisingly large cluster of older wood-frame homes, most of them small by modern standards, a visually arresting reminder of the halcyon past when Portal's mines produced most of the coal for all the rail routes west of the Mississippi. The town's economy may have shrunk, but its housing supply had remained constant. It would have been easy to own or rent a place in the heart of the community, but Will Tomson had apparently chosen otherwise.

She had to drive another two miles up a gradually ascending road toward Coho Corner, to a much smaller cluster of buildings that stood at the edge of Portal and Swiftwater's municipal boundary. The two towns had merged several decades ago, with their center of gravity located firmly in Swiftwater.

She found what she guessed was the place she was looking for, although actual house numbers were not easy to see. A medium-sized metal building fronted on a side road, behind it a small house that looked like an oversized cabin. Some of its finishing touches would have fit a larger home, and they gave an impression of solidity to a sturdy but not particularly welcoming structure. Heavy window shades blanked out all the windows, transmitting the message "keep away" just as effectively as an actual sign would have. She did not get out of her car to knock.

That was that. Her letter to Will Tomson had eventually been returned with a scrawl that might have been initials next to his typed name; she took those as proof that Will knew of his visitation rights.

About a month ago, she received a note with Will's name typed at the bottom, a brief announcement that he might be visiting the old house "to consult older records". No indication what those records were, or when he would be arriving. Bebe responded to the note, asking for clarification, but got no reply.

Then, maybe two weeks later, she had stayed beyond closing hours to complete a filing task when she heard what sounded like a motorcycle approach. She went down to the second floor and looked out a window. In the glow cast by the low-wattage night light above the entrance, she made out a tall figure on the cement walkway. Most of the face was hidden under a gleaming black motorcycle helmet. A long scarf made one turn around his neck, with one end trailing parallel stripes of red, yellow, and orange over the shoulder and down the back of a leather jacket. Apparently sensing something, the man's startled face pivoted up to stare at the window where she stood. He turned aside suddenly, and in a moment she heard his motorcycle drive away. If that had been Will Tomson exercising his right to visit his old home, he was sure acting in a strange way.

She hadn't told Officer McHugh about that interaction, but McHugh had been in a rush to leave. She could tell him if he came back, as she expected he would. At least she had lost some of her worry about him. He hadn't crowded her or tried overly much to help. He just did his job. At the same time, she had a sense, like the heightened hearing sensitivity of blind people, that he realized she had a disability. Not its exact or multiple nature, but enough to understand its essence and the distance it required. Very few people picked up on her condition as quickly as McHugh had done. And he hadn't shown any of the awkwardness that usually accompanied such awareness.

She felt a certain comfort in that realization as she opened her office door and let the rest of her little world back in.

"You have a positive that this is Will Tomson?"

Bill directed his remark to Greg Takarchuk, a fellow cop from Swiftwater, who stood near a body ready to be closed into a bag so the coroner's people could take it away. Others were there, too: techs from the coroner's office and a guy from the county Sheriff's office, where Bill had worked before transferring to the Swiftwater police department.

Bill and Greg had locked horns during a previous investigation, but had emerged with increased respect for each other. That didn't mean, though, that they'd become friends.

"Just a driver's license and motorcycle registration, both made out to Will Tomson of Portal, age 46. I understand he has a brother, and we may have to get him over from Seattle to do an ID. No one else seems to have seen him before."

Bill found that consistent with what Bebe had said about Will's solitary lifestyle.

"This going in as an accident?"

Greg registered surprise.

"What else? You got anything that says otherwise?"

"No."

How do you explain an instinct, especially one as faint as what he was feeling now?

Every scene was unique; but at the same time, if you were a cop long enough, there wasn't much you hadn't seen before. A one-vehicle accident, this time a motorcycle. Loss of control, collision with a tree, and death from a head injury. Time of death indicated that the accident occurred between one and three am, but the accident was not reported until just after nine am.

One-vehicle accidents were the most common kind in a sparsely-populated, economically depressed area. They usually occurred in the dark and were linked to drinking or drug use. In a high percentage of the cases, victims were on their way home. The only thing that made this accident unusual was that it involved a motorcycle. Car accidents were far more common, but they were also less likely to result in a fatality.

Bill walked toward the road and did a slow three-sixty, imagining what likely happened. The rider was approaching a curve on an unlit section. Most people would not have traveled this way, but if you were familiar with the area and you were traveling from Swiftwater to Portal, you might use it as a shortcut. In the dark, and even with the headlamp on the bike, a drunk, tired, or distracted rider might have mistaken the driveway of a house under construction as a continuation of the road. Beyond the construction site, the road's curve to the left was hidden by a stand of Ponderosas.

What happened next could have been close to inevitable. The house construction had evidently started months ago, then stopped, as many building projects did in the recession. Poured concrete had dulled to a dark gray, making it less instantly visible. The bike had traveled at speed down a short driveway slick with new snow. The driveway ended on a garage pad with a two-foot concrete wall at its rear, rebar sticking out of it. Hitting the wall, the bike's front tire would have popped. The rear end would have risen, almost flipping the bike over the obstacle, then slammed back down at an angle as the bike fell sideways and crashed once more into the wall.

Meanwhile, the disoriented driver would have started to turn away from the obstruction hurtling toward him, so when the bike hit, he was propelled off at an angle, unfortunately perfectly lined up with a medium-sized Ponderosa right behind the short wall. The rider's head hit the tree, either killing him instantly or leaving him for several hours at the mercy of serious wounds and a near-freezing temperature. An autopsy would determine the cause of death.

Greg's expression had returned to what Bill had come to think of as normal Ukrainian unreadable. The irony was not lost on him that that's exactly what many Whites had said about his Indian forebears.

Bill looked once more at the dead man. He appeared older than the age Greg had reported. Unkempt gray hair added years, but so did the deep lines etched in his face. Only his hands looked younger, with smooth skin and slim, gracefully tapered fingers. No wedding ring. A dark parka and blue-and-gray striped bib overalls, the kind that train engineers used to wear, were barely visible in the partially-zipped body bag. Next to it was a plastic bag with a black leather jacket. Light blue eyes with gray edging had clouded over, staring sightlessly ahead. A mouth, slightly open, added an air of astonishment. Finally, what Bill had seen first but pushed aside as he catalogued everything else: the obvious contusion above one eye, centering on a concave trauma about four inches across. The point of impact, most probably with the tree trunk. A three-inch gash had opened above it and some blood had flowed out, but not enough to have killed Will Tomson.

He'd seen many accidents where events and their sequences were much harder to reconstruct. This one looked cut and dried. A routine autopsy and further scene analysis would be completed, the pro forma requirements that would turn an unfortunate occurrence into a closed file.

He was done here, but not quite done at History House. He'd go back there now and clean up details. Then he'd check what else was on his plate for the rest of the day.

But he was finding it difficult to wrap his mind around any other work. There was a small but persistent feeling forming in him that something wasn't quite right. Doubt lingered, though Bill couldn't think of anything overt that he'd missed.

Bebe closed and locked the heavy front door, taking one last look through its hand-blown stained glass inset at the retreating figures of her two volunteers, both off to attend to family necessities. She was finally alone, a daily moment that always arrived with relief and, if it had been a good day, satisfaction.

It had not been a good day, certainly not one of those that flowed serenely from opening to closing, the best kind of day.

Loud ringing of the old-style rotary bell on the front door brought her thoughts back to the moment. She looked at her watch to be sure and, yes, it was after normal business hours. She could simply ignore ...

The bell sounded again, this time two rotations.

Reluctantly, she went to the door and, through the stained glass, made out a large uniformed figure with a round policeman's hat. She opened the door to Officer McHugh.

He stepped back, removed his hat, and held one hand palm up in her direction.

"I saw lights on inside and assumed you might still be here. Sorry about the intrusion, but if you have a moment we can wrap up what I need for the report on Will Tomson."

He must have noticed something in her face.

"Yes, I should have confirmed that first. The body at the accident site was Will's."

"I sort of expected that, though it's still a shock. Come in, please."

She tried to keep her voice calm even as she felt fear start its inevitable climb up some inner staircase. It had been one thing to meet Officer McHugh when she had fully prepared herself. But surprise always left her defenseless. She felt herself teetering.

Halfway back to a sense of balance, Bebe led the way to the parlor, circling to pull the chains on all three table lamps. It was still light outside, though shadows from two close-by Douglas firs dimmed the room. She took a straight-backed side chair while McHugh stayed standing in the opening from the entry way.

Her mind was partly on the memory of a man she had once seen in front of the house.

"Before I forget. I think Will Tomson may have come here one evening, though he didn't come in. I saw a man in motorcycle gear by the front door, wearing a long red and orange scarf. It could have been him."

He made a note.

"All right, we may come back to that if it's necessary. In the meantime, did you have a chance to look at the documents that had been disturbed?"

"Yes. We did a presentation for a school group after lunch and I just finished straightening up the third floor a half hour ago. No one else touched the papers until I got to them."

"Tell me what you found."

"Not a whole lot. First, I looked at what the documents that had been pulled from the cabinets were about. We don't have anything like a complicated coding of separate documents. Instead we've divided the archives into general categories like local news, local government, land ownership, personal accounts, and, of course, fairly large sections on this house and the Tomson family. Whenever a staff member consults files from different categories, we write notes or cross references and put them in both files. But we're real old-fashioned. Maybe we put off modernizing because we think an old-style system fits the house."

He didn't react, just waited.

"Truth is, the real files are here . . . "

She pointed at her head and saw a flicker of a smile in return.

" . . . and in the brains of a line of volunteers."

"And what did those brains tell you?"

His question carried no condescension. He moved deliberately to the settee across the room, muttering something about an injury and standing too long. Because of the overwhelming presence of her own phobias, it was good to be reminded that others had problems, too. McHugh hadn't moved abruptly, and he'd kept his distance. Her fears were down and manageable. She was encouraged to go on.

"I had a pretty good idea of which folders each document had come from."

She offered a smile, probably her first.

"Of course, I was already thinking about re-filing."

He nodded.

"You found a common subject?"

"Actually not, and that surprised me. Usually, if you're looking at a single subject, most of what you need would be in a single drawer, or at least in the same cabinet. But I found documents about railroad schedules in the 1920s; a scandal involving a prostitute and a visiting minister in 1938; the announcement that the Tomson family would be donating their home to the town of Swiftwater, along with an article reporting local reactions to that news; and the announcement of a new allocation of water rights above Portal in 1963."

She hadn't needed to provide all that detail. Some people thought her lists of information were just a way of showing off. But repetition was a mnemonic, part of how she remembered. McHugh's expression hadn't changed, so she finished the report.

"I expected that Will Tomson, if that's who it was, would have been looking mostly at documents that related to his family or to this house. Or he could have been searching for something related to his woodworking business and its sales."

She was unsure how much McHugh knew about the Tomsons, but it was better to tell him too much than too little.

"It's possible, too, that he wanted information on the lake property. About all we had on that was announcements of the annual powwow there, and we filed those under city events."

"You mean Tomson Lake? Why would that be of particular interest?"

Bebe now remembered that McHugh had moved to Swiftwater only recently.

"It's the Tomson family's main asset. Mrs. Tomson had a special interest in hosting Indians at the lake powwow every year, and I suppose it's possible she might have decided to return the property to the Indians when she died."

"You have anything on that here?"

"In the files, no. Besides, I've seen no public notice of any provision in Mrs. Tomson's will."

McHugh shifted his sitting position and changed direction.

"If it wasn't Will who made the mess upstairs, did you find anything else that might explain the circumstances?"

"No, but then I only was thinking about Will."

The scrap of paper! She pulled it out of her pocket and held it out to McHugh.

"I found this on the stairs."

McHugh silently read the words without touching the paper. He pointed at it.

"Anyone else handle this?"

"Not as far as I know. I doubt it."

He nodded.

"Doesn't mean much by itself. But hang on to it in case we need to examine it later."

She stepped to the wall and took a glassine slip from a shelf, put the paper fragment in it, and waited. After a long pause when he still hadn't spoken, she surprised herself by filling the void.

"Does what you've seen and heard seem significant to you?"

He replied cautiously.

"Not by itself. But alongside what was found at the accident scene, maybe it could be."

"The accident scene was also full of unanswered questions?"

He appeared to aim his answer more at his own thoughts than at her question.

"The opposite. It seemed to answer too much."

McHugh rose, looking uncomfortable.

"Please don't mention that to anyone. It's just incomplete thinking, and I probably shouldn't have said it. Thank you for your help. We're finished here. I can see myself out."

With those words he left, and she heard the closing mechanism snap behind him. That should have been the end of it; their conversation had been reasonably complete. Why then was her mind searching for more questions she could have asked Officer McHugh?

Not that the opportunity would likely arise.

MARCH 16, TUESDAY

S ara Winter glanced at the scribbled note in her hand, almost crumpled to illegibility from the way she had been clutching it. She rechecked the phone number of the cell belonging to Laura, the assistant who was temporarily fielding calls for Cascade Adventures.

Laura answered with her name right after the first buzz. Sara pictured her, a solid farm girl—stocky, some would say, if she were shorter. Her height must have helped when she rowed for UW. Sara skipped the small talk.

"You got a call about a tour?"

Laura's response sounded more tentative than usual, probably because Sara had not bothered to mask her impatience. She seemed to be impatient all the time, these days. As a teenager, she had been called Rocket, or just Rock; she could push herself along a rock face and through complex math problems with speed and daring that few others could match. The jets weren't firing now. Maybe they were completely burned out. She'd never know unless she tested them.

"Not a new one. It was the same people who called last month wanting a guided loop hike for eight over the July Fourth weekend. They repeated that their friends, the family we had last summer, said you were the best and that they wanted you if you were available. If not, they made it a point to say they wouldn't call again."

Well, at least they still got calls. But fewer all the time. And why not? Her husband Jeff was increasingly involved in legislative issues in Olympia. Neither of them had been readily available for the tour business since last fall, he because of an injury and she because of the time she spent caring for him. No wonder people had all but given up calling them.

Sara realized Laura was waiting for a response. For a moment she gave attention to the younger woman's feelings.

"Look, Laura. I know you're not making the kind of money you hoped to make when you signed up with us. That's not your fault. It's ours."

As she spoke, she looked out the kitchen window at a refurbished barn filled with skis, rafts, climbing ropes, and all the minor equipment needed for climbing and camping in the mountains. Beside the barn sat a large white van with a substantial steel rack on its roof. In bright blue and

31

forest green script, the name Cascade Adventures stood out crisply on its side. But Sara could also see the dust on the vehicle, and tires that needed inflating.

Laura must have heard a tone of dejection.

"It sounds like you're letting me go."

"Sorry if you thought that. Hang in there a little longer if you can. I got a few ideas about new directions. Maybe something up at Tomson Lake."

"That's nice of you, I guess. I've been looking, but you're as good a prospect as anything else I've found. There's no jobs available in Esterhill and, what with my mother being ill, I can't go back to Seattle."

Sara was well aware of Laura's situation: she had an MBA from the University of Washington and had given up a good job over the Cascades in Bellevue to care for her single and very ill mother. Laura had come on board with Cascade Adventures because its future represented her best option. The lengthy recession had hurt the tour business along with lots of others, and their hope that enough of the techies who scored big with Microsoft and the dotcom startups would keep them afloat so far hadn't turned into reality. It certainly hadn't turned into a role as Business Manager or CFO of a thriving small business that Laura hoped for.

She felt an obligation to Laura and commiserated for a minute or two. It was the best she could do for now, and Laura seemed to realize that.

Jeff was dozing in their bedroom upstairs. He'd looked so tired last evening that likely he'd be out for a while. If he woke, there was a sandwich on the table; and he could take that into the den and munch on it while he went back to his desk work.

Sara didn't need anyone to tell her that something had gone horribly wrong in their relationship after Jeff's injury. The fall he took was serious. Hospitalization followed the rescue, a trip to the emergency room and two surgeries. Physically, Jeff came through all that, and the surface elements of their life began to look the same as before. But in fact an invisible curtain had come down. Their conversations, which never deteriorated into real arguments, sounded just as reasonable as ever. But the light edge was gone: no more mild teasing or semi-sarcastic asides. Yes, a curtain had come down.

So what to do? She needed a new project. But, at the same time, her marriage needed attention. God, she wished she didn't have to give attention to that distraction at this moment. Her full attention ought to be on saving the business. But she was just kidding herself if she thought she could compartmentalize business and marriage issues so simply. Like it or not, they were intertwined.

Five years ago, when work was going well, she'd agreed to serve on the finance committee of the Esterhill United Way. She used her accounting background, did a public service, and got their business name out there, all at the same time. She put in two years on the committee, helped the town a bit, and met Calla Ogden, a county social worker who had probably been appointed—by Calla's own characterization—because she was part Native American. Calla had told her, with a smile, that her name meant "trout", and that when it came to numbers, she was, in fact, a fish out of water. She left the committee after a year. Two years after that, a major story in the media reported how Calla and her half-brother had been rescued near a back-country river, where an enraged drug maker had tried to drown them. Sara had tried to contact Calla to express relief at her escape, but her message was not returned.

Yesterday, Calla finally did leave voice mail, and Sara decided to try one more time to connect with her at her home in Swiftwater.

Calla's work was largely with people in trouble and, just as much, with the emotional problems that families and individuals developed when their lives spun out of control. As Sara's own relations with Jeff grew more strained, it occurred to her that Calla might help her on that front.

This time, she heard Calla's voice immediately.

"Sara, I have no decent excuse for not acknowledging your kind message several months ago. What can I say? A lot was happening."

Sara made light of the matter and steered the conversation into small talk, largely centering on Calla's recent marriage to Swiftwater's mayor, Phil Bianchi. Their banter quickly petered out, and Calla's voice took on a professional tone.

"Sara, much as I appreciate your call, I have a feeling it might deal with more than old events."

"You're right. Things have gotten pretty strained between me and my husband Jeff. It's part business, part personal. I remembered that you specialize in that kind of thing and thought seeing you could help me."

A long pause followed. Sara waited, wondering if she had accidentally crossed some informal boundary. Then Calla spoke thoughtfully, erasing any possibility that Sara had offended her.

"Often I'm faced with difficult emotional issues in my line of work. But I'm a social worker and only a part-time, inadequately trained counselor when I have to be. I'm certainly not a psychologist. Best I can do is learn a little more about what's going on with you and Jeff, and maybe steer you toward someone who can help you better than I can. I happen to be free right now, if you want to drop over."

Sara knew she could be there in about fifteen minutes; their home was halfway between Swiftwater and Esterhill to its east, while Calla lived in the center of Swiftwater. Sara left immediately.

The aura that flowed off Calla as she opened her front door was an encouragement in itself—calm, centered and strong. Here was an attitude Sara wanted to spend time with, maybe swipe some strength from.

They exchanged pleasantries and Calla led the way into the closet-like space that was her home office. Books filled tall shelves next to a functional steel desk, its surface neatly ordered. Sara's eyes flicked over the book titles. Most were about subjects you'd expect a social worker to consult, but one shelf was devoted to Indian lore and history.

Calla wore simple clothes in muted earth tones, but a brighter scarf of orange and teal, along with silver earrings, put an inner happiness on display. Calla was enjoying *her* new marriage. Really enjoying it, Sara surmised; a very evident swelling around her belly predicted a baby's imminent arrival.

Calla's time was bound to be limited, so Sara opened right away.

"You seem content. I wish I were. Things are not good between Jeff and me since his accident. He's been distant, uncommunicative. At home he's mainly at his desk, and he's spending more time in Olympia than before. Our business has been hard hit by the recession and even harder by Jeff's lack of interest. I've always done the major work, but we always talked together about our plans. It's like a hole has appeared where everything used to be seamless."

Calla shifted, leaned forward.

"Let me ask you something that may sound disconnected but could help me advise you. Tell me the most significant five events in your life. No details, just what they were."

Wow. That was out of left field. Okay. Don't argue the point. She let choices spool by, doing some rough rearranging. In a minute she had her answers and laid them out crisply.

"The first time my mom and dad let me make a solo climb in Colorado and I became the youngest person ever to summit. My brother's death in a climbing accident. Blowing the whistle on the rigged accounting in my old job at a major corporation and getting fired as a result. Meeting Jeff and deciding to go back west with him. Starting and successfully running our own excursions company."

She paused.

"And now Jeff's accident and our present problems. That makes six, but it's also the reason I'm here and I suppose it should be on the list."

Calla sat back and observed her for a moment. Her voice dropped in volume and sounded serious. But Sara also heard what she thought was sympathy.

"That's an interesting list. You've been through a lot."

She swiveled toward her desk, wrote quickly on a note pad, tore off the sheet and held it out.

"As I told you on the phone, I'm not the one to help you. Here's the name of a skilled counselor. She's equally adept with family and personal issues. She lives in Esterhill and, I think, could be right for you. She may or may not have space, but I would be glad to call her to see if she can fit you in."

Sara was stunned. She sat still, head down, trying not to erupt. The tone of sympathy she'd heard a few moments ago was gone. What a waste of time. She didn't need a counselor; a good friend would have been enough.

She raised her head and made an effort to thank Calla sincerely for her time. Behind the words she spoke, she came to a decision: push ahead. Find a project that engaged her. Support Jeff, but give him space to work things out for himself.

Calla's eyes replied with a curious expression, part resigned understanding, Sara thought. And part ... pity?

To hell with that! Sara's mind was already on how to revive that idea about the Tomson property. Concentration was the laser she counted on. She knew the dangers. Impulsiveness had never been her friend. Light up the after-burners. Taking a chance was exactly what she needed. Starting now.

She called Laura and set up a planning meeting for the afternoon.

Jeff Winter's cell rang and he heard Mac Champlin's voice in Olympia, two hours away by car, south and west across the Cascades.

"Yeah, Mac, I've almost finished all the reports and I'll have some recommendations on legislation about the proposed port expansion in a couple of days."

Phillip McMasters Champlin, a member of the state legislature, was, as usual, not satisfied until he had made his point at least three times. Jeff pretended to listen as he took a seat on a bench in front of his physical therapist's office. He'd just finished one more treatment for his injuries from the climbing accident. Each session left him with greater freedom of movement and absence of pain. At least that part of his life was going well.

Mac slowed down and Jeff responded, carefully masking his inner frustration. Disappointment would be more like it.

"Unlikely I can make it to Olympia until day after tomorrow, but for sure early next week. Meanwhile we've got cell phones and texts. I promise to get back to you any time you need my help. And yes, I'll take a close look at the energy costs of the new anti-pollution proposal right away."

That sounded good, but Jeff was under no illusions, pretty sure that Mac wasn't either. There was no substitute for being in Olympia, at the source of queries and actions. Information came at you there in pieces all the time—over coffee, during hallway conversations, and, often most accurately, from posture, tone of voice, or simply from whether someone would look you in the eye. At a distance, Jeff was only half as useful to Mac, if that.

What a contrast all this was to his life a decade ago when he was the chief aide on an environmental committee in the U.S. House. His life in D.C. had been comfortably triangulated—short walks from his apartment to his job and, on weekends, to the garage where he kept an SUV that carried him to skiing or climbing, even occasionally to surfing. Sure, frantic end-of-session activity brought around-the-clock interruption of his athletic routine; but that, too, arrived with comfortable predictability.

Then he met Sara. Their chance encounter was like a switch connecting two separate circuits into one with massively more energy. He had gone suddenly from being a public policy specialist who once thought he might have a crack at a pro surfing career to being a grown-up boy scout, an excursion leader-cum-hand holder who once had been something of an expert on legislative procedures.

Jeff walked to his Nissan Xterra, a couple of models newer than the version he'd had when he and Sara met. Everything these days seemed to bring up her name in one way or another. She was front and center in his thoughts. Those thoughts gave him a different kind of pain than his hip did, but they were growing in intensity even as his hip was beginning to heal.

The accident, and blame for it, was a big unresolved issue between them. He was just recovering from the flu and had not wanted to go on that trek, but Sara insisted. Not very far into the first day of a three-day hike with a family from Bellevue, his footing gave way and he fell. Not far, but fast, down a steep embankment. At its foot, he crashed into a fallen old-growth fir trunk partially covered with snow. The sharp, jagged remnant of a limb jutted out from the trunk at just the wrong angle. It had pierced the right rear part of Jeff's thigh, doing damage first to his hip, then to his knee, as it tore into him and then brought him to an abrupt stop.

The rest was a blur. He was in and out of consciousness while Sara and the family's mother stayed at his side, stopping the bleeding and trying to make him comfortable. A search and rescue team got him down to a waiting ambulance that took him to the trauma center at Harborview in Seattle. Weeks of recovery and rehab followed, and he could almost precisely remember each successive procedure, moment by painful moment.

It wasn't his nature to seek out and assign blame. But it didn't take much reflection to recognize that the root of what had happened—and the root of his current problems—was Sara's impatience to get their business up and running in the spring. She had hammered at him and his reticence. If they responded to every opportunity, she insisted, they would be able to use their early momentum to build a strong summer season.

He didn't need a shrink to point out that his current physical and emotional problems were intertwined. To look at him, an observer might see only a trim, tallish man in his early forties, with a full head of hair, blond surfer streaks now gone and grey creeping into the remaining sandy-brown mop. Someone who could get frequent comments about what good shape he was in when he actually wasn't. After the weeks of physical therapy there was some improvement. He could drive again. But that wasn't a lot of help. His other troubles—his Sara troubles—traveled with him, regardless of his destination.

Could he stay with Sara—especially in her current mood, where every issue became a major one—long enough to get his real points across? She hadn't bothered to speak to him when she went out this morning. Did he even know what his real points were, anymore?

Only one way to find out. They had to talk. He was the one who had to make that happen. Sara didn't sit still for long conversations; and when she decided to move, she ignored obstacles, even one as large as the gulf growing between them.

"Okay. I get it. So what have you got for me?"

For a moment, Sara breathed the oxygen of simple gratitude. Laura had her own problems, but here she was, smart and physically strong, offering help without guile. Sara made a silent vow not to let Laura down if she could help it. But there was no mistaking the fact that they were in a crapshoot and both of them knew it.

The truth of that last statement was all around them. They were meeting in a corner of the refurbished barn behind her house. She and Laura sat a space apart on one of two long, tan leather couches. The sofas were angled to face a large flat TV where potential clients could view professional-grade videos of previous tours mounted by Cascade Adventures. Sara had shot the videos and later, with Jeff's incisive suggestions to help her, edited them. He had done the final technical production. Most of the clients who laid out the substantial cost of an excursion were from the northwest, and many of them had shaped the details of their final choices while sitting on these couches.

Starting around the rear of the couches and extending into the unlit murk of the barn's interior were neatly-organized shelves full of the equipment that Cascade Adventures had accumulated in its eight years of existence: skis and their peripherals, fishing equipment, inflatable tubes and rafts, tents and sleeping bags, climbing gear. Impressive as the collection was, most of it had become useless overhead.

She waved toward the gloom, keeping her eyes on Laura.

"We've accumulated too much, can't use half of it, and aren't even sure what works, what's broken or outmoded."

Laura nodded.

"That means we should start throwing stuff out."

Sara smiled. Now they were getting into it.

"Some, yes. But we should try to unload as much as we can on eBay and Craigslist. Why don't you begin with an inventory and think about what we should keep, sell or throw away. Give me your first ideas as soon as you can."

Laura entered a note on the electronic pad sitting on her lap.

"I also want you to work on a parallel but related problem. If we cut down on equipment, we'll be cutting back on some of the excursions we can offer. Maybe the kinds of excursions we offer now aren't the ones we should be focusing on if we want to target a particular market. For instance—and I'm just riffing here—maybe we shouldn't focus on specific activities—you know, like fishing or hiking. Instead we could bundle activities that emphasize varied experiences. For instance, an excursion that shows you pretty vistas, gets you in shape, and introduces you to the benefits of different eating habits. There may be a large potential client group that wants the summer or spring break trip to be more than visiting well-known tourist attractions. Can you think about that, Laura? Look online to see if similar experiences are already marketed. A quick analysis of both possibility and potential competition?"

Laura, who had been tapping on the pad while Sara spoke, glanced up.

"I'll give you a report in a week, unless you need it sooner."

"A week will be fine. In the meantime, I have my own task. A couple of years ago I had preliminary conversations with Tomson family members about renting their place on Tomson Lake. We didn't get very far with that idea. Will Tomson wouldn't respond, and Tomson Enterprises, meaning Grant Tomson, eventually passed on the idea. But I did get some estimates of what it would take to refurbish the house into a lodge and make a smaller structure into overflow sleeping quarters. We could revive those ideas in a different form. I've already called Grant Tomson's assistant and hope to get a meeting with Grant himself."

She paused.

"Okay, I think that about covers it. We'll get back to it next week. Here, same time."

They both rose. Sara had been so intent on what she was saying that she almost missed seeing a shadow cross the TV. She turned and realized that the barn's small door closest to the main house was ajar. In the back light, she recognized Jeff's silhouette. As Laura departed, he advanced haltingly and stopped a few steps away.

"Sound like you've got something new going."

Sara heard the practiced neutral tone. Did Jeff have anything to offer other than passive open-endedness? But just as her thoughts were about to go further down that precipitous path, he moved closer and surprised her.

"I don't think we should go on with anything, much less anything new, until we've talked. I don't like the way things have gotten between us. We need to talk now."

Sara still vibrated with the energy she always felt when she contemplated a new challenge, but she held that tension in check. She, too, was tired of skirting issues. A detour was longer than a direct path, more time consuming, and much more tiring. She should welcome this moment as a chance to plow through obstacles and get past things, instead of living any longer in their energy-sapping and unsatisfying state of half-throttle.

She motioned toward the nearest couch, sat, and saw him take a seat that was closer to her than his recent habit, though still not touching. She began small.

"So where do you want to start?"

She looked right at him, at the way he glanced away, then back, settling himself, adjusting more than his physical discomfort. After weeks in hiding, his eyes seemed to open inwardly and she got a glimpse of real torment. He held her gaze, and opened his mouth to speak.

"Okay, Sara, let's begin . . . "

His cell phone buzzed and he punched off to voice mail. He returned his eyes to her, settled back, and then both of them heard the sound of an arriving text message, followed immediately by the ring of another call.

He looked at her questioningly, not realizing this had become a test. Her test.

"You better take that."

He was hesitant.

"You sure?"

His hand was already on his phone. He picked up, and she heard the return of his customary voice.

"I can't finish that today. Maybe tomorrow."

A pause, a quick flash of eyes toward her, then back into the shadows.

"No, I can't make it there that soon. Maybe day after tomorrow."

He hung up and covered with a stiff grin.

"Olympia. I put them off. Now we can talk."

The right words. But the old flatness was back in his voice, too. So much for new sincerity. She was already rising, resolve flushing out the sympathy and affection that a moment ago had begun to trickle in. A saying she once heard and hadn't quite understood came back to her: "There's nothing so hard as the softness of indifference". She got it now. Inner toughness and outer indifference was what would get her through.

"That's okay. We've both got things to do. We can always talk later."

She aimed at the open door, not waiting for a response.

It had been difficult, but Jeff had succeeded in putting further thoughts aside, at least enough to finish reading the most important materials he'd brought home. What remained was mostly a matter of assembling and writing, tasks he found easy and could do quickly. Besides, this was a preliminary report in a process that would cover the rest of the legislative session. Each subsequent report would focus on a piece of proposed legislation, and every report backing a new law would generate one or more responses opposing it. All he had to do now was survey the general terrain of the issue. The legislative trails through it were not his concern.

Jeff was under no illusions about why Mac was in such a hurry. He wanted to make a mark and make it quickly. His eyes gleamed when he looked in the direction of the governor's mansion. It was Mac who had interrupted his almost-conversation with Sara. It was Mac who wanted Jeff personally in Olympia, as if cell phones, email, and Skype couldn't keep the leash short enough.

His concentration shifted to how much his hip hurt. The tightness and occasional spasms were there even when he didn't think about them. Lately he felt like he was under assault from an unseen enemy lurking in a thick fog, attacking him from odd angles, retreating, then emerging again. No real enemy, only someone who increasingly seemed like one: Sara. Had it really come to that?

They had operated for most of their eight years together like a bond that flexed and gave room for decisions when times were tough, but one that was also endowed with the memory of a stretch fabric and could return to its original state when the pressure stopped. Now the memory had failed; there was no imprint of what they had had, and hence no original state to return to.

He'd tried, out there in the storage barn, to open a conversation. And then that damn call from Olympia. There was always a damn call or a damn PT appointment or Sara having to run or hike or snowshoe to some damn distant point that she'd set as today's challenge. Okay, he should have persisted, stayed with her, ignored the demands from Olympia. But it all happened so fast, and she reacted even faster. Besides, they had to have some income, and so far he was the only one earning it.

At least he should try to keep the boss happy. He punched in Mac's number at the Capitol. It was already Happy Hour in Olympia, and most of the legislative business was being done elsewhere.

While he waited for a pickup, he thought once more of Sara. If there was a chance later today, he'd try again for the talk they'd barely started. Or if that didn't work, he'd complete his current projects and refuse to take more until he and Sara found a way back to normal.

A recorded message started talking into his ear.

"You have reached the private number of Representative Philip Champlin. I want very much to speak to you, so ... "

Almost immediately he heard the bell tone of an incoming call and pushed a flashing icon. The recorded message changed to Mac's polished baritone.

"What's up?"

"Starting on your water rights report. I want it to be brief enough for people to read it, but I don't want to miss anything. Thought I'd lay out the outline so you can tell me now rather than later."

He sketched the dimensions of his task. First was completing the report on water rights in Indian treaties and how those rights jibed with subsequent agreements and modifications on the ground. The treaties had been around a long time, forgotten more often than they were consulted, casually and then habitually violated. But that was before the big population growth in the second half of the twentieth century, before the resurgent interest Native Americans demonstrated for their rights, and before the still-debated but increasingly inescapable effects of global warming reared their heads.

Water rights had become a hot topic for the first time in about a hundred and fifty years. In the State of Washington, the west side of the Cascades, from Bellingham to the Oregon border, spent more time fending off jokes about rain than they did worrying about water, while the biggest geographic part of the state—everything to the east of the

Cascades—worried about the fine line that divided an annual dry season from multi-year droughts.

For Mac's report, Jeff had organized those underlying issues under the usual rubrics—background, history, principal common attributes of water rights treaties, and special cases. He recited the headlines of each section.

Mac paused, thought, then gave a tentative go-ahead.

"Sounds as if you haven't missed anything obvious. I need a draft tomorrow so I can make changes if necessary."

"Sure, but can you please give me some uninterrupted time until then?"

"Just don't get too relaxed. We may need to present an immediate response to a proposed demonstration project at Tomson Lake. Once it's started, we can go to the legislature for official status, maybe as a pilot for several projects statewide."

Jeff ended the call. He still didn't know exactly what Mac had in mind. Did he want to back the Tomsons' water rights at the lake? Or would he want to include historic Native American rights in a broader agreement? His curiosity was piqued, but that could wait. He pushed the Tomson Lake project to a back burner, but immediately a different flame glowed. Sara had talked about some project that involved the Tomson property. Maybe he could make everything fit together: please Mac and regain Sara's favor.

But was that possible? Mac was predictable—or at least manageable. Sara was neither. What if he couldn't do both/and, but had to choose either/or?

He tried to shove that worry out of his mind as he got back to finishing the report in front of him.

MARCH 17, WEDNESDAY

Mashing the mixed undergrowth and stepping around small flowering plants, Sara strode up a hillock next to the parking area on the Tomson Lake property. From the top, she looked down a road that snaked upward toward her. A gleaming black blur was moving fast in her direction. About what she would have expected for a man of Grant Tomson's reputation.

When she heard about Will Tomson's death, she concluded that any proposal about the lake property would be ignored. But she had to do something, so she submitted a proposal anyway. She was, therefore, surprised when Grant's assistant called yesterday to say that Grant would be traveling the next day to Swiftwater, and could find time to meet with her.

By the time she walked down off the knoll, the black car had reached the parking area. It was an Audi, a top-of-the-line A-8, reputed to be one of the fastest production cars on the road, overpowered for city driving or even for the short haul on the interstate from Seattle. But that, too, fit the self-made Grant Tomson's reputation. On the chart of wealthiest Americans, he didn't show up alongside fellow Seattleites Gates, Ballmer, Allen, and McCaw; but regionally he was well-known as a deal maker and a rising force to be reckoned with.

From the first appearance of one shoe until he emerged fully from the vehicle, Sara recorded a meticulous attention to style. The shoes had long, squared-off toes. A black jacket looked casual over a dark gray mock turtleneck, and on first glance could have come from North Face or REI. But its cut suggested that the source would probably be a boutique with a label recognized by only an elite few. For business meetings, all he would need to do was swap to a suit jacket and a tie-less dress shirt. Overall, the result was an upscale version of Seattle's business answer to the more casual garb of its Silicon Valley cousins: Steve Jobs with Pendleton overtones.

Tomson stretched and did a slow turn, taking in the scenery. Only then did his eyes settle on Sara. Immediately she felt as if a falcon, perched on a leather-gloved arm, was assessing her value as prey. She shrugged off that silly image; she'd seen those eyes on the faces of plenty of ambitious men. It was a practiced gaze, mostly for show, though once in a while it signaled real power. Grant Tomson was for real. The kind of guy who could get

47

rockets to fire again. Her job was to convince him that he needed what she could offer.

"Mr. Tomson, thanks for taking the time..."

His response came out lazy and relaxed. He waved her off, no smile, his voice unhurried. Still, she sensed a message: let's get this over with.

But he surprised her.

"I don't have all the time in the world. But this is a place for forgetting that, for a while anyway."

He gestured at their surroundings. When he looked back at her, his eyes had melted to milk chocolate. She wasn't fooled. Business leaders and actors had a lot in common.

They both turned their attention to a clear-cut meadow surrounded by a deep ring of old growth firs, mountains rising behind, culminating in the massive distant presence of nine-thousand-foot Mount Stewart. Snow descended to about four thousand feet, hanging on in patches below that. Puffy white clouds hung near the peaks, lit from the south by a sun that was rising higher off the horizon each day as they approached the equinox.

The expansive scene was backdrop for the lake, glass-smooth on this windless morning, about a half mile long, shaped like a blunt-end football, perhaps five hundred yards across at its widest point. The trees and the mountains were upside down in its reflection. Back toward the trees at the end of the lake stood a large cabin that could have been called a lodge. Across the water, a smaller structure hugged the lake's long edge, two canoes upright against its side. Buildings aside, the place had a primeval feel, as if it had its own method of keeping time and could, whenever it wanted to, crumble insignificant human additions back into their original state.

Sara had almost forgotten about Will's death. She spoke softly.

"I'm sorry for your loss."

Tomson slowly pulled his gaze away from the vista long enough to look at her directly. She now saw shifting emotions, a kaleidoscope of grief, resolve and maybe other reactions that passed too quickly for identification.

He nodded, lowered his head, and turned away from her.

"Thank you. I doubt I'd be here if Will were still alive. I can't believe that he's gone. He had his furniture and his instruments, and I had business. With him gone, it's like a part of me went with him, a part I didn't know he still owned. That's a difficult and unexpected reality."

She felt as though she was eavesdropping on a private eulogy. He stopped and she waited. Eventually he returned his attention to her, wearing a composed expression, back in the world of business.

"Shouldn't have brought you into all that. That's not why you're here."

"You're right. But I meant what I said."

He nodded.

"Tell me about your idea."

She lined up the points she had thought through for this moment.

"We propose a long-term lease of the larger structure over there..."

She pointed.

"...which we'll renovate and use as the center of our revamped business. Up to now, we've focused on local hikers and outdoors people. There are lots of opportunities for them. So we want to reach tourists from other parts of the country. Some already stop here, driving to and from Seattle. We want more from there and other locations. They'll use the lodge as base camp for a package of activities: hiking, rock climbing, horseback riding, maybe even prospecting in some of the old gold mines. The focus will be on groups, family or otherwise. We can add other activities as we move forward."

He broke in.

"Will you be keeping horses here?"

"Maybe eventually. For now we'll rely on existing stables trucking them in."

"Go on."

"There's not much more to the general idea, and I'm not sure how much you want in the way of details. For instance, I assume you may want to keep a place here, and we'd be open to including some remodeling of the cabin..."

She indicated the smaller structure with the canoes.

"...to your specifications if you have interest in that. Mainly, I hope to find out whether you like the general concept. There are other locations, but for proximity—and, of course, for its phenomenal beauty—this is our best bet. Last time around, you were definite about not letting us onto your property. This time, we would offer a lease instead of rental fees. I know that this isn't the best time for you, but when the time is suitable, I would appreciate any reaction you can give to our proposition."

Tomson stared at her, eyes impenetrable. Then he broke contact to walk away and look out across the lake for a long time. She waited, giving him the time and space he needed—hopeful, but also realistic. She had not forgotten his impersonal, harsh refusal two years ago.

When he was ready, he pivoted slowly, maintaining the distance between them. His voice had the same mixture of accustomed decisiveness and unaccustomed reflection that she had seen before in his eyes.

"I used to think of this as the family place. My relatives got it through hard work and determination. It represented—represents—who we were. Change, or intruders, never subtracted from that. From us. Now everyone else is gone. It's not the family place any more. But it's still my place."

Tomson stopped abruptly and shifted his stance. His voice was softer.

"I wish Will were still alive; but, realistically, you and I wouldn't be here if he were. I now think of Will and what he might have wanted. Given a choice between signs that said 'No Trespassing' and the enjoyment that people could have here, Will would have voted for the people. I've got other obligations to occupy me, and it seems acceptable to let others use the lake, under the right circumstances. There are possibilities for other ventures here, one involving the bottling of our pure spring water. They seem compatible with your ideas. I may not agree to everything you propose, but I am willing, conditionally, to look at a more detailed proposal. Email me."

The high-flying deal maker was back, looking a little less aggressive than when he had arrived. Sara barely noticed. Her mind was on the decision Tomson had just made, however tentative, and on what it meant for her. She had a hopeful prospect, a concrete project. A goal.

Jeff's presence flitted through her mind. Maybe with real work to do, she could tolerate his mood. Maybe she'd support him even better now because she had something positive to balance out the negative energy she often felt coming off of him. They might do more than just get through the business downturn and Jeff's injury.

If their problems were too deep, she'd find out soon enough. What was needed now was to deliver a workable plan to Tomson. Then she'd concentrate on how to get all of her life back on track to better times.

Before leaving, Tomson routinely handed her his card. He was several steps toward his car when she turned it over and saw a phone number written on the back.

She really smiled, for the first time in weeks.

"You sure it's worth the trouble?"

Greg Takarchuk, standing two steps above him on the front porch of Will's cabin near Portal, held out his hand, and Bill passed over keys attached to a miniature red aluminum flashlight that still worked.

Bill knew from experience that Greg was naturally skeptical and had a nose for inconsistencies. Both good qualities in their line of work. Greg could also be stubborn; but, then again, so could he.

"The judgment all around has been that Will missed a turn and crashed. Tox showed traces of oxycontin, but not enough to seriously incapacitate him. He also had a small plastic vial in his pants pocket with two more pills. I figured we ought to check his place for drugs. It's one thing if he was just a solo recreational user, and another if he's got a larger stash."

Greg had the door open. He had come along in case they did find something significant and he could back up any report Bill would make. Technically no one had the official lead, but for the moment Greg was deferring. That didn't mean he didn't have opinions, which he was glad to make clear.

"Unless he turns out to be a major dealer, we're just wasting time. You really think he could be a major dealer and us have no suspicions already? Will's name has never come up on any suspect lists. This place is away from town, but not all that isolated. There are neighbors not too far away. You said you called Drug Enforcement and got nothing, no reports of traffic to his place."

Bill got it. His reply came out more heated than he meant.

"You got something better to do, go do it. A dealer doesn't have to wait for users to come to him. So no car traffic doesn't mean much. You can wait out here if you want and I'll call you if I need you. But I'm going to look around."

While Greg thought, Bill took a look up and down the road behind them. Portal was about two miles back down the slight grade, and Coho Corner, where there was a Forest Service substation and where a web of hiking trails took off into the mountains, was another five miles farther on. Scattered homes had been built in both directions. A few hundred yards toward Coho, he recognized a business that sold hiking and skiing gear and rented snowmobiles. Snow was still on the ground in the shaded areas, melting in patches. There had been hardly any until February, then several big dumps and little since then.

Greg stood calmly waiting. Bill toned down the touchiness; Greg had intended no challenge. That was just the way he saw things, and let you know. For a guy who was blunt about work, he was also real close-mouthed about anything personal. In that respect, Bill valued Greg; they both handled personal affairs the same way.

They entered and ten minutes later exited the cabin. A quick walk-through showed they would find nothing interesting there. The place consisted of one room with a single bed, neatly made, and beside it a writing table with a single drawer that held a few notepads and pencils. A book about Burmese musical instruments sat on the edge of the table, next to a reading chair. An upright lamp in the room's corner had a long retractable cord so it could be used to light the chair, the desk, or the bed. A chest of drawers, pushed against the opposite wall, held about a week's worth of socks, underwear, and T-shirts, all white. A larger cabinet with double doors served as a closet for overalls, long-sleeved shirts (blue and gray), three plain sweatshirts, and a collection of shoes and boots. Hooks, fastened to the wall by the front door, held coats of various weights.

An open doorway led to a tiny kitchen with a table and one chair. Open shelves above a sink displayed a single set of dishes, a few glasses, and three small cooking pots, as well as an assortment of dry cereals and crackers. A tall, narrow refrigerator had two vertical doors. The freezer side was filled with vegetables, frozen chicken and fish, and the other side with juices and half-eaten meals in covered plastic containers.

Bill and Greg randomly examined the contents of the food containers, finding nothing out of the ordinary. The same was true in the tiny bathroom off the kitchen, where a medicine cabinet held aspirin and a few over-the-counter cold remedies. Just to be sure, they looked for loose floorboards and closely examined the ceiling. If Will Tomson was hiding anything, it was not in this cabin.

Greg's look said "I told you so", and he added a question to go with it.

"Had enough, or do you think the big stash is in a violin?"

Bill blew by that question.

"We're done here. Let's check the other building."

Outside, they approached a steel pre-fab building, its long, window-less side parallel to the main road. A satellite dish pointed south from the center of a peaked roof. The building's main entrance, a roll-up metal door about eight feet wide, was on one of the short ends, secured with a large padlock to which Bill had the key. Nothing on the outside of the building gave any hint as to its purpose.

Inside, a small pickup truck with a covered bed was parked at an angle to the right. Judging by canvas on the floor with a few oil splotches on it, the motorcycle had usually been parked to the left. Behind that space and against the wall was a mechanic's work table with a rack of vehicle tools above it. The tools were well-oiled and in immaculate order.

When Bill flipped a switch by the door, multiple florescent fixtures, hung from the ceiling, lit the entire interior. Past the parking area, the remaining two-thirds of the floor space was given over to making furniture and instruments. Floor-to-ceiling racks near the entrance held hardwoods of varying lengths and thicknesses. Another rack held flat cardboard boxes and wrapping materials for shipping. A partly-constructed violin, two wood flutes, and what may have been the beginnings of a mandolin lay separated from each other on a large work table. A narrow compartmentalized box running down the middle of the table held an array of woodworking hand tools. More such tools were on a rack behind a workbench along the wall. Along one wall were the only power tools: a drill press, a table saw with wood extensions on both sides, and a rotary saw.

Bill voiced an obvious conclusion.

"So this has to be Will's workshop."

How Will had sold his creations and turned artisan skill into profit was not so immediately clear. Bill hadn't found a computer in the cabin and was pretty sure there had to be one in the work area. Greg, already making a tour of drawers and cabinets, must have read his mind.

"Laptop, over here."

By then, Greg was on his hands and knees, peering under the cabinet.

"Satellite hookup and modem down here."

Greg rose, removed the laptop from the drawer, placed it on the adjoining workbench, extended a cable that he found coiled in the drawer, and fired up the computer.

Bill walked over to him, and the two of them watched the computer come alive without asking for a password. So far, despite his initial instincts to the contrary, it was looking as if Will Tomson's death was accidental. They would inspect the computer, but there would probably be nothing of significance in its files. That seemed even more likely when they saw that the files were not password-protected.

They found records of furniture sales: tables, chairs, and bookcases, mainly. The dates of construction and purchasers indicated that most had been made for the local market a few years ago. The longer wood stored near the entrance must have been untouched for at least five years. Most of Will's work over the last decade had been on musical instruments, mostly recorders, viols, and lutes.

Will had amassed an impressive clientele for his instruments, scattered through most of the big urban centers of the United States, Europe, and Asia. Most clients came from big US and European cities. But Tokyo, Hong Kong, and Sydney were also well represented. Each instrument order included detailed specifications, a summary of the construction timeline, and billing and payment information. Files were organized alphabetically according to the name of the purchaser.

As Bill clicked randomly through the instrument files, Greg was looking over his shoulder.

"Wait, go back."

Bill glanced up at him.

"Which one?"

"The client list."

When the list reappeared, Greg pointed.

"Mostly you have names with countries, see: Santiago Morales, Chile; Gunter Haas, Austria; Evgeny Morozov, Belarus. But look at this."

He pointed.

"Lago Familiar. Looks out of place. No country designation, and, if I remember the Spanish courses I once took, Lago Familiar means 'family lake'."

Bill opened the file and found a single notation: Work Log.

He looked at Greg.

"Any idea what that means?"

"Maybe."

Greg went back to the drawer that had held the computer and lifted out a cheap notebook, about six by nine inches with mottled gray covers. It consisted of page after page of hand-written, informal notations. Bill riffled through a few entries about progress on various projects, reminders Will wrote to himself, and accounts of problems and their solutions. Some entries were dated, most not. Three pages at the rear of the notebook looked different, consisting of several rows of number and letter combinations. The first combination was JC/L/4/14/99. About a hundred such combinations, all identical in length and format, were strung together over two dozen lines. There was no explanation of what they meant. On the following pages were three lists: one of instrument clients, a second of cities, and a third labeled "chests". That list contained entries like "Salmon", "Snake", "Eagle", and "Bison", followed by initials that might belong to individuals. The buyers? Unlike the instrument lists, no prices or recognizable names were given for the chests.

Greg already had his phone out and began to take pictures of the notebook pages.

"Just in case."

"Good. I was going to do that. Could be nothing, but we'll see."

A list of Native American events and dates was the only other entry in the notebook of possible interest: council meetings, potlatches, weddings and other celebrations, and a few visits to sweat lodges. Obviously, Will Tomson had contacts in the Native American communities.

He and Greg looked around a little more, until, by mutual agreement, they decided they'd found all they were going to find.

Greg left, and Bill stood alone looking back into the workshop. There was still nothing to suggest they weren't looking at an accidental death. But his instinct had a life of its own and it was asking questions again: was the information in the notebook only routine? And if not, how could he find out what it meant?

"Good facts. You've proved before that you can lay them out. But where's the message? The passion?"

Mac had started out modestly satisfied with Jeff's report on water rights. But that didn't last long. His hand was raised now, thumb and forefinger extended, forming the universal image of a gun. Jeff had lost count of how many times he'd seen that gesture. The finger gun rose until it aimed directly between his eyes.

"If we're going to get anywhere with Tomson's new water use proposal and you want to be included in its success, get with the program. Everyone's as informed as they want to be. Legislating is selling, and selling is passionate message."

Yeah. Yeah. Instead of using the elevator, Jeff had walked up the stairs for the first time in several months. That had been a mistake, and he was paying for it. He pasted what he hoped looked like sincerity on his face while he waited for the throbbing in his hip to subside.

"Okay. I'll fix it. But where are we going with this? Passion needs a destination."

Mac kept up the intensity.

"Tragedy dealt us unexpected opportunity. Grant is devastated about his brother's death. His assistant told me as much when we talked this morning. Grant wants to keep Will's memory alive. At the funeral this afternoon—which I'll attend—he's going to pledge a large gift to the Spirit of Diversity Foundation. He's also willing to get completely behind the pilot water use project at Tomson Lake, because Will wanted it to go forward. He won't say anything about that at the funeral, but we should move fast with our legislation. At the right time, he'll throw the public support of Tomson Enterprises behind us. Now that's passion, and that's what I want you to get into your next draft, which I need ASAP."

It was hard for Jeff to drum up the enthusiasm that Mac insisted on. If anything, his years of staffing congressional committees had diminished whatever passion he'd initially brought with him. Dumbed it down. He understood exactly what Mac had meant about legislation and selling. Facts and analysis could be used to sell anything. Advertising agencies had perfected that art, and political operatives had adapted their techniques wholesale. But an inner voice still talked to him about the difference between truth and massaged truth, and he'd never been able to shut up that voice completely.

So if he was to find passion, it would have to be in the words and deeds of Grant Tomson. What did he know about the man? That he was rich, self-made and, by the tabloid standards that now defined most news sources, opaque. And what exactly was involved in this pilot water rights project that Mac mentioned?

When Mac left him alone, he spent two hours surfing the net, and after that ran what he had learned across his brain, movie style, trying to distill further the passion of Grant Tomson.

Tomson, he concluded, had a public presence and a visible profile, but not a high-voltage one. The media generally called him a "businessman" or "prominent businessman", yet "prominent" read like a conventional throwaway term, added more for color than accuracy.

The man had started with modest real estate acquisitions, managed them well, and sold consistently for a profit. He began diversifying after the dot-com downturn, and was now part-owner of businesses throughout the greater Seattle sprawl: commercial construction, new energy development, investment management, smaller banks, food distribution, trucking, and even a high-end, on-call taxi service. After the 2008 downturn, he was among the early rebounders. Grant personally was not listed on any of the boards of his acquired businesses, but apparently he had named surrogates, board members with the designation "Representing Tomson Enterprises", to almost all of them.

He gave money to several causes in amounts that put him in the middle of the donor lists. There was no single cause for which he was chairman of a major fund drive or listed among lead donors. In the case of controversial causes like gay marriage, abortion, or the legalization of marijuana, he made small contributions, often to both sides, and had given money to both Democratic and Republican legislative candidates. His name appeared among a large group of businessmen supporting a new basketball stadium, but Jeff could not determine Grant's opinion about the controversy surrounding its location. His charitable work consisted of board service for one hospital and, for one term, with the United Way.

Personal details about Tomson were skimpy. Stock stories usually mentioned that he had ties to Swiftwater and that his family home was now a museum. It was common knowledge that he had had two marriages and no children. In the few pictures of him at current cultural and social events, different sleek, beautiful women stood decorously at his side.

As he worked through official business documents and media stories covering a decade, Jeff's image of Grant Tomson hovered near the dim popular image of Howard Hughes in his later years. True, Tomson was not a recluse the way Hughes had been; but, like Hughes, his ambition to be successful was matched by careful control of what he allowed the world to know about him.

There was one exception to that rule. Tomson was willing to emerge from behind the curtain whenever the Spirit of Diversity Foundation was mentioned. There were probably more pictures of him at SDF-related events than all his other activities combined.

Yet for all of Tomson's willingness to be publicly identified with SDF, Jeff could find little about the purposes and work of SDF itself.

That's where he would concentrate, then. Mac wanted passion, and Tomson seemed willing to demonstrate passion for SDF. Now he needed more information about that foundation.

One other thought occurred: Sara said she had contacted Grant Tomson again about the use of his family's lake property. She might have current information on how a new water use project tied in with Grant's plans, and how, if at all, the SDF was involved.

Maybe the subject was neutral enough to help clear the air between them.

MARCH 18, THURSDAY

Sara looked up from the desk to see Laura standing silently before her. It took a moment to distance herself from the financials she was studying and reach for the paper that Laura held out: three neat columns listing equipment that could be kept, sold, or junked.

"Looks good. We can go over the details later. Have a seat."

They were meeting in the office of Cascade Adventures, tucked away in a corner of the cavernous barn. All the lights were on, and flames danced in the glass-fronted gas fireplace, combating the gloom outside the windows. March's fickle weather today offered low-hanging clouds and drizzle; the forecast was for a possible return of freezing temperatures tomorrow.

While Laura pulled a chair over by the corner table and file cabinets that Jeff had dubbed "headquarters", Sara acknowledged again what a gem Laura was. She deserved some kind of a break, and Sara added that motivation to her own reasons for wanting a new version of Cascade Adventures to take shape and succeed.

"Maybe 'Cascade Adventures' should have a makeover, too. If we're going to go in a different direction, we need a name that points there. Did you find any interesting models for what we can become?"

"You'll see that a lot of companies offer multiple adventure options, some of them quite different, and let their clients choose which ones they like. Some also allow mixing and matching. But I didn't find anything like what you're proposing—a fully planned and integrated experience. I found no real competition in the Pacific Northwest, though one outfit in British Columbia came close."

Sara half listened, already scanning the document on the table in front of her.

Laura went on.

"I don't know about the name; but, yeah, I think it would be a good idea to have a new one. You know, announce it when we announce the integrated adventure packages. 'Integrated Adventure Tours' would be clumsy, but we need something that gives that message."

We? So Laura was still invested. That's good. But finding backing for their ideas was the game maker—or breaker.

"Go on thinking along those lines. Meanwhile, I've got good news. Real preliminary, but it could be a start, maybe of something big. I met Grant Tomson and laid out the idea of leasing their big house on the lake. He's agreed to take a look at a proposal. Still pending is what he will say after reading it. We won't know for a while, and, frankly, it's still a crapshoot. Best case, the dice are no longer loaded against us. That's not a whole lot, but it's what we've got and what we've got to run with."

She half expected some skepticism or disappointment, but Laura stayed attentive. She expanded her pitch.

"So you can see how important it is for us to a have a compelling presentation ready. As you flesh out the 'integrated experience' that will be the center of our new business, think of what you would say to a single client, someone who's heard it all from other recreational companies, but has money to spend if he likes what he reads or hears. Think, too, of the publicity package we need to put together—how much print, how much internet, what kinds of visuals. Check out infomercials, though I doubt they would reach our best prospects. But still, look at that possibility."

Laura didn't glance up from her notes, but Sara saw the shadow of a smile in the way her lips turned up at the edge. She knew that while Laura was an undergraduate, she had been a member of UW's crew. She had a momentary flash of Laura seated in a shell, methodically pulling her oar, ready to pull harder when the cox demanded more. Hiring that young woman was a lucky break she didn't intend to squander.

"While you're building ideas, I'll be doing the same with costs and financing, what might need to be done physically to the lodge, that kind of thing. I know a couple of VCs, one in Seattle and one in Silicon Valley, who won't finance our kind of venture, but might be willing to steer me to someone who could. I'd also like to run our ideas past Grant Tomson and keep him informed as we progress. Without his approval, we go nowhere. So give me your input on the preliminary proposal in five days and I'll put everything together. Meanwhile, I'll also get on Tomson's schedule."

She'd see Grant again, this time with her pitch and on her terms. Back into the big time, or, if not all the way there, dealing with someone from that world. She felt a familiar rush—equal parts anticipation, fear of failure, and adrenaline. She was ready again to show the world what she could accomplish.

Sara pretended to consult the paper in her hand, checking that everything was covered, but she looked mostly at the number on the rear of the business card clipped to the top of the page.

Tomson's private phone line.

The phone rang. At close to closing time, Bebe considered letting the call go to voice mail. On the fourth ring, she relented and lifted the handset.

"History House."

"Ms. Sorensen?"

She recognized the voice and lightened her tone.

"Officer McHugh?"

"Yes, hello. I was wondering..."

Throat clearing.

"...last time I came over around this time worked okay. Would it be all right to come by now?"

She felt caught. Time to go home. Curio, her ridgeback/pit bull mix companion, still might have to go to the vet. He hadn't been himself in the morning, listless, lacking his usual curiosity. She depended on him, her real security system. Any stranger approaching the house would hear his deep-chested bark and see his muscled fifty pounds and square-jawed snout.

"I was just closing up a little early."

He must have heard her hesitation.

"Well, in that case, I could come by another time. Let you know sooner."

Bebe regrouped, replying quickly.

"Is this a matter of urgency?"

"Depends how you define that. I'm still wondering if we took questions about Will Tomson's death far enough."

"And somehow I might help you with that?"

"Possibly. The inquiry is close to closing down. Pretty soon I won't be able to keep going with it officially. But there's another line of inquiry. A person with access to records about recent history could do it."

Curio was whining at the back of her brain while she mentally scanned other possibilities. She saw a small quaver in her free hand, a sure sign that some thought had made her nervous, and extreme nervousness could lead to...

She began cautiously.

"My dog is sick and I have to get home. If he doesn't have to go to the vet, we can talk there."

He responded similarly.

"Wouldn't want to intrude... or cause you any other problems..."

Had he guessed?

"... so it's your call. What I want to talk about can wait."

Although her brain felt frozen, her voice stated a decision.

"No, let's meet. I'll go home and check on my dog, and I'll call your cell if he's okay."

As it turned out, Curio was waiting for her at the door, tail up and wagging. If not completely well, he was at least well along the road to recovery. She could still get out of talking to Officer McHugh, though. Could she manage a conversation with him here, in her home? That would be a first, and not a small one either. Over the years, only a handful of people had entered her private space. Several had been workmen to fix something she couldn't do herself; and two were women with who came as close to being friends as her condition allowed. She had nothing against men. She would pick out the ones who attracted her on TV or in magazine pictures. But that was always quickly followed by a retreat to reality, to the combination of embarrassment and fear that accompanied the thought of having an actual man in too-close proximity.

She could try to pretend that McHugh was different, in that he would be in her house for an official reason—like a workman—and she could terminate a conversation whenever she wanted. But she knew that that self-deception wouldn't hold for long. Maybe, instead, she was encouraged by the fact that she had already spent time alone with McHugh without a panic attack. If she could repeat that experience in her guarded living space, then getting through would be proof that she was making progress in controlling her fears, in expanding that part of her life she could call normal.

She still wasn't sure why she decided to lay out tea service for two and call McHugh. Another five minutes, and she heard a knock on her front door.

She opened the door, instinctively took two steps back, and crossed her arms, calming herself with deep, slow breathing. Only then could she focus on McHugh rather than on the overwhelming realization that a large man stood in her doorway.

He wasn't wearing a uniform, instead jeans, a sweatshirt, and running shoes. He stood still, shoulders relaxed, palms at the side open to her, waiting for her to take the lead. Finally she could speak.

"Please come in."

She backed away, motioning him to a chair, and turned only when he sat down. From the kitchen she retrieved the hot teapot and an assortment of teas, returning them to the living area where she placed them on the low table in front of McHugh and took a seat opposite. The table wasn't much of a barrier, but it was something.

He fixed a cup of tea. She waited until the cup was moving toward his mouth before she leaned forward and quickly fixed hers. He kept the cup near his head as he looked around. Otherwise he was very still, even as he broke the silence.

"Nice place. Not what I expected."

The two women friends who had been here had said the same thing.

"How do you mean?"

"No antiques. Kinda modern."

She allowed a small smile.

"Just because I'm interested in the past doesn't mean that I have to live in it."

She didn't add her opinion that people who tried to live the past through dress or decoration might actually have a harder time understanding it than those who looked critically at evidence. The past was never as pretty as nostalgia depicted it.

He returned the smile.

"What I should have said is that I like what you've done here, simple and comfortable, nice peaceful feel."

That was exactly her opinion of the room and the whole house. If he understood that, could he understand other things? The important ones? She took a deep breath, hesitated, and then spoke.

"Thanks. That's not only what I want; it's also what I need. I think you might have guessed that I have a problem."

He registered no surprise, started a small gesture and let his hand fall back.

"You probably can't take crowds or people that crowd you. And you're not comfortable with heights. So what? Everyone has problems."

Those last words opened a relief valve. She could feel the pressure of fear let up. A few others in her life had said they understood and tried to help her. But no one had ever used those exact words—"everyone has problems"—and she realized how much she had wanted to hear them.

She could only muster a nod, hoping that was enough. He waited and when she was able, she continued.

"But you're here to talk about something else."

He leaned forward to pour more tea, and this time she didn't flinch.

"Will Tomson. As I said on the phone, I have nothing concrete to go on. But when I put together his death in an easily explainable accident with his possible involvement in the break-in at History House, I can't help wondering if those two things fit together. Trouble is, I don't have any idea about how or why."

"I understand what you're implying, but where do I fit in?"

"The accident scene and evidence collected won't be of any help. Depending on it alone, we'll never know if there is anything more. Everything about the accident is being treated as routine."

"So what then?"

"Okay … as far as we can tell, Will kept almost completely to himself. I visited his place. Everything there pointed to a solitary life, including his furniture and instrument business. But there was some information in a log book that didn't fit with other entries. That's why I thought that maybe something in the history of the house, the family, and its dealings with other people in the area might be worth another look."

He glanced at her apologetically before continuing.

"It's farfetched, I know; and it sounds like I'm making a judgment in an area that you know much better. I only have an idea. Maybe you'll think it's worth pursuing. If not, I understand, and I'll drop it."

Bebe felt the little prick of interest. A good hunt was a reward by itself.

"Farfetched ideas sometimes lead to surprising discoveries. Otherwise why would unexpected results be so surprising?"

She'd never been a schoolmarm, but she caught herself sounding like her imagination of one. She went on without waiting for his reaction.

"What I mean to say is that I'm willing to look further. I don't like loose ends either. Tell me what to look for."

His face relaxed, looking slightly amused. His hand dipped into a pocket and emerged with a folded paper.

"Okay, a different-looking entry in Will Tomson's workshop log might lead to other information. Most entries clearly recorded clients, locations and prices, probably for the musical instruments he made. But here is a blown-up print of a strange string of numbers and symbols that stood out. I'll send you a digital file of all the images. I have no idea whether they're important, or how to start interpreting them. Maybe you can find time to have a look, though I still think family history needs to be studied, too."

She glanced at the list, seeing nothing more than what McHugh had described. Her teacup was nearly empty, but she raised it and looked over the rim at him. His hands clasped and unclasped, tried to find a resting place on his knees, then moved again. They'd both run out of things to say, but she waited for him to make the first move. It didn't take long before he stood up.

"Let's stay in touch about what we find. I'll be using my own time for anything that has to do with Will Tomson, so please contact me on my cell or on my private email. I'll do the same, if you prefer. Thank you for your time and for the tea."

"Agreed."

She went to a small desk, wrote down her email address, and walked over to hand him the slip. It happened so fast that she didn't notice how close she had gotten to him.

She hadn't noticed!

MARCH 19, FRIDAY

"Okay, four o'clock at Bingo's. See you then, Roper, and the beer's on me."

When Bill started considering how to find out more about Will Tomson, Roper Martin had come immediately to mind. Roper wasn't his real first name. Matter of fact, Bill wasn't sure he'd ever known what that was. The nickname had been around forever. Roper had been the best roper in Eastern Washington, working horse farms and winning events for many years in the big annual rodeo. At sixty-four, he was past competing but still put in a yearly appearance and got to hear the crowd roar one more time at his demonstrations.

Roper's other main activity hadn't slowed down either, from what Bill had heard. He was one of those guys who enjoyed people, especially in gatherings where liquor flowed. He could get high more on conversation than alcohol, and he possessed what Bill imagined must be the largest circle of friends in Eastern Washington. Because Roper was strongly attached to his native heritage, a big part of that circle included Native Americans from multiple tribes and bands.

Bill switched his attention to the pump at the gas station and, as the pump dials spun, tried to organize the rest of the day. His thoughts, however, wouldn't leave Bebe Sorensen so easily. He remembered the feel of the living room—slate blue, moss green, and cushions that were, what... like dusty rose. Everything subdued, but not lifeless or somber. There were touches of vibrant color in a painting or a bowl, adding a little sparkle here and there. He liked it. He understood why a person with Sorensen's make-up would need it: a place to relax in, one that didn't require energy and didn't fuel it either. From time to time Bill had wanted something like that, but he didn't know how to put it together.

There was another surprise. In her work space, Sorensen exuded the seriousness of a prim bookworm and everything else that designation suggested: detachment, physical weakness, a world made up of old things. In dim light, she looked mid-forties, at least.

In her home she seemed a lot younger, more like late thirties. Her arms, covered at work, emerged and revealed the taut healthy skin of someone who kept in shape. He had caught a partial view of an exercise machine

71

in what was probably a second bedroom, and of a bike on a covered back porch. Someone who used that equipment would likely make use of the trails that began behind her fenced property, running into woods that climbed a foothill to the mountains beyond.

The gas handle snapped shut at full. Bill replaced the hose and drove east two exits on I-90, then forty minutes south until he was near the edge of the Yakama reservation. He could remember going to a ceremony about twenty years ago, when the tribe reclaimed the rightful spelling of its name, dropping the "Yakima" which now designated only a city and a river. Roper Martin had been a dancer in that ceremony.

As Bill pulled into the parking area, part gravel and part rain-soaked dirt this time of year, he saw Roper leaning against one of the pole up-rights of the porch in front of Bingo's Bar. The place hadn't changed much in a decade, only gotten shabbier. There weren't many of these old drinking places left. Roper hadn't changed much either, at least from the distance of the parking lot.

Up close, it was a different story.

The face lines were deeper and the hair was gray now, all vestiges of a once glossy black mane gone. The bow legs might have stayed the same, but a previously straight spine had given way to a curve and a list toward the left. The old smile hadn't aged though; it took Bill back to early September days past, when he himself had milled with the crowds at the big rodeo in Esterhill. It was one of the top ten, right up there with the Calgary Stampede. In those days he had been a sponge for all the macho swagger a teenager could soak up.

They entered a room that, if it were better maintained, might have been said to have "character". It was old enough for that designation, but everything looked as though it had been replaced piecemeal over the years. Nothing matched or added charm. Even the condiments on the tables seemed to have been thrown down at random.

Handshakes over, and beers in hand, Roper asked the obvious question.

"Great to see you, kid. Should call you officer, but you're still...you know. Been awhile. So why the call? Is this official?"

Bill hoped his smile answered better than words.

"Hardly. Been several places, doin' the job. Kinda lost touch. Good to see you."

Across the table Roper waited on a real answer. Bill, for a second, wondered if there was one. What he was about to say was bound to sound vague.

"I'm looking into something and just wrapping up details. You know Will Tomson?"

"The guy who died?"

Bill nodded. Roper thought for a minute before he replied.

"Sorry about that. He used to come to some tribal events. Stayed quiet, off by himself. He did talk to people some. Never could figure out why he came. But he never made trouble, wasn't one of those White guys who wanted to prove how tolerant he was."

"When was the last time you remember seeing him?"

"Would have been maybe a couple of months ago. I was having coffee with a few tribal friends and he came in, asked if he could join us. Talked more than I remembered at any other time."

"About what?"

"About the annual festival up at his family's property and whether we were going to be there. That's how he started. Most of us hadn't thought about it. We went or didn't, depending on whether we had other plans. Never decided until close to the time."

"That was it?"

"Just about. Except he asked whether his brother had been around. That was a surprise. I guess most of us knew he had a brother; but none of us could have told you his name or what he looked like, except maybe as a kid, if our visits to the festival went back far enough. Guess we didn't say anything."

Bill waited to see if that was all. Roper shook his head.

"Come to think of it, then he wanted to know whether his brother had been asking about the property or had contacted anyone in the tribe about the lake use. I think we all said no, but I remember that felt like a strange question."

"And?"

"And he left and I didn't think nothing about him or that conversation. Until now. What's this all about really? He die accidentally or ...?"

Bill had to make a choice. He liked Roper and thought he was trustworthy enough.

"I'd appreciate it if you would keep this to yourself, Roper. I'm the only one who thinks Will might have been a victim of more than an accident, and I don't have much to go on. You still get around to see your Indian friends?"

"Maybe not so much. But, yeah, some."

"Good. I don't want you to go out of your way, but if you do hear anything about Will's brother—his name is Grant, and he's a businessman from Seattle—could you give me a call?"

"And keep quiet while I'm doing it? This information about Grant Tomson? That got anything to do with Will's death? You started with Will and got to Grant, see what I mean?"

Bill returned his steady stare. Roper had always been smart, and not only about horses and bulls.

"I don't think it would help either one of us for me to speculate about anything."

Roper smiled.

"Okay, I get it. Not the first time I've been asked to keep a secret."

He waved to get the waitress' attention.

"Got time for another beer? Tell me more about the kid I knew who became a cop and now needs information for something he can't talk about. I assume you're paying."

⚜

Caught up on the reports he owed Mac Champlin., Jeff had a chance to look into the Spirit of Diversity Foundation and to find out why it was so important to Grant Tomson.

Since the Foundation was privately established, Jeff had not expected to discover much about it from official records. He found a legal filing to establish SDF, listing Tomson as president; his executive assistant, Peter Runyon, as treasurer; and one Aaron Elkhorn as executive director and secretary. Neither the foundation's assets, nor any reports of gifts made, were listed.

There were other ways, informal ones, to find out more. Rex Ingals had been a reporter for the Seattle Post-Intelligencer before it followed so many other newspapers into the bone heap of print journalism. But instead of joining other colleagues in an attempt to keep the PI alive as an online presence, Rex had landed a job with the Gates Foundation. When Rex was covering state politics in Olympia, Jeff had met him in passing. The two of them had gotten together for lunch from time to time. Jeff still had his cell phone number and, toward the end of the working day, punched it in.

Rex answered on the fourth ring.

"I was heading out the door and had to dredge my memory for who this guy Jeff Winters is before it finally dawned. What's up?"

"Losing your edge in the soft lap of non-profit, are you? Hello to you, too."

He heard an amiable grunt in reply.

Jeff could picture Rex: fifties, neat but casual dresser, peering over glasses perched on the end of his nose. Or maybe he wore suits now and had changed to contacts. No matter. It was Jeff's dime, so he went right on.

"I'm still doing legislative consulting, and right now we're looking at a resolution that would commend the work of the Spirit of Diversity Foundation. I know it's Grant Tomson's baby, and I know about his enterprises. But it's hard to get beyond the boilerplate in the registration documents. What's SDF really about, and would the guy I'm working for get egg on his face if he fronts a congratulatory resolution? While you're at it, what can you tell me about Aaron Elkhorn?"

Rex grumbled a reply.

"Sounds hardly worth the call, so there's probably something you're not telling me. But okay, I'll play along. I can't tell you much about SDF. So far it has spewed out a lot of do-gooder rhetoric, but not much else. It feels more like a shell corporation, something put together for purposes to be named later."

He stopped, paused, and started again.

"Elkhorn, on the other hand, I know something about. Smooth, Harvard-educated, law degree I think, still young and never been with a legal firm. Tomson seems to use another guy—Runyon, I believe—as his main managerial assistant and an Indian, Aaron Elkhorn, as a kind of roving, special projects man. Elkhorn knows how to dress up or down. He can play the tribal card or be establishment. Approachable enough, but you leave him realizing he hasn't given you anything. His kind of style is a good match for how SDF appears."

"From what I've heard, that would also make him a perfect counterpart to his boss."

"And you are amazed by that?"

"Hardly. The brilliance of your portrait merely prompts me to express it."

Rex chuckled.

"If you find out anything, you owe me more than a compliment."

"So you're thinking about going back to being a hack?"

"Could be, some day. Foundation work is like journalism. Information is golden. Never sure when you'll need to know what a player like Tomson and his minions are doing. I like to keep my information bank full, and expect you to make a deposit."

"And there's always that book that might need to be written."

Rex's moment of silence was like a glower.

"Anything more you want to waste my time with?"

"Only with a sign-off. Thanks until the next time."

He and Rex had from the beginning framed their conversation with barbed banter. Rex grumpily enjoyed that style as much as Jeff did, but he was serious about wanting information in return.

Jeff made a mental note. There'd be a price to pay if he forgot.

MARCH 20, SATURDAY

S ara was in full campaign mode. She had always managed her major projects that way: assessing the forces lined up against her, making a plan, then launching a quick strike before the opposition was ready. Her project now was to set up the new adventure business at Tomson Lake, and if Grant Tomson wasn't an enemy—not yet, and she didn't want to turn him into one—he was still the main obstacle she had to climb over, burrow under, or get around.

She had once been successful in everything she tried. Nothing got in her way. That was true when she was rising in the internal auditing department of the meteoric energy giant EmCor. But she couldn't turn a blind eye, as all others around her could, to the massively deceptive practices that had become the core of that enterprise. She wrote a memo to the CEO, who invited her to discuss it, then almost immediately fired her. If she'd kept her mouth shut, EmCor would have imploded anyway, crashing from industry darling to the scrap heap. But then she would have emerged without the rat-whistleblower reputation that shut all other corporate doors to her. She might still have achieved the financial and reputational status she had set as a goal.

A short stint at the Securities and Exchange Commission after 9/11didn't turn out to be the road back. Management was bureaucratic and incompetent, so she probably would have left regardless. But she didn't stick around long enough to find out. She left because she met Jeff, because they fell in love in the course of a dangerous venture, and because they decided, together, to leave the east coast behind and return west where they belonged.

Or thought they belonged. On one count they did, and probably always would: the natural environment—the mountains, the vistas, and the space—was home in a way that the constricted feel of eastern hills and forests never could be. Unfortunately, that had not turned out to be enough. Children might have helped them build their relationship on a different level, but that was not to be. When she learned those things, maybe she should have looked for other opportunities. But failure was not part of her nature.

All that mattered now was that she would be financially ruined if she couldn't get the business up and going. Maybe she should be more understanding of how Jeff was feeling. Maybe not. Jeff, with his laid-back attitude, couldn't be counted on to handle the business. That was up to her. Business first, then fix the personal problems.

That was the only way she could see to succeed. Fear and self-pity were personal storms, something to wait out and then overcome.

Seattle, next week. Dinner with Grant Tomson. She'd continue to hone her presentation, even though it was basically ready. But her clothes weren't; everything she used to wear in the corporate world was gone, and would have been out of style in any case. She'd leave early for Seattle, giving herself time to get a new dress. Something serious enough for business, but... feminine enough?

That image crossed her thoughts like a shadow. What message would it send? She shook her head, clearing it. Leave that distraction alone for now.

Getting the contract with Grant was priority number one.

Saturday afternoon was usually reserved for exercise, but Bebe had decided earlier in the week that if she were to make good on her promise to Bill McHugh, she needed uninterrupted time to concentrate. High school students whose history projects were due had been drifting in and out of History House throughout the morning.

Now the old house was quiet and the big room upstairs, empty and orderly, waited like a friendly companion, inviting her to stir it into service. Everything felt momentarily in balance—a fitting mood, she thought, on the official first day of spring. Obviously the weatherman had not gotten the message. Outside, clouds hung low and trees scraped against the side of the building in a gusting and shifting wind.

What Bill wanted her to do was a long shot. "Bill?" They hadn't said anything about lowering the formality level of their exchanges. But in her mind he had stopped being an alien presence named "Officer". Several days had passed and she still was unsure how to proceed. Only one way to find out: try a possible approach, then see where you are.

She knew the Tomson family file well, if not by heart. Nothing pertinent would be in the archives' largest sections that covered the house's donation to the Historical Society, inspection reports, and bulky legal filing documents. All of that was important, but not germane to her current task. Even the permission for Grant and Will Tomson to have unlimited visiting rights to the house was only a single sentence.

The most likely place to start would be with the personal files of Grace and Lawrence Tomson, the parents of Grant and Will. Actually, there was only one such file, and it mainly contained information about Grace. Lawrence might just as well not have existed. Bebe, however, knew a few things about him. He was a pharmacist who had grown up in Swiftwater and had never left the family home where she was now sitting. He dabbled successfully in real estate and the stock market. Adding those earnings to the family money accumulated in the heydays of the coal mines and railroads, he was able to retire in his mid-fifties.

There was also a thin file on family finances. Bebe pulled it out, rereading information she already knew. When Lawrence Tomson had died more than a decade ago, the value of his estate, exclusive of the house, was about two million dollars. All of those assets, largely stocks, had passed on to his wife, Grace, along with the house. In the finance file, Lawrence was more visible. He had written occasional summaries of family assets. On the margin of one of them, he had added a handwritten note expressing a wish that the house might be preserved and eventually be used for some kind of civic purpose in Swiftwater.

Ownership of the lake and its surrounding square mile of land was treated as a separate asset. In another note, Lawrence stated that its ownership, too, should pass to Grace. Should the sons pre-decease her, Lawrence hoped that, upon her death, the lake property would be returned to the Indian tribe from which it had been purchased early in the twentieth century. A copy of Lawrence's will was in the file, and she found that Lawrence's hope had been confirmed in legal instructions.

So if the sons died before Grace, the disposition of Tomson Lake was clear: the land would automatically revert to the tribe from which the family had acquired it ninety years ago. If they did not, Grace had an option of passing the lake property to her sons. She also could have chosen to bypass her sons and deed the land directly to the Indian tribe. What she decided could possibly have influenced her sons' actions toward her or toward each other. That deserved a deeper look.

From an article on the Tomson family, written when the house was given to the Historical Society, Bebe picked up a fact that rang a faint bell in her mind. Lawrence Tomson was described as a Methodist and Grace as an Evangelical, though both had become members of a Pentecostal congregation presided over by Pastor Leonid Kuzma. Bebe also had rec-ollection of a nasty dispute within that congregation that had involved Grace, before her husband died.

Pastor Kuzma was a member of the Historical Society. Even if he hadn't been a member, she would have known of him. When the father of policeman Greg Takarchuk had been killed a year and a half ago, Pastor Kuzma became a suspect. He was cleared, but not before the whole town learned his background as a Ukrainian immigrant and a former soldier in the Soviet invasion of Afghanistan. Curiously, the whole incident had strengthened rather than weakened the church's stature in the community.

She expected to have to wait until Monday or Tuesday to talk to the pastor, but tried his office anyway. She let the phone ring four times and was about to hang up when she heard the familiar accent of his voice.

"Good afternoon, this is Leonid Kuzma."

"Pastor Kuzma, this is Bebe Sorensen. I hope I'm not bothering you."

"Ah, Bebe, for you it is never a bother. But can you finally call me Leonid? Just because I'm a pastor, I hope you don't think of me as more distant than your other neighbors. What can I do for you?"

"I'm researching the Tomson family. Do you have five minutes?"

"You catch me as I am reviewing my sermon for tomorrow. I'm glad to leave my words at this moment, let them settle and then go back to them."

His turned slightly more serious.

"I'm not sure what you may want to know, and will withhold my curi-osity about why this matter occupies you on a Saturday afternoon."

"Thank you. I have documents about the Tomson family's decision to deed History House to the Society. But it is difficult to determine why the gift was made. The historian in me wants to know whether the motivation for the gift came from one of the pair more than the other."

Bebe knew that reason sounded thin, and the pastor's tone of voice told her that he knew, too. She had learned enough about his background in the USSR to understand why suspicion was deeply embedded in an oth-erwise remarkably tolerant and accepting individual.

"On that matter, I could guess it might have been Grace that decided on the gift. But I don't know. Why don't you tell me what you are really asking?"

She began carefully.

"Leonid, you've undoubtedly heard about Will Tomson's accidental death. Officially accidental, that is."

"Yes, I have heard about his unfortunate death. Yes, accidental, I have assumed. Now you invite me to assume otherwise? And of what consequence would it be to you?"

She took a deep breath.

"I'm informally collecting background information for someone who is looking into the causes of death. I would just as soon not say who. And I'm only seeking impressions from the past, not information or opinions that touch directly on an ongoing investigation."

She listened to white noise during a long pause.

"I trust you, Bebe, and for that reason alone I am willing to continue this conversation. Ask your questions and I will determine whether I can answer them."

She took another long, slow breath, thought a moment, and began.

"I've come across hints that Grace Tomson might have held some unusual religious views that could have influenced her relations with other people, for good or for bad. Difficult personal issues can be at the center of larger disputes."

Kuzma took time to reflect.

"I have no information that will help you resolve the last part of your statement, but I don't see any harm in clarifying Grace's religious views. We spent many hours discussing them."

"Please go on."

She heard a chair creak and could imagine Kuzma settling back.

"Grace came to Washington from a Missouri community, where her parents had joined a small church that, from what I later heard, was different in its theology from other churches in the area."

"In what ways?"

"After World War Two, a young returning veteran, a member of a church in another town, had a vision that he believed came from God. God, he said, wanted his fellow church members to use 'Inspired Conviction' as their main form of worship. God would give instructions to each of them, and it was each individual's duty then to pass on God's instructions to the rest of the congregation in the form of 'Shared Conviction'. His congregation rejected him, so the young man moved to Grace's town where he started a Church of Inspired Conviction, and that was the church Grace's parents joined."

"These events are important in understanding Grace?"

"I would say central. The new church never became large, but its members fiercely believed in it and followed their pastor's teachings. When Grace married Lawrence, moved to Swiftwater, and later joined our congregation, the methods and messages of her church in Missouri stayed very much with her. She waited a few months before she came to talk to me about it. When she did, her message was very clear: we, in our Pentecostal gathering, needed to become more like her Missouri church if we wanted to attain salvation."

"But you didn't change?"

"Not exactly as she wanted, no. But I personally and, I believe, others learned something positive from her: the need to make our understanding of God's word both individually and communally explicit. The more we put that understanding into words and the more we shared it, the stronger we could grow as a community of believers. That fit well with what our members desired us to be."

"But?"

"Yes, there was a but . . ."

Bebe pictured the pastor's momentary smile.

" . . . what Grace wanted was to take a wonderful idea and put it into a rigid order of worship. Almost, I thought, like changing quiet worship into a business meeting. Her ideas didn't fit our communal spirit. So she confronted members individually. She disrupted our regular worship more than once to plead her case. Almost to order it, really. Very authoritarian. I tried to keep her with us, but it didn't work. She left."

"And Lawrence?"

"Left also. Followed her out the door. Too bad, because we liked his affable and cooperative spirit. But he always followed her, never led."

"Thank you for all this. I've taken too much of your time."

"Not at all. It's good to hear your voice, and . . ."

A slight hesitation.

" . . . if I may say so, I hear a difference in it, as if you are trying something new for yourself. Whatever it is, I wish you the best, and especially happiness."

His intuitive assessment, she suddenly realized, matched what she was feeling, even if she hadn't yet put that into words.

MARCH 22, MONDAY

Calling Chief Tom Cisek blunt was about like calling a scalpel sharp. He had a glower to match, and when Bill explained why he had asked for a meeting, that glower was on full display.

"You've done all this on your own authority, and you're just getting around to telling me? I don't know exactly how you operated when you were in the Sheriff's office, but I doubt that kind of freelancing was allowed there."

Bill had awakened earlier to the full realization that he couldn't continue to leave Chief Cisek in the dark about his private investigation of Will Tomson's death.

It was one thing to examine the lead officer's report, or the coroner's conclusions, and look for holes that might be officially investigated further. It was another to launch what could be construed as a private investigation without getting the chief's approval. Revealing a private opinion to Bebe Sorensen might have been inappropriate, yet still allowable. But when he suggested that Bebe look at old documents, and when he asked Roper to keep his eyes and ears open, Bill had crossed a line. If anything went wrong, he would be reprimanded. Or worse.

The scowling soon-to-retire Chief of Police of Swiftwater and Portal had been in office for so many years that he was already being referred to as a legend. A legend who had grown in girth as well as reputation. But some things, Bill had been told, had always been there: Cisek's bare, functional office; the always-clean desk flanked by the US and Washington flags; and the same oak swivel chair that each year creaked more with age and with the increased weight on it. Bill had never heard the chair speak louder than now, as if it were underlining Cisek's words.

"Around here, we go by procedure not just because we like it, but because it's the best way of staying out of trouble."

"You're right. I went too far in speaking to Roper. I'll call him off and I'll stop further inquiry if that's what you want, even though I've still got a strong hunch that there's more to Will's death than we've found out."

Cisek leaned forward. The glower was receding, but not gone.

"You do that with Roper. But just in case your hunch could be solid, what do you think points to more than accidental death?"

"Some of it's just instinct, but there are also vague details. Those documents that got messed up at History House might point to Tomson family problems that could build up to a motive. That's one issue. Who made the mess is unclear. The presumption is that it was Will, but that presumption could be wrong. Thin, I know, but maybe worth following up. Also, Will had no history that we know of with alcohol or drugs. The traces of oxycontin in his blood were too slight to impair him, and the pills in his pocket could have been put there by someone else. And last, from what I saw in the interview files, there's an anomaly in what one of the neighbors *didn't* report."

"What anomaly?"

"Twice before, when a motorcycle came near his house late at night, we got a complaint about excessive noise from Charlie Temple. Temple made no report the night of Will's death, and he told the interviewers he heard nothing. But the rider would have had to ride by Charlie's house, which is built right up to the road, on a rise—I checked it—and a vintage BMW makes a lot of noise, especially on a climb. He would have heard that, and ought to have made another complaint. But he didn't."

Now Cisek sat back, a faint smile taking over.

"Aw, hell, Charlie Temple. Behind his back some people call him Shirley. Retired postman, drove all around here for years delivering mail. Always came back with stories. Closest person we had to a town gossip. Some of his stories turned out to be true, but he was never strong on verification. Rumors and facts were about the same to him. Lately his wife has become real sick, maybe terminally. Charlie's tired and nervous all the time. We didn't really have to, but we went through the motions of checking out his complaints. But with Charlie, a report of motorcycle noise could be just a case of his wanting attention. Does that answer your question?"

Bill had to admit that, if he had known what Cisek just told him, he might have come to the same conclusion. His face must have said as much, because Cisek's tone changed.

"Look, I'm still pissed off that you went beyond what you should have done without checking with me. But I know your record and hired you in part because, according to the Sheriff, your instincts turn out to be more right than wrong."

He paused.

"Tell you what. I'll ask Takarchuk to take the lead for one last look at the Tomson accident. If he doesn't come up with anything confirming your hunch, I'll let the accident finding stand. Okay? Meanwhile I've got some other cases for you, mostly routine, but they still gotta be looked after. Take care of them, and what you find out about the Tomson case on your own time is up to you. But report to me immediately if you come across anything significant."

"That's clear enough and it sounds fair to me."

Cisek picked up a sheet of paper from the credenza behind him and handed it over to Bill.

"Here's what I want you to look into right now."

Bill glanced at a short list: a reported vehicle theft, a report of domestic violence, possible shoplifting of tools at the hardware store. All seemingly routine.

"I've got a last physical therapy appointment mid-morning, but I can get a jump on these before then."

He stood, nodded at the Chief, and walked out.

Although he absolutely meant that he would call off Roper Martin and that any additional investigation on the Tomson case would have to be limited, he still held something back: he'd made no mention of Bebe Sorensen.

And why was that? Technically, he had not asked Bebe to investigate anything, just to look at the already existing documents of a family history. That distinction was cutting it pretty fine, he knew, and not everyone would see things the way he did.

Something else was at work, too. He didn't want to involve Bebe publicly, or expose her to pressures and hassles that would be difficult for her to handle. He respected and understood her need to live a life apart from those intrusions.

And there was still more. He felt a need to protect her from anyone else's heavy-handed oversight. If she needed supervision, he would do it informally. And, curiously, he realized that he didn't mind that prospect at all.

MARCH 23, TUESDAY

Jeff awoke alone in the king-size bed. Sara must have gotten up early for her run. They used to do that together. There'd also been times when they got in a quickie before the run and would laugh at the idea that there was no way they could finish five miles after *that*. But that was then, and this is now. He almost spoke out loud to a room that, in its emptiness, seemed to have gotten smaller.

He rose carefully, needing morning stretches before he could get his left side working. It was improving, but still far from what it had been. The other ache in him, though, had no easy path to relief. His accident and all that had followed had ruled out lovemaking. At some point, one or the other of them could have suggested baby steps that would lead them back to full pleasure. But neither of them did. He knew why he held back: there was a different feel to Sara, a frostiness perched on a lip of anger and impatience, no longer about specific things, but about their life in general.

Last evening he had tried to draw her out on what she knew about Grant Tomson's plans to change the water use at Tomson Lake, but she'd balked. Then he had tried again.

"I'd think you'd want to know about that, in case it affects the new project you're planning at the lake."

She had relented a bit.

"Grant said something about bottling water, but that it had no bearing on the project we're discussing. That was enough for me."

He'd tried to move toward some of the other things he was learning about Grant, but she'd turned impatient again and cut him off.

Putting those thoughts aside, he made the bed. After a solitary breakfast, he could move with less pain. An hour and a half after that, the PT specialist had finished with him, and Jeff could feel some lessening of the residual tightness. He'd go home now and work on two reports he'd take to Olympia tomorrow.

He had almost reached his car when he heard a voice call out.

"How's it going, Jeff?"

He turned to see Officer Bill McHugh heading his way. Jeff knew the media stories from over a year ago: McHugh had been severely injured in a confrontation with a killer up in the mountains, and had endured several

93

surgeries and lengthy physical therapy. They met when Jeff began his own PT and McHugh had dropped by the therapist's office for what he called his occasional "tune-ups".

Jeff wiggled his left leg in McHugh's direction.

"Getting there."

McHugh stopped in front of a coffee shop in the strip mall where the PT office was located.

"Just going to get a cup. Want one too?"

Why not? Soon Jeff was nursing a short latte, and McHugh a tall one, at a window table that looked directly at the grill of Jeff's five-year-old Xterra. Jeff got the conversation going.

"Time enough for morning coffee, huh? Calm around here, crime-wise, I'd guess."

McHugh's reply carried some gruffness.

"It takes something big for me to miss morning coffee. My next stop is the hardware store, and I'll get there soon enough."

Too late, Jeff saw how his opening might have sounded like criticism.

"Did I ever mention that you guys do a great job?"

They both took long sips. McHugh allowed a quick grin.

"I told myself that I'd learn to be less touchy. Thanks. So how are things going for you and your wife?"

It was Jeff's turn to wonder whether he needed to look for a second meaning. No reason, though, for McHugh to know about his personal problems.

"I'm getting more involved in Olympia, and Sara's tending to business."

McHugh responded with a curious look, quickly replaced by neutrality.

"Then what's new in Olympia that a small-town cop ought to know about?"

"Put that way, not much. Same old same old: politicians talking a lot to hear their own voices. Promises of the birth of giant new ideas. Long, contentious pregnancies and midgets to show for it. Meanwhile, behind the scenes, protection of the rich guys who got you there. And promotion of yourself, of course."

McHugh raised his paper cup.

"To cynicism."

Jeff tried a smile.

"Touché. Okay, that's about half of it. Blame it on my leg. There are some good men and women who try to get good things done—and occasionally succeed. But it's hard to win against a stacked deck."

McHugh nodded slowly and Jeff realized, again too late, that he was talking to a person who had met stacked decks all his life.

"But my work with Representative Mac Champlin has enough questions floating around that at least I can say I'm not bored."

"What kinds of questions?"

Was McHugh really interested? Or just filling time?

"You know, like any politician he always has a bucketful of things he claims he needs to handle. He's only interested in a few of them, but he has to say something about most of them. So the work I do for him is all over the map. A lot of what he wants done recently relates to Grant Tomson. I guess I pay special attention to that name because his brother's death makes me more conscious of it."

The way McHugh leaned forward without raising his head gave Jeff the impression that his interest level went up.

"Why Grant Tomson, would you say?"

"He's a player in many of the projects that are reshaping Seattle, like the new basketball stadium south of the city, and the way business interests and public spaces will be decided as downtown gets impacted by the new tunnel."

"That I can understand. Even our media out here pay attention to those big projects. But how about anything that connects back to Swiftwater?"

That was odd. Was McHugh interested because he was looking out for the fortunes of his city, or was he after something else? Jeff decided to give the cop more than the question called for, to see which way he would go.

"Tomson has a guy who works on legislative issues and keeps an eye on public reactions. He's part lobbyist for Tomson's interests and part PR guy. My boss has mentioned him: Aaron Elkhorn. Part Indian. Know him?"

McHugh looked up, nodded, his face betraying nothing.

"Know some of his family and have heard of him. Who hasn't? Local Indian makes good—big time. Is he especially involved in things that will make a difference to us up here in the mountains?"

"Hard to tell how much because I don't have many details. If there is a major project in the works around here, no one has told me what it looks like. All I know is that Mac has asked me to look into what he could do to help a constituent change the use of his water rights, if the constituent wanted to bottle part of his allotment. That kind of action is possible, though not easy. My guess is that Tomson is the constituent, and that the rights pertain to Tomson Lake. The lake is fed by a mountain stream and a large nearby spring. It's this spring that would be valuable for bottled water."

Jeff gave Bill a chance to absorb that information and got a nod in return. He waited another moment, deciding whether to reveal a hunch. Why not?

"I doubt that anyone like Tomson would go to the trouble of bottling water from the spring unless that venture's the tip of the iceberg. A larger venture could mean a hotel or condos, which in turn would mean road improvements, different land-use permits, and several types of economic and environmental assessments. Lots of work that couldn't be accomplished without lots of money. A major investment, in other words. And catnip for guys like Mac Champlin."

"You didn't mention negotiations with Indian tribes."

"No. Because that would not be something I would work on. But you're right."

"Anything else?"

Jeff hesitated, partly because he wondered if McHugh would really be interested, and partly because he would now be revealing even more speculative matters to someone he hardly knew. But the absence of those daily conversations he used to have with Sara had created a hole in his thinking, even a hole in his confidence to act on his conclusions. Back in the old days, in DC, he'd learned to deal with difficult issues by skirting them. Talking with Sara had made him more proactive. Her challenging questions had helped. Who knows, McHugh might give him useful feedback. He sure wasn't getting any from anyone else.

"Well, as long as I'm at it... I think it's likely that Grant Tomson has more than just pet projects in mind. Politics, maybe. Part of that guess comes from watching Mac Champlin. If there were such a thing as an opportunism Olympics, Mac would be a winner. He's also like the canary in the coal mine; he senses trouble early and runs from it. So when a guy like Mac gets cozy with Tomson and his plans, you can bet that Mac thinks they're for real."

"And you think some of what he's doing will involve the Swiftwater area?"

"I haven't heard enough on that to say for sure, but I hear Aaron Elkhorn has been going to the tribes and testing ideas to get their reactions. Of course there are tribes all over the state, but he might be talking to those around here."

McHugh sat back, swiveled his gaze out the window. He spoke as if he were sending a reminder to himself.

"Could be something interesting there. I'll keep it in mind."

They shook hands and went their separate ways. At home, Jeff found a note from Sara, cryptic, without greeting or tender words.

"Off to Seattle for a meeting. Probably back tomorrow, but could be longer. I'll let you know."

She didn't say whom she was meeting and, for the first time Jeff could remember, didn't tell him where she would be staying.

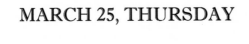

MARCH 25, THURSDAY

Sara checked her new dress in the hotel's full-length mirror, doing a pirouette so the gauzy pale-lavender pleats flared and settled again. The sales lady at Nordstrom had said it looked stunning on her, and a glance at the image in the mirror confirmed that she was right. Clothes for Sara had usually meant mountain gear, when it was not the business look of the day. She had rarely shopped the way a lot of women do; her mother had been the one who picked out her dress for the high school prom in Boulder. And anyway, Esterhill didn't provide much in the way of boutiques—simple, durable garb and a rancher look were more the style there.

The hotel phone rang, and she was informed that a gentleman was waiting for her in the lobby. Sara had chosen the Roosevelt as a compromise between trendy new boutique hotels and the stuffy elegance of the Four Seasons. The Roosevelt was old Seattle, but modernized enough to meet the needs of today's go-go high tech city.

Grant Tomson stood by the registration desk, his slim black suit a hat-tip to the old, and his open white shirt a statement of the new. They shook hands, but Sara was more conscious of how his eyes looked her over. Vigilant, acquisitive eyes. Used to singling out the best part of any offering. She wondered whether she should have stuck with a business look. As if he had read her mind, he spoke.

"Very nice. I like the color and it suits you well."

He was already motioning toward the door, beyond which she recognized his dark Audi at the curb. At a restaurant not far away, a valet parker was beside the door before the car stopped moving. At her suggestion, Grant ordered for both of them. She was positive that the food was excellent, though she tasted nothing—too nervous about the presentation she would be making. And about something else that she knew the shape of but didn't want to name.

When the second bottle of wine came, he jumped right into the business at hand.

"So what is it you're proposing?"

For a moment she relaxed, back in her element, encouraged by the wine. She took a bound presentation from a slim portfolio she'd brought along and opened it to a double-page summary graph. From then on she spoke from memory about building modernization, equipment needs, and projections of clients by type and time of year, all reflected in a rising revenue stream.

She might just as well have mailed him the printed presentation. He never looked at it, his eyes unwaveringly, disconcertingly, on her face the whole time.

She finished and neither of them moved. She needed desperately to regain some control.

"So in general, do you have a reaction?"

He smiled—a little.

"I never have general reactions. What you propose makes sense and is in line with the kind of partnership I'm looking for. I'm encouraged, but I'm also enjoying myself, so let's discuss this in depth later."

"Thank you. I'm gratified."

"You're welcome. Now we can get beyond the formal necessities. My city place isn't far from here. I'm told I have one of the premier views of the city. It'll be at its best with the full moon and clear sky we have tonight. With snow still on the Olympics, you'll see a panorama that's breathtaking."

Sara tried to keep a smile on her face. Inside she was in turmoil, part of her a block of ice, other parts cracking like a spring thaw. Ice in a raging river could tear up anything in its path. She knew that and still craved the cleansing feeling of that rush, the flirt with danger. She also heard a quieter voice that matter-of-factly told her of hurt to come, for her and, mostly, for Jeff. Poor Jeff. Down on his strength, his ambition, and his luck. It had been a good try the two of them had made, and they had had a gratifying share of good times. But things change. She and Jeff had changed. It was time to move on.

"I'd very much like to enjoy that view."

MARCH 26, FRIDAY

Bebe scanned her notes on the Tomson family history. Not much to show.

Six generations of Washington residence were inherited by the Tomson twins from their father's side. A mother from Missouri lived in Washington long enough to bear and raise them, but decided to return to her roots when her husband died. There were hints about unusual elements in her background, yet nothing definite enough to be worth further investigation, and especially nothing that could be linked to a possible crime after her death.

If anything, the family seemed unlikely to have been divided by passions of the kind that could lead to violence or murder. Quite the opposite. Donating their home to the Historical Society and allowing their lake to continue as the site of an annual Indian celebration spoke to generosity and public spiritedness.

Now she was wondering if it mattered at all—the time she had put in versus the meager results her effort showed. Only . . . something startlingly new had happened as she worked. It was as if a presence encouraged her, looked over her shoulder, in her solitary endeavor. She had always worked alone, yet this time she welcomed an imaginary presence that generated no negative vibrations, no disruption, no panic.

And that presence was very specifically Bill McHugh, a man who had been careful, official even, who had been scrupulous in maintaining his distance, never crowding her physically or verbally, letting her lead. She was glad when it had been time to update him on her progress.

His voice had felt like a wave of warmth that started at her feet and moved upward.

"McHugh."

"It's Bebe, to let you know what I'm finding."

"Great to hear from you. I was wondering how you were doing."

She heard, or thought she heard, warmth in those words and added some in her own as she summarized her meager results. Toward the end of her report, consciously concise, she heard papers rustling. Bill's voice gradually modulated to neutral.

"Well, thanks. Not much to go on. But I appreciate your work."

After a pause, she heard him speak again, back to warmth and adding a small apology.

"I really meant that—that I appreciate how you've tried to help. I thought of calling to tell you that my boss is not very enthusiastic about my spending any time on the Tomson case. So I'm loaded up with routine cases and am on a tight rein. My suggestion is that you wait before doing anything more..."

Then she heard another phone ring.

"...for now I'm alone and covering the phones. Gotta pick up the other one. I'll call you if there's anything new to indicate you should spend more time on Will Tomson."

With that, he was gone, and had stayed away since. Rationally, she knew there could be many acceptable explanations for his silence. There was no doubt, she chided herself, that she had let her expectations rise too rapidly.

That left one loose end which she would tie off, completing her investigation, such as it was. She had found out that Grace Tomson, in her last months, had become increasingly reliant on an assistant, Gretchen Cox. Bebe had placed a call to Cox's home phone in Missouri two days ago, but so far hadn't gotten a reply.

It looked as if "so far" was morphing into "forever" on all fronts.

Time to stop thinking she could be anyone other than who she had always been.

"Let me get this straight. You asked me to keep my eyes open and now you want me to shut them? Not listen and look around about what Grant Tomson and his slick new Indian, that Elkhorn guy, are up to?"

Bill could see that Roper Martin wasn't really mad, just playing with him. But there was an undertone of curiosity. If something juicy was going on, Roper wanted to know. Bill tried to broaden the smile he'd purposely brought into their conversation, even if a big grin was not natural on his face.

"Aw come on, Roper. I already told you and there's no more to it. The chief wants my attention on other things, and no one's sure that there's anything worth knowing, anyway. Like I told you, Greg Takarchuk might reach out to you from our department, but that depends on how busy he is."

"So I ain't deputized no more."

"Never were."

They'd run out of banter, but Bill didn't want to leave it there. Roper might be useful some other time.

"Could be, if you or Greg thinks that whatever Tomson or Elkhorn is doing would impact tribal relations with the state or the counties, then he might want to ask you to take a real close look. Any time things get tense, there's an increase in conflict between the people involved; and we wouldn't want things to go any further."

"You mean like bar fights?"

"You know what I mean—seeing White and Indian relations get worse. The next step would be lawsuits, lots of publicity, and a situation where all our lives get harder."

Roper stared at him, turned, and walked away, tossing his voice behind him.

"Later."

Well, that was done. Bill wasn't sure how Roper was feeling, but right now it didn't matter. He'd done what the chief wanted.

That left one more thing, and it felt harder. Bill stayed where he was, in Bingo's Bar, an untouched beer near his right fist, and gave it some thought.

Uncharacteristically, he had no idea how to act with Bebe Sorensen. No, actually, he knew exactly what he ought to do: just not call again. It was his style, the most direct way to finish what was no longer important to the job at hand. Or he could make one last call to confirm that there was nothing more to look for. But she already knew that.

Fact was, that call could be troubling for him. He would be able to get across what he needed to say about the Tomson family in a sentence or two. And then what? Then the question of whether they might see each other again would hang there between them. But why should they? Sure, he enjoyed her company, though he wasn't certain how she felt about him. Maybe—probably—she would be glad to be rid of the intrusion. She had built a private and protected life. She'd been cooperative and broken her own rules to help out with an investigation. If the investigation was finished, of course she'd want to reestablish the simple life that made her comfortable.

It would be best for him not to call. He didn't want her to feel pressured by the thought of his continuing to hang around. Not to call her would be the most humane thing to do.

Whatever the feeling was that was bothering him, it would probably pass if he left it alone long enough.

MARCH 27, SATURDAY

Waking late and alone in the king bed, Jeff gave in to his misery. What other choice did he have? He'd neglected the prescribed daily stretching and strengthening exercises during his last stint in Olympia, and was paying for it now. The last two nights back here over the pass yielded restless tossing and no real relaxation.

His injury now had an equally demanding partner: an inner voice that had risen in volume and insistently shouted for attention. Sara, Sara, Sara, it yelled. Things aren't right, man. Where had she been? What could she be thinking? She's changing or you're changing. Or both of you. And it's *never* going back. Get your head out of the sand. Think! Do something!

He'd tried for too long not to listen to that voice when it was smaller, less strident. Maybe things would be different now if he'd paid attention then. But that was no longer important. *This* moment was. *This* situation. Just paying attention wasn't enough. What could he *do?* Watch passively while life changed around him, and hope for the best? Fat chance that would do any good. Change? Himself? That he could do, or thought he could. But into what? Right now, here in this house that had once seemed so secure and right for both of them, he was no longer sure who he was, much less able to conceive who he should become.

They had met in the maelstrom of complicated times, a period of colliding events that had impacted each of them and thrown them together. They became casual, surprised lovers. They survived a dangerous encounter with a deluded and powerful man. Maybe it was only euphoria over their survival that encouraged both of them to quit their east coast jobs, drift for a while, and challenge each other on mountain trails and in Pacific waves before settling down. And what did settling down mean? An adventure company that succeeded mainly in keeping their adrenaline levels high.

Coming down from that high, he could see now, had been gradual. The first bump hadn't seemed like one at the time: their realization, after numerous and joyous attempts, that they could not have the children that both of them wanted. It hit him hard at first. He suggested adoption, then adjusted when Sara said no to that. He pressed her to find out how she truly felt—okay, maybe not enough, or in the wrong way. But he'd tried.

When she said she had come to terms with barrenness, he'd believed her. In retrospect, he shouldn't have.

In fact, throughout their relationship, any discussions they did have had focused mostly on what needed to be done. They were a good team: she the fearless, intense plunger and he the laid-back sidekick, ready with humorous caution and the willingness to pick up pieces, if necessary. That arrangement had worked so well that it never required much examination. And what examination did occur was almost always attached to the implementation of some project. Implementation, he realized, was their style of communication.

Well, that realization was a starting point. They had time now to fill in gaps in reflection and communication. It would be good to fill those gaps before their new project at Tomson Lake got too far down the track that Sara was constructing—or before he made any more commitments in Olympia.

He was trying to flesh out the bones of these new thoughts when a key rasped in the front door lock. Was she back?

"Sara?"

She must have heard, because he made out a low, indistinct reply. After that, he heard the staccato sound of her shoes on the stairs.

A moment later, the shower started. He listened as it went on for a long time. Longer than efficient, rapidly-moving Sara usually allowed herself.

Longer than he could ever remember it lasting before.

TWO WEEKS LATER

APRIL 12, MONDAY

Sara watched the sun flash its first light over the Noble firs. Brashly, it blotted out the pink penumbra that a moment ago had rimmed scattered clouds, and gave her a momentary sense that the meadow and the lake had receded into deeper shadow.

She had gotten up early to experience this moment on a hill by Tomson Lake. Plans for Best Fit Adventures—the cool name that Laura had come up with—were progressing, but were still confined to the stylized language of business plans and draft contracts for service providers. She wanted a birds-eye view of the place where things would happen, where she could summon up a visualization of the real activities of BFA. Then she might feel a sense of the old excitement and, with it, fresh ways to turn ideas and dry language into a vital, marketable product.

The dimensions of the lake and the locations of buildings were becoming clearer in the expanding light. However, Sara wasn't getting the rush she came here to experience. She greeted that realization with a combination of disappointment and anger. It was all those other, undetermined parts of her life that were getting in the way.

Yes, this was *her* project, no longer *our* project. Jeff didn't seem to object. In fact, he encouraged her to proceed, but in words unmoored from any apparent feeling, expressed as much in what he didn't say as in what he did. She might be reading him wrong; but, if so, he had taken no initiative to reopen their previous attempts at communication.

She'd left him at five am, still asleep. He'd always preferred to stay up later and sleep in longer. Over most of their marriage, they had developed a kind of easy compromise. Weekdays they used to be up early, while on weekends she would wake and wait for him to do the same. Now they attended separately to their schedules, tacitly recognizing that conversation would be awkward at best.

Ever since her return from Seattle, they seemed to have even less to discuss. He had his slow, dutiful attention to physical recovery and his work in Olympia. Regardless of whether he was out the door or at his desk in their home, she had come to think of him as always away. He probably thought the same of her, always buried in the details of reshaping her business. She had to admit that, for now, she welcomed the silence. She had enough else on her mind.

Grant Tomson was part of what was weighing her down. A major part—or, as she put it in her most analytical mode, two big parts of it. One aspect was purely business, and that was mostly in good shape. Not quite up to what she had hoped for, but encouraging. Grant supported a partnership that would merge his long-term plans for the Tomson lake property with initial steps that put Best Fit Adventures in the lead. He subjected her suggested plans to detailed criticism and constructive improvement. On those matters, they communicated frequently and easily. Grant endorsed the refurbishing of the family lodge and the more radical remodeling of the small cabin as first steps leading to major development down the road.

She only wished that he would be specific about the other part, about how her business could fit into his long-range plans. Would she and BFA continue as an independent operation? Was it his intent to buy her out and make her a partner in a new corporation? Or—she didn't like to think about this possibility—would he use her hard work and marketing to garner initial attention and then simply get rid of her when she was of no further use?

So far, there was nothing in their personal relationship that pointed to the last option. But neither was there anything that ruled it out. At first she'd felt guilty about how their first dinner together had ended. But Jeff's silence and withdrawal had tamped down the guilt to the point where she hardly felt it at all.

So, on the whole, she was satisfied that she'd experienced first the unlimited views from Grant's fortieth floor penthouse on Second Avenue, and then the practiced way he introduced her to his expert lovemaking. Everything about the man was expert, carefully chosen, honed to a relentless perfection. She hadn't expected anything less.

She imagined herself to be single again, in the business world, where she had regularly met men like Grant who were rich, worldly, and powerful—or aspired to be. This time she'd commit herself to the game. Let someone else blow the whistle if they wanted to face the consequences. She was under no illusion that she was the first to savor Grant's favors, but she yielded to him anyway, using him as much as he was using her. Thoughts about Jeff weren't entirely absent, but she found ways to slide past them, concentrating on the fact that he knew as well as she did that their relationship was crumbling. Thank God neither of them had to deal with the complications of children.

The lake and the lodge were by now in full sunshine. Sara tried to conjure up images of people arriving, parking their cars in hidden parking areas, sitting on Adirondack chairs facing the mountains, cavorting on a sinewy climbing route laid out among large rocks, or slinging skis over their shoulders. She could do that much visualization. But where was the excitement she had come here for?

That never quite materialized, no matter how hard she tried.

As Bebe made her usual early rounds of History House, the insistent sound of the telephone was an unwelcome intrusion. There was still half an hour until opening time. Local people should know that. Let it ring, she thought. But after two more rings, she gave in and lifted the receiver off the kitchen wall.

"History House. May I help you?"

For a moment she heard only an empty echo and was about to hang up when a hesitant female voice spoke.

"I was trying to reach a Ms. Sorensen."

"You've succeeded. This is Bebe Sorensen."

The voice continued, now carrying a note of apology.

"This is Gretchen Cox in Morrisville, Missouri. I'm returning your call of several weeks ago. It came in just after I left to help my mother in St. Louis, and I forgot to check for messages."

Ah, Gretchen Cox. Grace Tomson's longtime assistant. Bebe had almost forgotten she ever placed that call. She hadn't expected to learn anything significant from Cox, but she'd reached out, just in case. After Bill put the brakes on further investigation into the Tomson family, even that weak intention had faded.

"Thank you for calling back. At the time, I thought you might be able to help me fill in some details about the Tomson family, but the need has passed."

"Okay, then, I guess we don't need to talk. Except... except you've got my curiosity up. What kind of information were you looking for? I've heard that Will died."

"Yes he did. From an accident. I wanted to write an account for our historical records and it occurred to me that you might be able to fill in our rather sparse history of the Tomson family."

"Family history?"

In just those two words Bebe heard rising interest, along with a note of caution. She waited for more, and when Cox did not go on, her own curiosity spiked.

"I was interested in the relationships that Grace had with her sons. A few things I saw in our files here at the old Tomson house made me wonder if they weren't a bit tangled."

Cox paused, then spoke.

"'Tangled' about covers it."

"What do you mean ... ?"

Cox politely interrupted her.

"I'm sorry, but after Grace died I took a job with a local insurance company, and I'm calling you on my break. Maybe we can talk later, if you still want to."

She read off her cell phone number before hanging up. Bebe, repeating the number to herself, rushed back to her office where she jotted it on a scrap of paper.

Further inspection of the house was out of the question for today. Her mind was busy running her limited knowledge of the Tomson clan against Cox's enigmatic remark. Cox obviously had more to say. But did she herself want to find out more? The investigation was over. Will's death was officially an accident, and nothing that Cox said was likely to indicate otherwise. There was her curiosity, of course, but she was curious about a lot of things.

What she *wanted* to do was the harder question to answer. Any answer, she realized, took her back into contact with Officer McHugh. Should she run the idea by him before speaking to Cox again? Normally, that might not be necessary. But her involvement with the Will Tomson case had been a special circumstance, which was a roundabout way of saying that it involved her with a man she was now trying to forget. Go on talking to Cox and she was probably setting herself up for more faint hope, followed by its opposite.

On the other hand, suppose that what she had just heard was important? Should she ignore it just because her feelings might get hurt? Put that way, she knew where her duty lay. Duty, and the other fact—that despite any possible hurt, she really wanted to hear Bill's voice.

A few minutes remained before she had to unlock the front door. She used her cell phone and dialed a number she had not forgotten. He answered on the third ring.

"McHugh."

"It's Bebe Sorensen. I got a call back from a woman in Missouri about Grace Tomson. It might be something, or nothing. Thought you might want to know."

"I'm not able to respond to that information at this time."

An official tone encased his voice, and she realized that she had caught him in the middle of something. Or maybe he was just blowing her off, making sure that she got the message. Bebe was ready to end the conversation when he went on.

"Please name a time when I can pursue this matter with you."

"Five-thirty pm. I'll be home."

"I will try to reach you then, or slightly later."

So she had done her duty. The information about Cox might be of interest to Bill McHugh, but that was probably it. By the time they wrapped things up later today, it would really be all over.

Bill tried to concentrate on the details of the domestic argument that was being reconstructed for him. Each time the woman returned to the moment her boyfriend attacked her, the details in her account escalated; a chair he lifted in one version became a gun raised in the next telling. The boyfriend, in turn, sullenly upped his defense by changing a story of a woman headed to the kitchen to get a knife, to having her hold a knife "right by my eyes".

The case so far wasn't too bad, in some respects. This was a first call at this address and for this couple. The damage to one lamp, a chair and one wall was repairable. No blood had been drawn, though the man had angry red stripes across one cheek and an area around the woman's eye was already turning purple. Beer cans were everywhere and there might be hidden drugs. But this was not a drug case. It was just one more sad example of what jobless twenty-something drop-outs in a poor county had for a life, and there were all too many such examples.

A social worker would soon take over. Bill would file his report and add this address to an informal watch list. On the surface, the incident was manageable. The peace and daily life of the town was not threatened by it. But real damage lay in the scared eyes of the thin five-year-old boy who was hiding in the next room, and who answered questions only with movements of his head. What damage would stay on inside that boy? What hurtful influences had the child absorbed that would take years to emerge? Bill knew about all that; he'd been there.

The social worker arrived and Bill conferred with her. Most likely, since this was a first incident and there were no major injuries, counseling and a few visits to check on the boy would be mandated. Bill could put his own responsibility behind him, at least officially. This was no longer a police matter. Though, from what he saw, the police might be back to this house soon.

He left, already focusing on what came next, but the boy's eyes kept appearing in his thoughts—like other eyes he had seen, whose anguish occupied a permanent place deep inside.

It was an easy side-step from thoughts of anguish to thoughts about Bebe Sorensen. Anxiety was a daily part of her life, though Bill had never before met anyone with such personal burdens who bore them so matter-of-factly. It was that ability to cope—not just to survive, but actively to live a productive life—that he hadn't wanted to interfere with. That's why he hadn't called her. Better that she should maintain what she had than that he should become a disruption. At least, that what he'd told himself.

Then *she* called, and he faced unexpected nervous anticipation: he was looking forward to seeing her. That's the only way he could sum it up now, and he didn't know what it meant—not friendship yet, but maybe the potential for it. He'd once acknowledged that he wanted to protect Bebe. That was still true; but then, he also wanted to protect five-year-olds with hurt in their eyes.

He had obeyed Tom Cisek's request to leave Will Tomson's death alone. But that didn't mean he couldn't think about it. In preparation for talking with Bebe, he played over in his mind the last conversation he'd had on the subject, with Greg Takarchuk, about ten days ago. Greg had his own ideas about the Tomson case.

"Yeah, I looked around like the chief said, whatever that meant. Not that I was so busy I couldn't fit it in. But what was the big deal?"

"You're right, maybe nothing. But what did you get?"

"I talked again with Charlie Temple. That is, I asked him questions and tried to keep his answers on track. The guy's like a broken main wanting to pour out all his stories and opinions, whatever he thinks is important, no matter what you ask him. Hard to interview."

"Nothing, then."

"Not quite. I did get a look at his house and where his bedroom is. The bed's right up against a front window. He convinced me that he's always been a light sleeper and that sleeping is harder now because of his wife's condition. You and I know that a big, older BMW is a noisy bike. Charlie's reports of previous disturbances were full of detail, so I'm pretty sure that no bike passed Charlie's window that night. Unless, of course, he had a rare night of deep sleep, or maybe went to the bathroom at the exact time the bike passed. Both unlikely."

"Okay. Anything else?"

"I reviewed the accident report. It was routine. There was a partial examination by the ME that confirmed Tomson's head wound as the cause of death, exacerbated by exposure to cold. Time of death is consistent with that finding. Wood particles in the head wound were consistent with Tomson's body ramming into a tree."

Greg had paused.

"But ... and here's the only real hole I could find. If someone else was involved in Tomson's death, no effort was made to find evidence of their presence because there seemed to be no need to do that. The individuals who found the body walked around and obliterated any footprints. Snow after midnight also covered surface indentations. So there's no evidence that points to anyone other than Will Tomson being at the scene. But neither is there evidence to say with certainty that nobody else was present."

Bill had thanked Greg and left. He was sure now that with no additional evidence to go on, it was only a matter of time before the case was closed for good and whatever else may have happened out on those back roads would be lost to time. Maybe there still was evidence out there, just not at the scene of the accident. Maybe the information Bebe had could be the start.

At five pm he called her cell. Bebe answered cautiously.

"Yes?"

"This is Bill McHugh. Is this a good time to talk?"

"As good as any."

He was about to start what would have been a semi-official interview, or at least would sound like one, when, almost as if it had a mind of its own, he heard his voice take a different direction.

"Some matters are better dealt with face to face. Would it be inconvenient if I dropped by?"

The phone was silent, and he wondered whether they had been cut off. Finally she spoke, and he heard the protective cover of caution and indecision.

"All right, I guess."

"We can continue on the phone, if you…"

"Just come."

Bill lifted his tea cup, then returned it to the saucer on the table beside him. At almost six pm, the sun would still be up for another hour. It shone obliquely through the west window, illuminating one side of Bill's face more than the other.

Bebe had made tea. He'd liked that the last time, or said he did. Mostly, the act of boiling water and setting out cups gave her something to do, something to take her mind off of a combination of anticipation and lurking dread.

Apparently, Bill was unencumbered by emotions. His work face—or at least the half she could see well—was set to complete one more task in his daily routine. Neatly-combed black hair punctuated the formality of his posture, knees lined up, his back ramrod straight. He could have been just any police officer on official business, except for the fact that he had brought no hat into the house, and that his khaki uniform shirt was covered by a loose-fitting sweatshirt from the ski lodge up at the summit.

Bill's only real movement was occasionally to reach down and scratch Curio behind the ear. Her dog lay calmly by his leg.

The cup settled on the saucer without a sound. His words tiptoed as if around something fragile. She heard him in mid-sentence.

"… and apparently you learned something from a source that has a bearing on Will Tomson's death."

She forced herself into research mode, precisely trimming yards of information down to millimeters of significance.

"It would be up to you, officer, to decide its relevance, but in my opinion it is not much. Mrs. Tomson, in her last years, used an assistant, Gretchen Cox, whom I was able to contact briefly. When I told her about Will's death, she didn't exactly say she wasn't surprised. But she did reveal that the Tomson family relations were, in her words, 'tangled'. That's all I have, except that Cox left open the opportunity for me to call back, which I have not done."

There. She was done. They were done.

Bill started to reach for his tea cup but stopped, clasped his hands across his thighs, and leaned toward her.

"Tell me what you really think."

"I've told you all I know."

"I appreciate that you didn't begin with speculation. But I'm guessing that you have an intuitive conclusion to go along with those thin facts."

Bebe was surprised and, at the same time, noticed that some of her tension was seeping away. She considered what she might say and realized that the words were already there, just waiting to be spoken.

"All right. I'm not saying that my intuition, as you call it, necessarily says that somewhere in a complicated family history you will find a motivation for murder."

He was unfazed by her comment.

"I get that. But what does it say?"

"Putting together Gretchen Cox's comments with Pastor Kuzma's description of Mrs. Tomson's religious beliefs, I come up with a mother whose controlling presence may have been a disruptive influence in her sons' lives. That's not much. But it could, potentially, have produced strong negative reactions on the part of her sons, both to her and to each other. Those reactions might have resulted in violence."

She shrugged.

"Or, of course, they could also have been mild and had no effect at all."

Bill sat back and was quiet for a while. When he spoke again, all the official overtones were gone.

"I guess you're asking me whether you should follow up with Mrs. Grant's assistant, Cox?"

"She did leave the door open."

He went on, now thinking out loud.

"I've also got to make another follow-up decision. Grant Tomson has an assistant who's making the rounds of some of the tribes on Grant's behalf. There may be no connection at all, but it might not be a coincidence that Grant's brother died when Grant began to show increased interest in a family property. I thought I was done with puzzling over this case, but I guess it still bothers me. I think I should hear what Grant Tomson's assistant is willing to tell. Could you call Cox back and find out what else she knows? Both are likely dead ends, but I think we would both feel better if we found out for sure."

They would probably have to meet one more time. Despite her resolve, she could feel wings of hope testing a timid flutter as he stood to leave.

He took a step in her direction. She rose and he took another step.

His voice changed, deeper, just loud enough to cross the small space between them.

"Thanks for letting me come over. It was worth it ... "

He looked down, then at her. The sun lit both of his eyes now as the obsidian melted into something softer.

" ... and I think you look very nice."

Very nice? When he invited himself over, her first reaction had been to change into something more attractive, but she'd stayed in the clothes she had worn to work. She hadn't even run a comb through her hair.

And now he says she looks very nice? She was so wrapped up in that message that she didn't notice his big hand move to rest on her upper arm. She was taken aback, yet pleased. Momentarily afraid, too, then reassured by the absence of instant panic. She stood still, keeping her eyes on him, trying not to shake. A tremor went through her anyway, not fear, something else. He must have felt it, because instead of pulling away, he put his other hand on her free arm. No squeeze, just the light presence of a touch that felt more protective than threatening.

She thought they were both motionless until she realized that he had been leaning in, stopping before his body touched hers. For what seemed like eternity they stayed that way. She could feel a current like electricity closing the gap. Before she could react, he squeezed her arms gently and stepped back.

There was a smile on his face and there might be one on hers. He turned away and headed for the door, waving with a hand at the small of his back.

APRIL 13, TUESDAY

Mid-morning, and an hour after a solitary breakfast, Jeff finished his second set of leg raises on the Bowflex, dismounted, and wiped the sweat off his face. The exercise machine sat next to a Nautilus orbital and a small array of free weights. Along with a floor mat, that's all they needed to make a space-saving, efficient home gym in a corner of the barn. In the full-length mirror on the wall behind the equipment, his image—hunched forward, arms hanging down—was a picture of indecision.

Despite his new resolve to confront Sara with the questions that would not go away, he'd found an easy collection of excuses to procrastinate. Confrontation had never been his style. It felt awkward and uncomfortable, like trying to fit a right-hand shoe onto a left foot.

He'd always been called laid-back. Laid-back was an attitude in the air you breathed growing up near the California coast. It was what you lived as you biked your board to the break after school when the waves were up, and skipped school if there was a humongous swell in the morning.

In the waves, laid-back made it easier to become part of a closed group. But it wasn't enough for full acceptance. Surfing, like everything else, had a pecking order that began with skill but ultimately depended on aggression.

He had started with the disadvantage of a name that had "III" attached. At first he was "Turd"; then, as late-developing surfing skills moved him up in the pack, he became "Tres". He thought he'd finally arrived. But the most aggressive surfers told him the same joke over and over, that Tres stood for "vanish without a trace". One of those guys with whom he'd gotten mildly friendly explained it to him in surf Zen: he might be a dude *on* the waves but not *in* them.

Side by side, once in the break, he was as good as anyone. But waiting for the break in the swells, when he should have been grabbing the best position, he was a pushover. Lesser surfers took advantage of his skill in reading the waves and positioned themselves near enough to watch his moves. But they also shoved him aside or cut him off when a good wave arrived, knowing there would be no payback. It was easiest to float at the edges, grabbing the waves he got and not fighting for the ones he didn't.

He had carried that same attitude into work in DC. He'd learned the ropes of legislative work quickly and soon had a reputation as a competent and trustworthy aide. He'd advanced, but only so far. The top rungs belonged to the aggressive battlers who identified stars in the Congressional firmament and hitched their wagons to them. The top-rungers poached his information, knowing he didn't have the connections to take revenge, and that, too, had been all right with him. He met Sara; they left DC behind, she as point person and he as the rear guard. She plunged, he protected, and they built themselves a better life. A winning combination.

He shook himself out of his reverie. There was no point in remembering what he had been. He needed to discover what he should be now. He needed to figure out how—maybe even if—he could confront Sara. Laid-back had fit their relationship well for several years, matched by Sara's inclination to be the opposite. But, face it, just because a style had worked once didn't mean it would always work. It sure wasn't working now.

He still hadn't arrived at any decision when Sara walked in. She glanced at him.

"Getting back on the machines. Congratulations. Means you're making progress."

Before he could think of what to reply, Sara was in the middle of a set of leg raises.

She didn't look at him, though he knew that this particular exercise did not require the level of concentration that she was pretending. He couldn't help noticing how she'd lost weight, exhibiting a body that had always been trim but now was actually lean, showing defined muscles and sinews without any of the softer symmetry that had always attracted him.

When she finished her set, he spoke.

"We need to talk."

"Who needs to talk? I don't have time right now."

She was already picking up light free weights and beginning rapid squats.

As he had guessed, she would resist or run away from any direct approach. Indirect, then, and try for the hard stuff later.

"I know you're making plans with Grant Tomson about a venture at Tomson Lake, not that you've told me any details. But just in case you're talking about more than a simple rental or lease agreement like the one we worked up before, maybe there are some things about Grant that you ought to know."

She looked at him without revealing any level of interest. After two more reps she spoke impatiently.

"Don't just sit there. What is it?"

"Tomson's pushing for technical changes in his water use permit."

Exasperation showed.

"Tell me something I don't know."

"All right. Tomson has a mixed reputation: part business success, part humanitarian, and a big part shit. He uses people, steps all over them. I worry that he might be doing the same with you."

She dropped the weights and fully faced him, breathing hard.

"What proof do you have for that last part?"

"I hear the same information from various sources. Behind his public image, he's ruthless."

Sara continued to stare at him. Then she leaned over, picked up the weights and slowly positioned herself for a different exercise.

"Let me see. You have 'information' from people who did business with Grant. Your so-called concern doesn't extend to real facts, does it?"

A note of disappointment joined in. Or was that contempt he heard?

She dropped the weights and took a step forward. Anger replaced any remaining attempt at civility.

"This is the business world we're talking about. A world you don't understand and will never understand. You can't win in it without taking some people down. People who just aren't as good as you—and who then make up accusatory stories to cover their inadequacies. You have your 'information' and I have *facts* gained from knowing Grant and seeing how he really operates. If you get *facts* to the contrary, I'll listen. Otherwise, don't bother me with rumors."

The weights were moving again.

Jeff looked down, girding himself. What about communication or partnership? What about infidelity—too harsh? Okay, then, cheating? There, he'd used that word. But he still couldn't bring himself to speak it out loud.

He'd peered over the edge of the caldron and gotten a peek at Sara's bubbling fury. He didn't think he could endure a closer encounter with its crippling heat. When he looked up, he caught a glimpse of her back exiting the door. Fear had won out again.

Or had it? His body had cooled enough so that the now-accustomed fatigue and pain began to return. But, on reflection, he had more energy than two weeks ago. Not enough, but more; and less pain.

And he noticed another change, a new and fully unaccustomed one. He was mad. Maybe he faced a solitary and dreary future. But, on the wave of that future, he was not going to sit there and give up what he'd worked for.

This time, not without a fight.

Sara drove above the speed limit, not aware of any particular destination, just wanting to put distance between Jeff and herself. Before she knew it, she was on the interstate, with Swiftwater ahead. She was still in her running clothes, topped with a dull brown fleece jacket that didn't match. But who would care?

When the occasion merited, she could and would dress for success. There were lots of those occasions ahead, but not now. Now she was just getting away for a while to think, to regroup before making the final push to launch Best Fit Adventures. To leave Cascade Adventures behind and start fresh.

She pulled off at the south entrance to town and drove past the downtown businesses, older brick or wood buildings which, along with a few newer structures in the same style, tried unsuccessfully to keep alive the heyday of the railroad town of a hundred years ago.

Goddamn Jeff! He was part of her life and yet he wasn't. She knew they needed to talk. But each time she considered how to start, one look at the anguished-eyed shadow of the man she fell in love with would convince her that he was not even capable of conversation.

She passed the town's popular coffee shop, avoiding the parked cars that signaled a good-sized crowd inside. Not a place to be alone. Beside the bike shop was a new sandwich place she had visited once before. It had a few tables, and they weren't likely to be filled at mid-morning. She'd met the owner, a former successful businessman in Seattle who was now running the small establishment he'd always dreamed about. He'd decorated it with photos of the town in the old days, pieces of crockery, old window frames, all assembled into a harmonious whole that never slid into kitsch. The photographer in her awoke to interesting opportunities for still-lifes. But when was the last time she had used a camera?

As she entered, a young mother, babe in arms and toddler energetically circling, was getting ready to leave. Irrationally, another pang gripped her. Yes, there had been a time when she had pictured herself as that young mother, wanted to be her. But now a hardened inner voice squashed those images. Forget all that. It's not going to happen. Toughness, determination, the will to succeed. That's where you have to be.

And if succeeding meant being the moth to Grant Tomson's flame, well, that was just part of the deal. Plenty of people she knew traded sex for favors—a necessary exchange that could be altered as other opportunities arose. She herself had never adopted that attitude, even in the years before meeting Jeff when she'd played around. But it was high time she joined the big boys if she wanted to succeed, and she did. No illusions. Danger, yes, but also the possibility of a home run. She was ready.

The café door opened, and she saw Calla Bianchi on the porch. Calla's husband Phil, Swiftwater's mayor, lingered there long enough to give his wife a goodbye kiss, then left. Calla entered alone, now so obviously pregnant that Sara wondered whether she might have to assist a birth before she finished her coffee.

Calla recognized her and looked uncertainly at the four empty tables. Without thinking it through, Sara waved, her circular gesture signaling that she welcomed company. Actually she didn't, but it was too late to back away from the casual invitation.

Calla ordered a cappuccino while they exchanged pleasantries and Sara learned that the baby could arrive at any time. In a lull in the conversation, Calla looked at her with friendly concern.

"You seemed unhappy the last time we met. Did you decide to speak to the counselor I suggested?"

Ah, yeah. That again.

"Actually, I feel great. I've found a new project that is really going to challenge me."

She launched into details about the future of Best Fit Adventures. As she talked, she watched for some sign of enthusiasm or, at very least, of support from Calla, who listened intently, her eyes never wavering until Sara finished.

Suddenly, Sara realized that Calla was answering her comments with courteous skepticism. She quickly brought her account to an end and Calla nodded.

"That's quite a plateful. I hope it brings the satisfaction you're seeking."

Wow! How's that for passive aggressive? If I don't do it the way she suggests, she can't congratulate me on finding my own way, on my own terms. Okay, two can play.

"Very nice of you. I hope your baby comes soon and is healthy. Goodbye."

She got up and left without looking back.

APRIL 14, WEDNESDAY

"**D**o you think he's capable of violence?"

Bill watched Aaron Elkhorn's body language closely to help interpret the words that followed. But Elkhorn had the calm of a veteran poker player, despite the fact that Bill knew from an internet search that he was just shy of his twenty-eighth birthday. His smooth words were a perfect match for his demeanor.

"You're asking the wrong person. I've worked for Grant Tomson for less than six months. I've spent what might amount to one full working week in his presence. But your question prompts one from me. Why do you ask?"

The two of them sat in the far corner of the dining room of a winery/restaurant on the grounds of the nearby resort Heliopia, a ten-year-old up-scale enterprise that locals were hoping would deliver a big economic boost to the community. The recession was partly responsible for Heliopia's slow growth; also, it would take a while to fill up six thousand acres. Meanwhile, the site offered large tracts of undisturbed forest, intruded on only by roads along which future homes would someday sprout.

The winery, built with heavy dark beams, wasn't Bill's kind of place. Old mining tools were hung on the walls to make it look as if the place had been there for decades, although he knew it had opened less than a year ago. Its cavernous main room suggested a hungry beast in the shadows, waiting for its feast of dollars. Maybe there was more life here in the evening hours when the wine flowed, but Bill had no intention of returning to find out.

Right now, he was glad not to be crowded by the distractions of other people. Only two waiters came and went, setting up for the breakfast service that would begin in half an hour. Elkhorn got points for working in such an early meeting and for arranging the pot of coffee that sat on the table between them.

At first, Elkhorn had seemed reluctant to meet, until Bill played the common heritage card—something he rarely did, and almost always with a sour aftertaste. Bill was proud to be a Native American while acknowledging both the achievements and the tribulations that designation carried

135

with it. He felt comfortable within his cultural heritage but distrusted those who traded on that history for special favors and for excuses when they ran afoul of the law. He hadn't asked Elkhorn for anything yet except for this meeting, and he didn't want to start down a slippery slope, having one favor turn into more favors until you don't realize how fast you're sliding.

Bill assessed the man opposite him before answering. Tall, slim, perfectly if not expensively dressed with dark slacks, a brown shirt open at the neck, and hiking boots. A zippered outdoor jacket over the back of his chair added another northwest touch. All in all, Elkhorn looked just right for a weekend conference featuring seminars and long breaks for golf.

Bill hadn't forgotten the short leash that Chief Cisek had attached. But, hell, he was already partway over the falls.

"In answer to your question: there was an accident, the death of Grant's brother Will. The accident might have been more than it seemed. Before you ask further, I will admit we do not have proof that a crime occurred. We only have hunches and coincidence. I'm just checking possible leads to be sure."

"And you consider me a lead?"

"No. Not any more than I consider you a confidential source. I realize that you have the option of reporting this conversation back to your boss."

Bill paused.

"I thought you'd have an interest in getting to the bottom of anything that could be damaging to other concerns you might have. See, I'm not officially involved in the investigation, but people with common interests can help each other out. Maybe you have a perspective that could point in the direction of possible leads."

The common heritage card, face down, now occupied a center space on the table. Bill just wasn't sure whether Elkhorn could see it.

Elkhorn looked away before he answered.

"It would help if you gave me something more specific to work from. Grant has widespread interests, and I do a lot of things for him."

"Such as?"

"In-depth checking on possible acquisitions and potential business partners, for instance. It's one thing to check legal records, even use a private investigator on personal financial histories, but entirely another to meet people face to face."

"Any special reason he's using an Indian to do that work instead of someone else?"

Time to stop the sparring. Elkhorn might have thought the same. After a glance at his watch, he put his coffee cup down and left his arm resting on the table. His face was that much closer, and Bill could see how acne had left his cheeks with slight scars. His dark eyes made a small shift from inscrutable to challenging.

"Tell you what. You show me yours and I'll think about showing you mine."

Bill held his stare and began again, giving Elkhorn a chance to decide how far to take this conversation.

"How's this? Grant Tomson has plans for the Tomson Lake property. You probably know details I don't. The property was formerly tribal and the Tomson family, particularly the mother, invited tribes to a powwow every year. She also wasn't too strict about who came to fish the lake and when. There's some incomplete evidence that one of the Tomson twins had differences of opinion with their mother, maybe over the future of the lake property. Maybe over something else. Depending on who was disputing who and about what, tempers could have gotten out of control, and . . . "

There was no mistaking the new interest in Elkhorn's eyes and in the way he sat up straighter as he spoke.

"Are you the only person collecting information on that issue?"

The cautious side of Elkhorn had returned, as Bill continued.

"Someone else is also working on it informally, doing research."

Elkhorn sat back and looked across the nearly vacant dining space as if, Bill guessed, he was looking for the limits of what he could say. Finally his attention returned to their conversation.

"I can give you this much, and it's only for you. Frankly, I'm not sure people on the outside would make much of it, even get it. As to how important my responsibilities are to Grant, I can't say. He runs a very compartmentalized shop. He knows everything but keeps all his help in separate boxes. That way everything has to go through him."

Bill waited. Elkhorn surprised him with his first smile—more like a grin, really, the kind that people use with each other before making a comment they would ordinarily not make in public.

"I'm supposed to inform Grant about possible Indian reactions to his business ideas. As if an 'Indian reaction' existed! You and I know . . . "

The brotherly ethnic card lay face up now.

"... there's no such thing. There are lots of individual opinions, different tribal views and, for sure, often differences between what the tribal councils see and what the individual tribal members want. Differences that are hidden from outsiders as much as possible."

Elkhorn was right that no explanation on that score was necessary, so Bill just nodded encouragement.

"My impression is that Tomson likes the councils—that they think bigger and longer term about tribal benefits. And there are council members who don't mind looking at what they personally will get out of any deal."

A questioning look from Elkhorn, and another nod from Bill. Sure, he's seen that kind of behavior plenty of times.

"Grant Tomson has a special interest in what happens at the lake. He's never said that in so many words, but I can tell by the way he keeps bringing it up."

"What can you tell me about the plans?"

"Not much, and that has been a problem for me. Tomson wants feedback about those plans, but won't give me specifics that could sharpen my investigations. That's part of his compartmentalization technique. Very inefficient, but that's the way he wants it."

"Understood. Has he ever mentioned anything about his family's interests in the lake project? You know, any potential conflicts within the family or potentially with the tribes?"

Elkhorn shook his head, a hint of caution entering his eyes.

"No mention of anything like that. But look, your question comes close to crossing a line. I was in law school for two years before I decided to switch to an MBA, and I got part-time work with tribal councils at the same time, some of it dealing with legal issues. There are tribal people who think I'm a lawyer, partly because Tomson occasionally introduces me as his 'Indian lawyer'. We've never really talked about the nature of our legal relationship, but I've erred on the side of maintaining an informal attorney-client privilege. Regardless, I lean toward discretion as good policy."

"Okay. I understand the line you're talking about. It's your call."

They were back in a more awkward formal face-off mode, and Bill was sorry to note the change. He shifted in his seat, pointing at the clutch of other people who entered as the restaurant doors were opened.

"That's it for now. Again, thanks for your cooperation."

He started to rise and Elkhorn motioned him back down.

"I can tell you this. Grant treats the lake project differently from all the rest of his projects. He's more personal about it—not, it seems to me, because he likes it more, but maybe because he wants to prove something. Don't ask me what, because I don't know. There. My memory bank is empty."

That wasn't a lawyer talking. Bill thanked him again, and then left the table.

Beyond the restaurant, the winery's lounge area was filled with over-stuffed furniture covered in new but purposely faded period fabrics. The view out the window was genuinely a reminder of what changed and what didn't. A large hill, built from tailings of Portal's last coal mine, dominated the foreground. Behind it rose a ridge that had been a familiar hunting and fishing ground for his ancestors long before the Tomson family purchased a lake. Unexpectedly, he found himself wondering how Bebe would react to the view in front of him, and what they would be talking about. That was something new!

He felt a movement of air and glanced over to see Elkhorn standing by him. They watched the scene change while advancing sunshine washed brightness across it. Elkhorn spoke. His voice was soft, and in it Bill heard for the first time the submerged lilting cadences of their common background.

"I love the land around here. Someday I want to do things to preserve and restore it. Right now I'm learning, and a man like Tomson is worth studying. I'm not with him to become like him."

Bill let silence be his answer. In their culture, silence could mean a lot of things, agreement being one. Elkhorn dropped his voice further.

"Tomson's teaching me a lot about how the business world works. That's why I hooked up with him. But I'm less sure about his real motives for cozying up to the tribes. I've got real limits there and I'm watching him closely in that regard."

Elkhorn moved to leave. No handshake. Their eyes met in silent understanding about something deeper than a common social gesture.

APRIL 15, THURSDAY

Jeff looked out the window and through his open office door in Olympia at scenes that were at once familiar and wholly new. Ample lawns and spring flowers, early this year because of a spate of warmer weather. Varied rhododendrons welcoming a brilliant cloudless day. Carpe diem was good advice, though. Tomorrow could bring rain, and a late snowstorm was not unheard of this time of year.

Down the hallway, the weather had no effect. In fact, a snapshot of what he saw would not, by itself, identify its location. It could be a hall in any of the US Senate and House office buildings in DC. Or the legislative houses in Saint Paul, Salem, or Pierre, for that matter. Doors down the side, aides in a hurry to get out and go home, or at least to get a meal before returning to prepare for the evening session. He'd been in a lot of these halls and could vouch that they all smelled the same too, infused with palpable energy and invaded by an invisible pall of acrid disagreement.

Anonymous or not, the particular hallway before him had a different feel today. He had something important to investigate within it: the real reasons behind Grant Tomson's desire to amend his water allotment at Tomson Lake. Though the mechanics of the task might be familiar, his motivation and the consequences were getting personal. Sara was affected and, probably for that reason, he felt his dislike of Grant Tomson growing. His job now was to get beyond that feeling and use impersonally the skills he'd developed over the years.

He already knew the broad outlines of the task. Washington DC, Olympia, and other such places were two-faced, permanently schizophrenic, both public and private at the same time. Yes, the public business got done and even—once in a while—there were aspects of that business that deserved the label "public service". The other face, the one that everyone conspired to keep shadowed, was every bit as real and alive. The state capitol was also an auction house for private interests, including those of the state's duly elected and appointed representatives. In that house, special advantages were up for silent bidding. And advantage almost always meant money.

The money in that auction house was tracked as precisely as transactions on Wall Street. But whereas the Street eventually was forced to make most of its transactions public and transparent, the government auction house worked to keep private transactions away from public knowledge by disguising them as acts of public service. So a bill that trumpeted new public housing in Western Washington could also hide clauses that would help a developer in the eastern part of the state avoid costly environmental impact studies. This developer could make a bundle of money and, at the same time, help collaborating legislators gain credit for the appearance of a civic gift to the poor of Western Washington.

All right, most legislative work was routine, not sinister. But the routine provided cover for those secret deals. Not so secret, however, if you knew where to look, where to go, where the tracking took place.

In DC, when he'd first gotten started on The Hill, the places to look were bars with specific clientele. You went to one if you wanted to meet Democrats, another for Republicans. There were bars where lobbyists congregated, and several favorite haunts for journalists. That's where the dealings of the auction house were discussed in hushed allusions that only the in-group would understand. Say K Street, and you didn't mean one of DC's important urban corridors; you meant the lobby shops and think tanks that had been put in place there in order to further particular agendas, allocate power, and line pocketbooks.

Olympia was a smaller city and there were fewer hangouts. Their number had actually declined in recent years—not because the auction house was less busy, but because Twitter and texting made face-to-face encounters less necessary. Still, new technology didn't give you a chance to show off your cynical smile or to watch the expression on someone's face change when you told her something she didn't already know.

Rick's Dock was a hangout that had survived in Olympia and still drew regulars from the Capitol crowd. Jeff actually liked its food and atmosphere and, on infrequent visits, had overheard parts of conversations that confirmed how active this annex of the auction house remained. He decided to go there now.

During happy hour, Rick's was doing good business. The tables in front of the long water-view window were full, but not with the people he was looking for. They preferred the dimmer light of booths and tables by the windowless walls near the entrance, below mounted game fish in various action poses. At the bar, where he stared at a mural of fishing boats in a rough sea, Jeff ordered a beer and nursed it. Two seats away sat his target, an aide he knew in passing: first name Page ... Bentley. That was it. Been around a while. Not far up any ladder, but one of those useful bottom feeders that were a necessary part of any political operation. The Bentleys of the world scooped up and digested information that they could sell later for favors and job security.

After waiting a minute or two, Jeff moved over one stool.

"Page, how's it shakin'? Jeff Winter."

Bentley looked him over carefully, gauging his potential, flashing an automatic smile.

"How's it goin' with you, Jeff? Surviving the final sprint to the end of the session?"

"Doing okay, except for one little problem."

Bentley perked up, adding a sympathetic look that encouraged more.

"Yeah, I know the feeling. What's up?"

"Just trying to find out how a particular developer's plans might impact S-123, you know, that omnibus bill on environmental protection."

"Maybe I can help. You know my guy does a lot in that area. Who are you looking at?"

Jeff stared at Bentley, then looked away and looked at him again before lifting his beer and taking a swallow. He hoped he wasn't laying it on too thick.

Bentley hitched his stool closer.

"C'mon. It's just you and me here. Who's the developer?"

"Grant Tomson."

"Sure, he's a well-known player. But what plans?"

"Up at the lake property his family owns. Know it?"

"Tomson Lake? Yeah, I know it. Go on."

"Well, as you know, the Boldt decision in 1974 reaffirmed Native American fishing rights that had been violated over time. Later Congress added reparations, including dollars to reconsolidate land that was repurchased so that it could be administered by the tribes, as originally intended in the treaties. You with me so far?"

Bentley waved airily.

"I knew most of that. But thanks for the reminder."

From what he had heard about Page's entirely political approach to legislation, trading horses even when he didn't own them, Jeff doubted the response. But then he hadn't expected anything different. He'd upped the level of detail to give his words the feel of authenticity. That way, what followed later was less likely to be questioned.

"Okay, so we now have a situation that's playing out gradually in the implementation of the 2010 appropriation. Our new governor wants to be sure that she shows quick results of the implementation in Washington State. You've probably seen that S-103 includes supplementary funds for the state AG to assist the tribes in reacquiring and consolidating original tribal lands."

"I'm up on all that. So what's your problem?"

Jeff added an expression that he hoped looked conflicted.

"Good question. The guy I work for thinks he has no problem, but wants to be sure before taking anything further. And that's where Grant Tomson comes in."

"Explain."

"Here's one possibility. The Tomson family's water rights specify that a certain amount of water must pass through the lake so further down-stream it's available for public use. There's some indication that Grant may be looking into a change, maybe to bottle water and maybe to re-duce the flow-through. That would be legal if he gets permission from the Department of Ecology. No problem with that. But municipalities or tribes downstream might not be happy with such a change. My guy doesn't want to be connected with an outcome in which he might be accused of not having protected the rights of interested parties to have a say in the matter."

"So he might be worried about the consequences of a last-minute rider?"

"You got it."

Jeff didn't miss the calculating gleam in Page's eyes.

"I may have something for you. But first, your word that you'll keep me informed how this deal plays out. My guy's got skin in the game, too. Wouldn't want him to be vulnerable either."

Jeff didn't care about Bentley's "guy". His willingness to deal was all that mattered. But he tried to look mildly shocked.

"You'd expect anything different? Look, you're going out of your way to help me. Of course I'll keep you in the loop. You didn't need to ask."

Bentley slipped for a second, allowing a smug smile that Jeff might have missed if he hadn't been looking for it. He waited until Bentley, after a somewhat theatrical look over his shoulder, leaned in.

"On the far left as you face the back wall there's a man alone at a two-seater. Mike Zerbe. He works on quotas and licensing. No one knows more about this water rights stuff than he does. Prickly guy. Better catch him before his second beer or he'll never talk to you. Don't mention me. We have a history. And don't forget your promise."

Jeff laid a fiver on the bar, pivoted away and began a slow circular stroll around the outside of the room until he stood over Zerbe. He leaned down.

"Mike Zerbe?"

Zerbe glared up at him with armored hostility.

"Not here, I'm not. You want to talk to me, I have an office and office hours."

"I do apologize, Mike. I'm Jeff Winter, and as a legislative aide I know exactly what you mean. I work for Mac Champlin and I've got a deadline. See, my work is mainly on the other side of the mountain, and I have just one question."

The glare did not change, but Zerbe waved at the seat opposite and shifted his gaze out the window. Jeff took the seat and went directly to the point.

"Have you heard anything about Tomson Lake wanting to change the use of its water allotment?"

Zerbe rolled his neck back toward the table and looked directly at Jeff. Most of the glare was gone. Two minutes later, Jeff had the confirmation he needed. He thanked Zerbe and headed directly to the exit.

He glanced toward Page Bentley, who had been tracking his progress. Jeff nodded, and Page lifted his drink off the bar a few inches.

He'd done what he could. Now to see if his act would produce a full play.

APRIL 17, SATURDAY

Grant could have been a rigid statue, his eyes twin inset LEDs, almost too glaring to look at. Not even a greeting. One extended hand pointed at her accusingly, the thumb and one finger pinching the corner of a single sheet of paper. A breeze from an open window made the paper move, adding emphasis to his congealed fury.

Yesterday, Sara got a curt call from him that he wanted to see her. Now they were meeting on a Saturday morning in the large living room of the lodge at Tomson Lake, allegedly to discuss renovation plans. If the rest of the house was like the living room, she'd have to raise her estimate of necessary changes. The place was sizable but disused in the way that any place left alone for long periods becomes. The sight and smell of dust accentuated outmoded furniture made of alder and pine with the bark left on. She'd come here to discuss details; instead she encountered a furious Grant.

His expression turned everything into a menacing tableau, forced all cogent thought from her brain and locked down her tongue. She had no idea what message was in the air.

They were standing a few feet apart, his arm still pointing, when he finally spoke. His voice was practically a whisper, and she could hear the massive control it took him to keep from yelling.

"Give me an explanation for this."

How could she do that without knowing what was on the paper?

"I have no idea what's on that paper."

He continued in the same near whisper.

"Oh I think you do. You may be surprised to see it on a printout from a blog. But you know the subject matter. Outside of a lawyer who understands the meaning of confidentiality, you're the only one around me who knew about the possibility of a bottling plant at the lake. Let me rephrase. Why did you want to publicize my plans?"

Her mind raced through a catalogue of recent contacts and conversations. Nothing.

"Sure, you mentioned tentative plans for bottling the spring water, but give me a break. I know why business plans are kept secret. It's a cutthroat world. I have nothing to gain and a lot to lose if I reveal any part of our joint venture. Think about that and I know you'll agree. So what was in the blog post?"

Grant relaxed enough to lower his arm, glance quickly at the paper, and hold it out to her.

She read through the printout quickly. The blog came from a site unknown to her, called "itsyourhome.org". There were hundreds of blogs in this general space, which she privately had dubbed "civic progressive activism", ranging in emphasis from "save the whales" to "nuclear is good for you". She and Jeff had worked cooperatively with some of those bloggers as they grew Cascade Adventures. On the whole, the post was unremarkable. After paragraphs on the proposed new basketball stadium, and a weak attempt to drum up resistance to the done-deal of the huge downtown tunnel, the blog concluded with a brief and, Sara thought, fairly innocuous reference to Tomson Lake.

The only possible target for Grant's wrath was a single sentence: "Any effort to change the water use permit at this location, including opening a bottled water business, should be scrutinized carefully, both for its effects on local water use and to make certain that, as it is implemented, it continues the welcome emphasis on tribal rights contained in the landmark Corbell case (see our earlier post on this issue)." A hyperlink to another post followed.

She handed back the sheet of paper, expecting more criticism. Instead, Grant turned away.

Waiting, she glanced briefly out the window at the shimmering lake and the tall ring of firs that rimmed it, then back at Grant. She knew he didn't like to be contradicted, a blemish that was countered by his incredible ability to make things happen. But this reaction was over the top. In any entrepreneurial venture you had to accept irritating bumps in the road. In the first place, who was going to read the third paragraph of an obscure post anyway? And secondly, the bottling venture had always seemed to her like a decoration, or maybe a marketing device, for a project with much more significant dimensions. Why sweat this little problem so much? His mood should have been more like the equivalent of a bad hair day.

A small inside voice repeated what she had said to herself before: Grant had a personality that would not wear well. No, not quite that. The warning didn't come from the strict internal governor that kept his warmth from rising above a certain level, nor from the way his success drive ignored collateral effects on others. If anything, those characteristics together made up the most successful personality type in the business world.

But in Grant's case, below the business drive she sensed something deeper, a compulsion or obsession which might or might not have anything to do with business. It had never surfaced enough to worry her, before. She saw it only as a small red flag that would keep their extra-business relationship within bounds. She wasn't seeking anything deeper anyway. Nothing like comfort or tenderness; and, God, for sure nothing like that soul-mate crap she'd once bought into. Success pure and simple was the uncomplicated medicine she needed to align herself again. A place in Grant's wake would pull her all the way there, and all she really needed to worry about was maintaining that position.

He finally faced her and spoke to her again, voice tight, but rinsed of threatening overtones.

"I'm not dropping this. It's up to you now. Convince me absolutely that you aren't directly or indirectly the source of this damaging statement. If you can't do that, we'll reassess all our recent conversations. Understood?"

Yes, she did understand. Unmistakably. He shouldered her aside, exited, and slammed the door behind him. Their meeting, such as it was, was over.

Amazingly, her next thoughts were of Jeff, how opposite he and Grant were, how Jeff would never dream of treating her so roughly. Of treating anyone that way. In fact . . .

Some mental circuits rearranged themselves, and she saw clearly why Jeff had entered her thoughts. When she told Grant that she hadn't discussed the bottling project with anyone, she forgot what Jeff had told her about water use at the lake. Well, she hadn't exactly forgotten, but certainly she had not considered Jeff as the possible source of a leak. An act as simple as leaking information meant taking action—something Jeff seemed to have lost the will for. Or he could simply have been careless, a condition that would have been consistent with his total loss of motivation.

In either case, she hadn't leaked the news. Jeff had, and that was unacceptable, damaging her chances for the success she was planning and—could she admit it?—desperately needed.

When she thought about how she would confront Jeff, she imagined her eyes looking like the ones that, a minute ago, had been trained on her.

"I know we agreed to talk. But I thought it over, and now I'm not so sure."

Gretchen Cox's voice came through clearly over the speaker phone, and Bebe couldn't miss its intention.

"I can understand a reluctance to talk about Grace Tomson, if she were still alive and you were working for her. But both those things are different now."

"I have friends who claim to have gotten messages from beyond the grave, so I'm not sure about that first part."

Bebe recalibrated.

"I don't imagine you would be breaking any confidences if you just told me more about Grace herself. You know, as background. I understand, for instance, that she was quite religious."

Cox's voice lost some of its nervous edge. Bebe pictured her at home, relaxing on a Saturday. Her voice sounded tired, though the hesitancy disappeared in a soft snort.

"Quite religious. I suppose some would say that. I'd say religion was her life. You see..."

Bebe waited as Cox shaped her thoughts.

"...you see, I used to be part of her church until I got married. Up to that time I was working for Grace, but she let me go when my husband couldn't stand the church's demands, and I chose him instead of the religion. To finish that story, my husband later left me and I went back to working for Grace. I got to see her up close through all of that, and I can tell you she had more than one side. Several, I'd say."

Bebe now got the impression that Cox was beginning to welcome this chance to unburden herself.

"The church believed in direct, individual communication with God and that God answered with new commandments. Not as important, in general, as the first ten, but almost on the same level for the people who received them. We were supposed to tell others about the commandments we got, as a form of teaching. But what God told us individually to do was sacred law."

Her summary was in line with what Pastor Kuzma had said.

"I see. So the church was very important to her."

"That's an understatement! Grace never forgave me for leaving the church, or for not coming back to the fold after my husband left me. I never knew when I would get a lecture about that, and sometimes she was so harsh I wanted to quit. But she paid well and I needed the money. She must have had a commandment from God about business relations or whatever you'd call them, because she'd stop whatever we were doing exactly when we agreed. She never asked for extra work unless she told you in advance what she'd pay for it. She also never gave a tip or a bonus. On business matters she was clear and respectful, but in the next breath she'd criticize me about my duties to God, church attendance, and the right way to live. Like I said, she had several sides."

Bebe took a chance.

"Did she ever talk about the lake property she owned?"

"Not often, but she said she had a mission from God to keep including the Indians in the protection of the land. The annual gathering was a big part of it. I got the impression that she didn't care about the big house in town and was glad to give it away. But the lake property was different."

"That's a vivid portrait. With those kinds of special requirements, Grace must have had complicated relations with everyone, including her sons."

Cox's reply had an edge again.

"I don't have anything to say about that. I told you so."

"Sorry, I wouldn't want you to say more than you feel you can. Out here in Washington, Will Tomson is still dead and there are still questions about his death. It's up to you if you want to say any more."

Through the phone, Bebe heard breathing for so long that she was beginning to wonder if it was just static. Then she caught Cox's voice clearing.

"I've only got impressions. Things I've pieced together over the years."

"I understand. Please tell me what you can."

Cox's voice grew more decisive.

"I guess the most important thing is that I'm pretty sure that Grant was not actually Grace's child."

Bebe's excitement demanded an outburst. It was a struggle to keep her voice calm.

"Go on."

Cox continued.

"Grace came back from Washington State to have her baby, leaving her husband out west. A few months before she arrived, Grace's cousin Agnes, maybe a few years younger, also came to live with the family. I know that for a fact, because Grace would speak openly about how her cousin had come to visit and died suddenly of illness. But, from little things that Grace let drop, I'm pretty sure Agnes was there for an extended visit because she was pregnant out of wedlock."

Cox stopped for a moment, then resumed.

"I don't know whether you're thinking the same, but you might be. How the Tomson family handled Agnes' pregnancy sounds more like the 1930s than the 1960s. I would guess that abortion was out of the question by the time Agnes arrived and, anyway, the pregnancy itself and what to do with the child was considered to be a family matter, period."

"I can understand that."

"All right...well...now I'm putting things together, not reporting. Agnes died, there's no disputing that. But I think she probably died in childbirth or from complications right after. Will, for sure, was born at home, with a midwife assisting. The family had always done it that way. Agnes' baby was no doubt delivered the same way."

"And you believe that Grace decided to take the baby as her own? Tell everyone that she'd had twins?"

"Decided or, more likely, had instructions from God to do so. She was already a member of the new church, as most of us called it. Accepting a relative's child and raising it as your own would have been very much in keeping with the values of the Tomson family. And adopting without calling it adoption would have been an easy way to cover up the shame of Agnes' sin. This I do know: Grace spoke of her 'second twin' as a 'grant from God', and that's why she named him Grant."

"But wouldn't there be the matter of registering the births? Someone, maybe the midwife, would have had to attest to the birth of twins. To say otherwise would have been perjury."

"You have to remember that this was a small rural community, much smaller then than now. Out here, certain matters were thought of as optional, not required. I had reason to look it up when I was tidying up Grace's papers a few months ago. The twins weren't registered at birth. Neither were my parents—I asked them. They both put in for Social Security numbers when they needed to work, and then later used their numbers to get driver's licenses. I would guess the twins did the same, even got passports using their driver's licenses in the years when security and nationality weren't such big issues."

"So, however it was handled when they were born, Will and Grant grew up as twin brothers. Did they get along all right?"

"I don't know how it was for them growing up out west. You'd have to ask people out there about that. They'd come here for visits occasionally, and they seemed okay with each other. Of course, I was about fifteen years younger."

Bebe heard a return of the caution in Cox's voice that had disappeared during the course of their exchange.

"So, no reason to think that bad blood between them could explain what happened to Will?"

Now Cox replied in a tone that sounded put upon, if not angry.

"You're pushing me beyond where I'm willing to go."

Bebe tried to be soothing.

"Not my intent, just following up on what you were saying."

Cox went on, now sounding slightly desperate.

"You put me in a difficult position, you know. I really want to help you. Someone needs to know what went on. But I'm not the one. I worry, too, about myself."

"There's information that will put you in danger?"

"I hope not. Probably not. But sometimes my imagination takes over. I worry about what would happen to my boy if anything happened to me."

"Please, I'm sorry to put you in that position. You've given me a lot. Just one more thing. Do you remember the name of the midwife?"

"She's not with us anymore. Passed on. Her name was Mary Lamb and she was quite obese. Us kids used to call her Little Lamb and we'd sing 'Mary had a little Lamb' when she was around. Kind of mean."

Cox took an audible breath and paused.

"Sorry. I rambled."

"That's all right. I truly appreciate your willingness to say what you have said. Is there anything else you want to tell me?"

"Maybe I shouldn't, but I think I'll feel guilty if I don't. You ought to look into Grace's will—or wills, I should say. There's a lawyer in Kansas City. He knows. Promise me you'll say you got his name from some reference in Washington, not from here."

Bebe promised, and Cox said the name "Sanford Gordon" slowly and distinctly before hanging up without a goodbye. The dead sound on the line was a door closing for good.

If she was going to learn any more, Bebe knew it would not be from Gretchen Cox.

Still...

She took a minute to search the net, found only one lawyer named Sanford Gordon in Kansas City, and noted down his office telephone number. For Bill McHugh, in case it would be useful.

Bill accepted the iced tea. This far north, mid-afternoon was often the warmest part of a day; and this year April had gifted a rare one. Nighttime would be cool, but for now a wood gazebo in the middle of an open lawn offered welcome shade.

J.P. Chavez slotted himself into the chair opposite. Bill had found him after a look at old issues of student newspapers on the Internet. Chavez had played on sports teams with the Tomson boys at Swiftwater High; one picture showed him on a homecoming committee with Grant.

The two men had never met before, so Bill began from the edges of what he really wanted to talk about.

"Nice farm you got. You been here long?"

Ripening Timothy hay grew right up to the sides of a modest and well-maintained pre-fab house over Chavez's shoulder. He looked relaxed in brown low-top Timberlands, jeans, and a tan work shirt with a Carhartt label. One leg was lifted over a side of the chair, so he was canted in Bill's direction.

"My folks came up here from Mexico to pick vegetables, then started working for the hay growers. So did my brothers and I. About fifteen years ago we all put together enough to buy this place. My brothers liked the Seattle side. I bought 'em out and stayed put."

"Thanks for seeing me. Things goin' well?"

"Well enough, but not so well I can sit here while there's still light. Work never stops. So what do you want to know about the Tomson brothers? I told you on the phone I know Will died, and I haven't seen Grant in years, though I do hear about how big he's gotten. So what's a cop like you want to know?"

Bebe's call last evening had been welcome. What she'd gleaned about the Tomson brothers was intriguing, but didn't provide anything solid. Getting the name of Grace's lawyer held out more hope. Bill would try to call him soon. That's why he was here now, sipping ice tea with Chavez and looking at Timothy hay fields and thinking about Bebe.

Something in her voice had allowed him to imagine that maybe she just wanted to talk. Good thing, because he wanted the same. The personal warmth of their conversations stuck with him now.

He brought himself back to Chavez' question.

"We're trying to build a picture of the Tomsons as boys, how they were back in the day. You spent a lot of time with them growing up?"

"Not that much. Sports together, little league, then high school ball. We crossed paths some, took a lot of classes together. But I wouldn't call them friends. We didn't hang out with the same groups. I'm not sure they hung out with anybody but themselves. But I could be wrong."

"What was your impression about how well they got along?"

Chavez swung his leg back down so both feet were on the wooden floor.

"You didn't answer my question. Why are you asking?"

"Asking about the brothers? Because I'm trying to find out if anything in their background might be relevant to a case I'm working on."

"Relevant, huh? Like Grant could have had something to do with it?"

Chavez was paying attention.

"I'm only collecting information, not making conclusions."

"Yeah, maybe. But okay, I'll tell you what I remember about them, and then I gotta get back to work."

He motioned to the fields around him. The sun was just beginning to dip toward the horizon.

Bill nodded.

"Fair enough."

Chavez settled back in his chair, mostly looking across the fields and off and on back at Bill.

"In some ways they seemed alike—partly, I guess, just because they were twins. They were the same height and build, though Grant had dark hair and Will was lighter. But I think now what made them seem the same was that they were always separate from the rest of us, like they had been told to stay that way."

"Told?"

"Yeah, probably by their mother. I was at their house once—that place that's now History House—for their fourteenth birthday party. Only time they ever invited us, and I doubt any of us would have gone a second time. It was no fun. No games, just sitting on that old furniture and having cake and juice after a lecture from Mrs. Tomson about not spilling anything. The father wasn't around. I got the impression that she ran everything."

"Anything else?"

"Just one thing. In the basement there was a small shop area. Grant took me and one other guy down to see it. There were wood pieces all over this workbench. Will came down and got real mad. Lost all control and yelled at Grant for showing us the shop. No one had touched anything, so I don't know why Will was so mad. Grant kinda took it, but I could see he was angry at Will and tried not to show it."

"Did you see anything like that at school?"

"Nah. Will was a loner. He did some sports and was good at them, but he didn't seem interested. Grant wasn't as athletic, but he worked hard and became one of our better soccer players. Same way with school political offices. Will had no interest, but Grant ran for everything, even though he didn't win very often. You know, high school politics is all about how many friends you have."

Chavez stopped, mulling things over. Bill gave him time. Then Chavez stood abruptly, gripped by some decision.

"Basically, I didn't particularly like Grant, but I distrusted Will. There was something sneaky about him. That's about it, and now I have to get back to work. You can decide whether anything I said is helpful in a murder investigation."

Bill had never used the word "murder". Interesting that Chavez would go there without prompting. He started to thank Chavez for his time, but the farmer was already striding across the wide lawn and back to his fields.

Back in his car, Bill pondered: what next? He could almost picture Chief Cisek's eyes glaring at him. Wondering if I'm doing my regular work with full attention, Bill thought. Cisek was right about not spending time just on hunches, and Bill had to admit that up to now he hadn't found anything suspicious about the Tomsons more than speculation about their relationship during adolescence.

There was still the lawyer in Kansas City. Could be just another dead end. But maybe ...

He checked the time difference, pulled a receipt with a scribbled number out of his wallet and dialed Kansas City.

The law firm's receptionist picked up right away. Bill provided his name and full police title along with a request to speak to Sanford Gordon. After that, the wait was so long that he had started to punch off when he heard a deep male voice.

"Officer McHugh?"

"Yes."

"Normally I wouldn't have taken your call, but your location in Swiftwater and Portal fueled my curiosity. Is this about Will Tomson? I have been informed of his death."

"That is correct. We are still looking at circumstances, and have information that some provisions of Grace Tomson's will might be relevant. Can you shed any light on that?"

Gordon's tone turned frosty.

"Officer, your call on that subject without written notification is irregular. Furthermore, the will has not yet been probated, and until it becomes a matter of public record I must maintain strict confidence."

Bill tried to lighten his tone.

"I apologize for the irregularity but thought you might be able to provide an informal, non-legal perspective on any aspects of the will that could have affected the relations between Grace's twin sons. I cannot go beyond that except to say that their relationship might be relevant to our investigation."

Bill waited through another long pause during which he imagined cold, empty air. The pause was shorter this time, and Gordon's voice sounded more neutral than offended.

"It is taking more time than usual to send the will to probate. That is because the will contained an unusual provision in its execution. We are erring here on the side of caution in case any additional document relevant to the will has still to reach us. That's it. I can tell you no more. Good luck with your investigation."

Was that useful? Or just another irrelevant, though tantalizing, piece of information? For sure he had no way of knowing. He'd pass it on to the chief and let him decide.

"Godammit, Jeff, I trusted that you wouldn't interfere. Grant's plans to bottle water at the lake were his business and didn't affect our ventures—until this blog came out. Now we could be screwed, thanks to you."

She stopped for a moment, gathering steam.

"You told someone. Maybe you thought it wasn't important, or just didn't pay attention. Wouldn't be the first time. Or maybe you want me to fail."

Her voice rose.

"Whatever trust there was between us is gone."

"Sara . . ."

"Don't even try. What is it you don't understand about the word *gone?*"

She had stormed in before dinner time and went straight upstairs without a word. Only when he followed her to their bedroom had she pulled out a piece of paper and flung it at him. He glanced at it and saw it was a blog about Tomson Lake. When he began to explain, she had released a blast of anger.

Lately, Jeff had seen Sara angry a lot. She exhibited that mood in many different ways. There was her instant mad, like a comment tossed over the shoulder. Her "let's get organized" mad, a boost of effort. Her "why didn't I see that coming?" cautionary mad. And her "don't get mad, get even" mad, after which she got down to business. He'd come to the conclusion that her various mad moods were an intrinsic element of her thought process.

But, up to now, her various mad moods had ranged from warm to hot. This time Sara seethed in bitter cold, the look in her eyes like an invitation to enter a giant freezer, locked away.

Jeff was still searching for a response when he heard a noise and saw her pulling down a suitcase from her closet shelf. He took a step in that direction and she swung her arm like a hatchet.

"Go on back to your work. I'll only be a minute. You've got the place to yourself now. I'll let you know when I need to get the equipment out in the barn. The legal arrangements can wait."

Cold had changed to cool, and efficiency was back in her movements. Despite the return of some surface familiarity, she was already far away.

True to her word, she was soon gone.

The full weight of her words and her departure crushed him into a hunched position in a side chair from which he stared bleakly at the half-empty closet.

What had he been thinking? He knew Page Bentley's track record and that there was every chance he would take the information about Tomson's water rights at the lake and try to shop it for advantage. Maybe the person who wrote the blog was his first call, or maybe that person heard it from someone Bentley contacted. It didn't matter. The information got out and his Plan A, designed to make Grant react and reveal himself, had worked. Wearing blinders of his own, he hadn't even considered other consequences.

He'd run out of options at the precise moment when things couldn't be worse. Rolling that thought around, checking it from different angles, he found only confirmation of this hopeless conclusion. The armchair began to feel like a prison cell.

He heard his phone's ringtone. On the fourth ring, he watched his hand listlessly lift the object.

"Bentley. Seen the blog?"

Saturday evening and hearing from Bentley? Those two things didn't belong together. He nodded automatically before remembering he had to speak.

"Yeah."

"More interest in that information than I thought there'd be. I owe you one."

That was one asset Jeff would never collect. What was there to say? Bentley waited a couple of beats before speaking into the silence.

"I already got a call from a legislator wanting to know if I had more details. I'm calling to see if you've learned anything more about water use permitting."

Jeff said he hadn't and punched off. So his attempt to prod the hornets' nest had worked. Only now it looked as if he would be the one who got stung the worst.

The ringtone sounded again. Probably Bentley again.

"Yeah, what else?"

To his surprise, he heard Mac Champlin's voice.

"You fucked up big time. Remember our first conversation, when I told you that we'd get ahead if we knew more than anyone else and kept our heads down? You were supposed to be this DC genius who knew all the ways to pull the ropes and open doors, all without being seen. That's why I brought you on board."

Mac took a breath. Jeff tried to recall a conversation where any of that had been discussed. They had talked only about workload and how to find political gold in a river of messages that never stopped flowing. Whatever. Mac was talking again.

" ... and he actually called me personally, on a Saturday. Grant Tomson, a guy who was clear that we should never talk directly. And why did he call? Because he's decided that if it wasn't your wife, it was you who passed information to some blogger. I don't give a shit whether you did. The only thing of relevance is that Tomson thinks you did. I hired you because you were supposed to be smart enough for that kind of a leak *not* to happen."

Jeff heard hard breathing, then one final deep breath.

"Fuck it. You're done. You can make one more trip here to get your things. Then just piss off."

Jeff couldn't have cared less.

APRIL 19, MONDAY

Grant pointed at a chair, raised a buzzing cell phone to his ear and turned his back to her. It was all done in the fluid way you only get from practice. How could such obvious affectation have escaped her up to now?

Sara had come to Grant to figure out where they could go from here. Did their partnership have a future or not? She was in Grant's office for the first time. The fact that they were here and not, as usual, back at his condo, was a message in itself. There he entertained the chosen. A conversation in this office was a demotion.

The office had a view, too, one of South Lake Union, an area in transition where new office buildings vied with low-rise apartments waiting for the wrecking ball. If media reports were accurate, this area would soon be Seattle's new "in" place. Grant's condo opened to the sky and, with views in all directions, flaunted the power and excess of a private domain that the world might see but never reach. The office in which she now sat was, in contrast, little more than a vantage spot for following a project. It was no more than sixteen feet long. One end held a small sitting area, the other a rosewood desk and two chairs.

Grant finished his call, sat and stared at her, waiting. After a few beats of silence, he verbalized his impatience.

"Well?"

His tone made Sara bristle. Behind the desk hung the room's sole wall decoration: a large abstract painting of tightly-grouped cubes at its center. The colors of the cubes radiated outward, passing through each other to form new tones that reached the rectangular rim of the painting. There they again became cubes of the same color as those at the center. In the mutation and rejoining there was beauty, logic, and an almost boastful control.

Even with a quick glance Sara saw how the painting matched the man. Had he consciously searched for this portrait of himself—openly displayed, but inscrutable enough to keep the viewer at bay?

Grant was waiting for a response. She willed herself to speak calmly, laying out factually why she had confided in Jeff and revealed Grant's plans for the lake property. Near the end, he broke in, his voice devoid of sympathy.

"How disappointing. Apparently you tried to be gentle with a husband you're about to ditch. You didn't pay the right kind of attention. You let feelings, feelings that you yourself knew were dead, lead you to revealing something that could be used against you. Against a deal we were working on. Against me."

By the time he got to those last words, anger was resurfacing. She'd seen his anger before and ignored it. Now it bothered her. She'd concentrated so much on how inadequate Jeff turned out to be as a business partner that up to now she'd not examined the ways in which Grant's defects might not be ideal either. He went on.

"I've already started countermeasures. Objectively, what your Jeff let out of the bag was revealed to such a secondary source that it can probably be contained..."

He stared at her, his dark eyes now transformed into twin hammers looking for nails.

"...but even if that works out, there remains the matter of your trustworthiness. I liked the idea of a partnership on the lake venture. That still could be a significant part of my strategy going forward. You have the skills to make partnership a success. But to regain your rights, you still have to prove to me that I can trust you."

The hammers went back into their tool box. Something else had changed, too. What? Sara raced through Grant's last words and found it: Grant had up to now given her the impression that the lake venture, though important to her, was only a convenient first move for him. He'd never framed it as a central business objective. If it was not central, how could it be a significant part of a strategy? She tucked that thought away as he went on.

"I have a way to get us back on track. There's a piece of information I need to have before taking next steps at the lake. I don't need to tell you that it's in your interest to help me get it."

He was right about that, anyway.

"Go on."

"Upon my mother's death, all her property passed jointly to Will and me. In case he predeceased me, the entire property, obviously including the lake, would be mine. However, in conversations I had with Will before he died, he brought up some issues that may interfere with a clean probate of our mother's will. What my brother said is not important. I just need to know whether any additional documentation relative to a will exists. I have already looked in Will's home and his work building and found nothing."

Okay so far.

"Where else is there?"

"History House. Have you ever been there? You surely know it's the old family home. They have family records on file as part of the archive."

"Sure, I know where it is. But I've never been inside."

"Well, here's your chance. The archives are on the third floor. I want you to give them a thorough look to see if any relate to my mother's will."

"There must be a lawyer handling the estate. Doesn't he have a copy?"

Grant's hands rose off the desk and immediately slipped back to a clasped position in front of him. That movement betrayed nervousness, the first time Sara had seen any hesitation get past his careful façade. His voice shifted to a smooth and practiced tone that didn't square with what she'd just seen.

"Of course, and so do I. But there's a possibility that informal commentaries on the will may exist, which could cause difficulties. I don't want to have to face those difficulties until all my major plans are in place. At very least, I don't want to be blindsided."

His tone up-shifted to decisive.

"We could sit here all day wasting valuable time. This is a simple job, and I want you to do it. You *need* to do it if we are to continue a joint project."

Her expression must have revealed some hesitation, because his forcefulness gathered strength.

"No more questions. Look at the files in History House. Don't miss anything. Report back to me. You've got two days. Simple. Are you in or out?"

Now an alarm rang. Something's wrong here. What else is being left out? Sara examined her options. Drop Grant and his project right now, this minute. Start over. Even go back to Jeff. She could do those things, but then she'd just be back again in the life she was trying to escape.

She closed a mental door so that the alarm was barely audible. Be smart. Get what he wants. See what's next. Be more careful, and don't lose sight of the fact that you can drop out and go back to other options any time you choose.

She tried to put on a convincing smile.

"Of course I'm in."

APRIL 20, TUESDAY

"Are you sure there aren't any other files where I could look?"

Bebe chose not to read criticism or insult into a question that implied she didn't know her archives. She was glad to help Sara Winter on a morning when nothing major was scheduled at History House.

"The files I laid out for you upstairs are everything we have that relates directly to the Tomsons. Perhaps I could be of greater assistance if you could tell me more precisely what you are looking for."

Sara repositioned herself in her chair on the other side of the desk and seemed to think about an answer. While she did, Bebe took a closer look at her. She saw a fit woman of what she guessed to be late thirties, dark-honey hair and intense blue eyes. Bebe put Sara's height at five-nine, about two inches shorter than she herself was.

But those externals, including the fact that she was in jeans and running shoes, didn't define the woman opposite her. When Bebe first started making the rounds of therapists, the one who helped her most had left her with a piece of advice she had used ever since. Everyone has fears, he'd said; get to know your own, and you'll be very good at recognizing what other people are afraid of.

Sara Winter was afraid. Her rigid posture and clipped, rushed words were giveaways. Her greyhound-thin frame looked like the remainder of a once healthier person. She was making an effort to appear calm and businesslike, even though flashes of panic came and went in her eyes. Most of all, her presence gave Bebe the feeling that, for the moment, History House had become a battlefield.

Sara began talking, a faint note of pleading creeping in.

"I was only partly upfront with you. It's true I want to look at the Tomson family records. It's also true that I'm doing it partly on behalf of Grant Tomson. Grant would have come here to search for himself, but he's very busy. I'm not looking for anything out of the ordinary, but I think Grant would feel better if my connection to him were not made public. Can I count on you for that?"

Despite herself, Bebe could no longer hide her reaction and heard an audible huffiness creep into her voice.

173

"We don't have a reputation for gossip. Many people make inquiries on different subjects and we never give out information about anyone."

Sara held up a hand.

"Sorry if that came out wrong."

Bebe tried to sound mollified.

"All right. Then tell me what you're looking for."

Sara glanced at the door behind her. It was cracked open, but all other visitors had left at least half an hour ago.

"Grant is working on a major business deal involving Tomson Lake, and he doesn't want to get deep into that deal only to find out that there are problems with the property ownership. The brothers were to be given joint ownership of it when their mother died, and it's not impossible that their mother might have added additional provisions in case one of them died. There's no expectation that she did. I'm here just to double check."

"Has Grant checked with Grace Tomson's lawyer?"

Sara looked a little startled but nodded an affirmation.

"Well, then I'm afraid I can't be of further help. I've given you everything we have."

Sara didn't move, hands clutched in front of her. Her expression was hard to read. Bebe thought she detected relief, only to see that replaced by a glint of determination.

"I suppose you've shown me and I can tell Grant there's nothing in the files about the will. But as long as I'm here, is there anything else? Maybe more than the documents you showed me?"

Bebe had made sure that the document collection available to the public was well organized and up to date. However, she hadn't yet finished doing the same with other items—photographs, for instance. She rose, opened a closet door, pulled down a large cardboard box from the upper shelf, and placed it in front of Sara.

"This box contains unsorted family photographs. We've used a few for specific exhibits. If you wish, we could see what's in there. The kitchen table would give us space and good light."

At the table, Sara opened the box and pulled out the item on top.

"Lots of photos here, but what's this?"

She held up the glassine slip with the unexplained paper fragment Bebe had found on the stairs weeks ago. She had put it for safekeeping in a box with other unfiled items.

"I found that on the floor a while back. It looked like trash, but given the name on it, I decided not to throw it out right away."

Sara looked at the slip again. When she spoke, it as if to no one in particular.

"Looks like the kind of entry Grant makes on his daily list of to-dos, but then, probably half the world uses the same software."

Bebe made a mental note to pass on Sara's comment to Bill.

For the next hour they sat opposite each other in the kitchen, looking at pictures. Almost from the start, they created a system. They divided the photos into four categories: shots that were taken at the house, at the lake, of family members in other settings, and all else. They worked easily together. Bebe sensed that beneath Sara's current tense state was a woman who organized things very much the way she herself did.

Nothing remotely pertained to the will. But Bebe hadn't expected there would be any such connection, and doubted Sara had either. Their quick scans and sorting began to take on an automatic feel when seven pictures, some apparently taken in front of an open garage and others at the lake, abruptly caught Bebe's attention.

Lawrence Tomson, the twins' father, was pictured with two teenage boys, enjoying what appeared to be a serious hobby. In four photos, a garage door stood open to show a bench and two professional-grade tool boxes, in front of which stood a proud father, his sons, and two identical large black motorcycles. The shots were of Lawrence, Will, and Grant on or beside the bikes. Lawrence, obviously enjoying himself, hammed it up a bit. The boys looked simultaneously awkward and dutiful. A following set of three photos showed the three of them in indifferent poses, standing between the two big cycles with the family mountain home and the lake clearly identifiable behind them.

Sara must have noticed Bebe's reaction. She put an index finger on one of the pictures.

"Something special about this one?"

"You may have noticed that there are very few pictures of the boys' father. I think he took most of the others. So these that show him are different and also ... "

Sara was looking at her intently.

" ... I think Will was riding one of these same motorcycles the night he was killed. That gives me an eerie feeling."

Sara said nothing and went back to sorting.

The two women finished and Sara prepared to leave, thanking Bebe once more for her help. As she held the front door open, Bebe felt an unexpected compulsion to say something more.

"You're a nice person, Sara, and you seem to be under stress. I hope you've helped yourself today. Though it may be beyond what you wanted to find here, I feel I ought to tell you that it's possible that Grant's relationship to his brother Will might not have been very good when Will died."

Sara looked back at her, masking any visible reaction.

"So you're still working on Will Tomson's death?"

A moment ago, Bill's cell had buzzed. He was waiting on two other calls, so this one from Aaron Elkhorn took him by surprise. He paused on the flagstone steps leading to a low rambler in poor repair. Its owner had called the station to report a possible break-in, and Bill was responding on his way home. Chances were slim that the call would amount to much; the break-in had occurred the previous evening, and the owner waited until this afternoon to report it. Interviewing the owner could wait another two minutes.

The last time he talked to Elkhorn, Bill thought they had both discovered the beginnings of trust. Not enough to lean on, but maybe enough, he decided, to test further.

"I thought I was clear that I am not officially on the case. But, between us, little bits of information here and there make me even less sure it was only an accident. Nothing provable, though."

He heard the muffled sound of Elkhorn clearing his throat.

"I thought long and hard about whether to call you. Besides the ambiguous confidentiality issue, it's not my inclination to volunteer information unless I'm sure it's important."

"So why are you calling?"

"Conscience. And because I thought I could trust that you will handle what I tell you carefully. I hope I'm right."

He still hadn't gotten to the point.

"I guess neither one of us will know unless you get more specific."

"That's part of the problem. Getting specific with an impression. But here it is: Grant Tomson has changed. He's different now. Not all the time, but often enough that I'm beginning to wonder if he might do something extreme."

"Are you talking in general, or about action?"

"What sets him off the most is anything related to the Tomson Lake project. Until the last two weeks, that project was one among many. Now it has become his main focus, maybe his only focus. This just doesn't square with all the previous planning. He has larger projects—several of them— with much more money at stake. But recently he can't seem to focus on them. Everything comes back to Tomson Lake."

"I appreciate the heads-up. But I'm not sure what I need to do with it."

"There's more, though it's harder for me to explain by just describing it. You would have to be there with me to hear his tone of voice change, or to see the way he paces, when the lake is mentioned. Most startling of all is the look in his eyes. His whole demeanor shifts, like he's focusing on something I can't see. Irrational is the only word that comes to mind."

Elkhorn paused. When he spoke again, Bill heard some of his native intonation join in.

"I'm not meddling in your job, but I thought if Grant was involved in his brother's death, there could be another part of him that I hadn't seen. Now maybe I've seen it. That's really all I wanted to tell you."

"I appreciate it. I'll do all I can to repay your trust. No attribution of any kind to you. You have my word on it."

"Thanks for that."

Bill had another question.

"As long as I have you, can you identify anything in particular about Tomson Lake that sets him off? Anything that occurs to you might help me."

Elkhorn was silent for a while before Bill heard his voice again.

"Have you heard about the blog post?"

Bill didn't follow any blogs closely and said so. Elkhorn explained, and Bill's level of interest jumped several notches.

"Got more? How did Tomson react?"

"He's proud of avoiding media scrutiny, so I would have expected some irritation at the blog post. But the degree of his anger was way out of proportion. He just wouldn't stop. He was particularly mad at the source of the information. He wouldn't tell me, but I got the impression he knew who it was. And revenge was on his mind."

"Anything else?"

"Yeah. I told you before that one of my jobs has been to assess tribal reactions to any possible changes at Tomson Lake. I hadn't been able to discover much of anything specific. But the blog changed things. I hear a new buzz in the Indian communities. I told Grant about a couple of calls from tribal representatives asking for clarification on the blog, and Grant went ballistic again."

Bill waited to see if Elkhorn would add more. He heard a sound like a chair leaning back. Elkhorn's voice returned, closer to the mouthpiece, but softer.

"That other matter we spoke about—his motives toward the tribes?"

"Yeah?"

"I overheard two of his other assistants talking. One said that Grant said something to him about limits in working with the tribes 'once we're over some political hurdles'. That rubs me wrong in its own right, but I think it could also explain the feeling I have that he's not confiding in me even as much as he used to. You got any other sources talking about Grant?"

"I once asked Roper Martin to keep his ear to the ground, but had to caution him not to be too aggressive or obvious. After all, I wasn't officially interested."

Elkhorn guffawed.

"I remember Roper. If there's a rumor, he'll be the first person to know. So if you're looking for someone to talk to about the tribes and Tomson Lake, you've got the right man there."

That sounded like Elkhorn opening the communications door wider. But he was done, and his voice switched to the lawyer tone again.

"If anything new develops on this end, I'll inform you. May I assume the same applies to you?"

There was no time for a response before the line went dead. Bill lowered his cell enough to punch in another number. Roper Martin answered on the third ring.

"So there, Bill the cop, how's it hangin'? Why you callin'? Thought you told me I was done with whatever you asked me to listen out for."

"I told you the chief wanted me to work on other cases. Things got busy."

"You mean your White man's chief."

"I've had two chiefs for a lot of years and I can tell the difference."

"Good for you. Whacha want?"

"You remember I didn't want you out looking for information all over the place on my account. But now I wonder whether you might have gotten wind of reactions on one specific issue."

You sure change your mind a lot. Okay, about what?"

"You seen a blog about Tomson Lake?"

"You mean the one about Grant Tomson and water rights? Not personally. Computers and me don't get along. I know some of our people seen it. Not everyone picked up on it. But more than I would've expected."

"What kind of reactions do you hear?"

"'Bout what you'd imagine. Tribal leaders want to know why they weren't consulted. It's not like they have legal rights to be consulted, it's just the usual first reaction. Any discussion of treaty lands—even those that got sold a while back—and they look at compensation. Same everywhere. Noses go up when there's money in the air."

"But no action so far?"

"Calls, maybe, wanting information. Anything more than that usually takes a while before it means much."

They finished the call on better terms than when they started.

So the fact that tribes might want to take a closer look at new development ideas for Tomson Lake could account for Grant's mood change. But in his gut, Bill felt that that news was not enough to explain all that Elkhorn had described. Tomson was no newborn in the business world, and he'd been working statewide for several years, so there was no way he would plan development on tribal lands, present or former, and not expect some kind of scrutiny. He must have already thought about the possible complications and slowdowns.

There's got to be something else.

His cell phone chimed. Jeff Winter had texted, wanting a meeting. Bill replied, suggesting coffee tomorrow at two pm at the Sunrise.

It was hard to return mentally to where he had been. Once readjusted, he mounted the steps up to the door of the rickety rambler. A hung-over man in shorts and dirty T-shirt finally responded to his knock. Bill stepped into a living space that matched the man. A few sullen answers to his questions quickly established that the possibility of a break-in was a hazy, inconsistent part of almost incoherent recollections. Bill made a few notes for his report and let the man go back to sleep.

APRIL 21, WEDNESDAY

"Naw. Didn't know Will Tomson at all. Saw him once in a while on his motorcycle or at a store in Portal. Pretty much kept to himself."

Jeff could barely see eyes under a ball cap pulled down low. The house door began to close, shutting off any further view of a neat, almost tiny man, probably around sixty. He'd opened the door cautiously to Jeff's knock and had courteously done his best to end the conversation as quickly as possible.

The same had been true at another house near Coho Corner, a remote jumping-off place for hikers in the summer, and cross country skiers and snowmobilers in the winter. The woman who spoke to him through a crack in the door, cigarette dangling from her lips, was close to hostile.

Two more houses to visit, after which he'd probably have nothing to report back to Bill McHugh.

He had met McHugh at the Sunrise Café earlier that afternoon. They sat in a corner booth with high partitions, an emergency exit on one side and a pass-through from the bar area on the other. The dining room, a place decorated with large framed photos of bygone miners, railroad workers and cowboys, was sparsely occupied. A gas flame flickered soundlessly in a huge fireplace rimmed with river rock. This booth where they sat practically belonged to Chief Tom Cisek, and often served as an informal second office. Bill shrugged and said he knew Cisek was at a conference in Seattle when he asked to be seated there.

There had been some awkwardness to begin with. Jeff's words must have sounded like verbal shoe shuffling, explaining that his wife was involved with Grant Tomson in a new venture at Tomson Lake. McHugh had listened for about two sentences, then said he wasn't going to get involved in marital difficulties. Tomson, however, was another matter. The policeman proceeded cautiously to sum up his informal inquiries about Grant Tomson's possible role in his brother's death. Jeff had pushed him a little.

"You got anything new going on there?"

"More like the opposite—winding down. Officially, at least."

"Then any offer on my part to help wouldn't make a difference?"

McHugh had brightened a bit.

"Just out of curiosity, what could you do?"

Jeff had improvised. If there *was* a way to bring down Grant Tomson, he wanted to be part of it. And to protect Sara if she was in real danger, regardless of how she had treated him.

"Suppose I ask the people who live up by Will's place what they know about him and his relations to his brother. I've done some freelance writing. It would be easy enough to say I'm writing a human interest story on Will Tomson—contrast the decency of a skilled man who didn't bother anybody with the tragedy of his untimely death. You get the idea."

McHugh was getting comfortable enough with the conversation to smile.

"I'd toss you out on your ass..."

He'd waved that away with a broader grin.

"...but, what the hell, maybe it wouldn't hurt. If you want to try, see what you can find out. Just don't overdo it."

Up here on the way to Coho, Jeff hadn't gotten far enough into any conversation to use the sales pitch he'd prepared; and he expected the third house to be as barren of useful information as the other two. A log house this time, older, much closer to the road than houses would be built nowadays. The yard was a mess, overrun by what once had been decorative plantings, mixed with random forest intrusions. The house itself was surprisingly well maintained.

An overweight, balding man opened the door to Jeff's knock, reading glasses low on his nose and an open book still clutched in one hand. He jovially introduced himself as Ezra James, his smile broadening below a deeply receding hairline after Jeff gave his pitch.

"Sounds interesting. Don't get to meet an author every day. C'mon in. Coffee?"

Jeff accepted and sat down, sinking low in an upholstered chair that matched his host's well-worn jeans and baggy red sweater. One other chair, with a good reading light, stood by a stone fireplace nearly clogged with ashes but still sustaining a low wood fire. Only when his eyes had adjusted to the low lighting in the room did Jeff realize that every bit of wall space was covered with bookshelves.

James returned with two mugs of coffee. He handed one to Jeff and waved around the room with his free hand as he walked to the other chair.

"You're looking at my hobby and main entertainment. I buy books in lots. Keep what I like and give the rest to the county library. So what do you need to know?"

Jeff opened the notebook he'd brought along.

"I'm confident I can eventually find out a lot about Will Tomson the furniture and instrument maker. But it's harder to write a description of Will Tomson the man. I'm hoping you might have known him, and can help me create that description."

James rocked back and forth, his face appearing and receding as it passed in and out of the reading light's cone of illumination. His voice turned thoughtful, almost distant.

"You're right, Will would be difficult to describe. Despite the fact that I would wave to him on his motorcycle or run across him buying groceries in Safeway, I never really met him . . . "

Jeff got ready to rise.

" . . . until, one day, Will came knocking on my door."

He settled back down, only then noticing James' mischievous grin.

"Please go on."

"For a number of years I was a general handyman all around this area. Mostly a carpenter. Before that, I was a physicist; but that's another story, only relevant in explaining my reputation as someone to go to if you have a particularly difficult problem in making or fixing something. I think Will must have heard about that, because he came to ask me to help him on a project."

"What kind?"

"He wanted me to help him build a woodshop up by the lake."

"Why would Will possibly want that? Didn't he already have a big shop just down the road?"

"My first question, too, you bet. He wanted to stop making the same kind of furniture he made at his workshop down the road. He had a new project: small intricate chests. He'd still go on with his musical instruments. But he wanted to keep those two activities separate. Later, he talked once about why making chests with hidden compartments and opening mechanisms required solitude and closeness to nature. Never made sense to me, but he paid the bills on time, so what did I care?"

Jeff thought out loud.

"Sounds like it might have been a lengthy and expensive project."

"Both. Took about four months, pretty much full time. He'd found a place at the foot of an escarpment, back about half a mile from the Tomson house on the lake. First we had to hack out a trail to the base of the escarpment at the back of the property, then into a thicket of trees. That's where Will wanted his cabin. We had to cut down several big trees just to get started."

"Quite a project. How did you get the materials in?"

"We welded together a narrow trailer that could negotiate the trail and hooked it to Will's motorcycle. Took lots of trips for the lumber and shingles, but luckily the cabin was only about eighteen by fourteen and there was no electrical or plumbing. Grubbing the trail around big boulders, setting logs in low places, and adding a layer of gravel for drainage took just about as long as the cabin itself."

"What was the final result?"

"Pretty handsome, if I do say so myself. Oak on the outside, and finished inside in some Costa Rican hardwood. A long work table and a big rack for hand tools. Plenty of uncluttered floor space. Shutters that can be raised almost the whole length of both sides. When those shutters were up, the forest was right there; when they were down, they were strongly secured from the inside."

"Sounds rewarding."

"When I was finished, I was just as glad."

"What do you mean?"

"You're trying to find out what Will was like? After four months of working side by side you end up with a pretty good idea. On the one hand, Will worked hard. He had lots of skills: metal work, masonry. Best finish carpenter I've ever met. But there was a bad side."

James stopped, regrouping.

"I don't know how to put it, exactly. He was more than just a loner; I think basically he looked down on people. Not on particular people, more like on the whole human race. There was some serious hatred in him. Once I figured out that that included me, I buckled down and finished the job; but any pleasure I took in the project was gone. I was glad never to see or speak to him again."

Jeff tried to look casual, but his mind was a blur. He was ready to leave, though a specific question remained, the one McHugh particularly sought answers to.

"Did you get any impression about how he related to his twin brother Grant?"

James made a sound that was part snort and part bitter laugh.

"Impression? I only saw them together once, and that was enough. We were about halfway through building the cabin when Grant showed up at the work site. I heard him yell something at Will about asking his permission to build, and Will yelled back that he could do what he wanted. Then they went off a ways and I couldn't hear, but sure could see what was going on. They were arguing when Grant suddenly hit Will. More like a hard slap than a fist shot. Now, Will was still holding a hammer and he swung it hard, hitting Grant in the upper arm. Grant went down on one knee and eventually got up, clutching his shoulder. He walked away without a word; but if revenge had a face, I'd say it was pasted on Grant at that moment."

"And Will?"

"Went straight back to work as if nothing had happened. Never mentioned it."

McHugh would want that information. He might also want to look at the cabin.

"The cabin? Still there?"

James laughed.

"Nothing else I've worked on is so over-built. It would take a big fire to destroy that thing. And we haven't had a major fire in the area for years."

"Guess I'll take a look."

"You can find the trail without too much difficulty, long as you're looking for it. Start at the big house and go toward the mountains along the lake a couple of hundred yards and keep a lookout for the trail on your right. If you want to look inside the cabin, you'll need the key. To the left of the trail, where it begins, there's a big Noble fir, taller and skinnier than the others around. A birdhouse hangs on it at about ten feet. You can reach it by standing on a boulder at the base of the tree. Will had a key of his own, but kept a spare in the birdhouse. Maybe it's still there."

Jeff thanked James for his time and left. As soon as he was in his car, he pulled out his phone to call McHugh, then realized his cell connection would be chancy at best at this location. Tomson Lake was less than twenty minutes away, and cell phones worked better there. He drove in that direction. A thought occurred: as long as he was up here, why not take a look at the cabin? Then he'd have even more to report.

Bunched clouds had parted and, a couple of months before the solstice, the late afternoon sun was about ready to slip down over the mountains to the west. The lake was glassy calm, mirroring the surrounding mountain peaks, still topped with snow. No indication yet of a late snow dump that the weatherman had said was possible. Jeff stopped for a minute to take in the view, feeling a pang of sorrow as he remembered other times, similar views, and the peaceful, easy feeling that had risen inside him. A fragment of the old Eagles song arrived softly, only to be shoved away by the emptiness of loss. Of innocence. Of Sara.

As James had predicted, the trail to the cabin was not hard to find, especially after Jeff spotted the Noble fir with a birdhouse on its trunk. Standing on a boulder at the base of the tree, Jeff could just reach into the birdhouse. The key was still there, a long-shanked implement with a complicated blade featuring dimples and z-shaped cuts. He slipped it into his pocket and reached downward with his good leg, jumping backward from the boulder.

It had been a long day. That last maneuver intensified the ache already growing in his hip. He started up the trail to the cabin, but soon decided the pain was too much.

Better go home, clean up, and call McHugh. The policeman could examine the cabin if he wanted to.

Jeff was in his car when he noticed the extra weight in his jacket pocket. That key—he hadn't put it back. Oh well, he'd turn that over to McHugh, too.

APRIL 22, THURSDAY

Bebe rubbed her eyes, caught herself in the act and reached instead for the small bottle of eye drops by her elbow. She stood and looked down at a small stack of notes, trying to decide whether the hours that had stretched to three am had produced what she thought they had before she'd dozed off at her desk.

After her meeting with Sara Winter two days ago, she'd begun to wonder whether she had learned all she could about the Tomson twins. Just as the picture of the two motorcycles had startled her, could there be something equally surprising lurking in the information she already possessed? Something that she had overlooked?

Last evening, she realized she could no longer ignore that question. Soon, the excitement of the hunt started to energize her, and so did the thought that she might find something that could help Bill. She started with a source that still remained mysterious: the photocopies of Will's workshop log. Previously, she hadn't been able to crack the code of the number-letter strings. She'd give it one more try.

The folder held two photo files, one with shots of hand-entered information in Will's notebook, the other showing the inside of Will's workshop. She spent most of her time with the notebook entries, particularly with one item that was different from the rest. For all other entries, she found a connection between initials in the entry and lists of client names and cities at the rear of the notebook. Thus, DS/B/6/6/05 was Diego Salazar of Barcelona, involving a transaction on June 6, 2005. So what was the unexplained entry "DF.L6.8X10.7 "?

Nothing popped out at her. So, as much to relax her mind as to find a new approach to the numbers and letters, she'd turned to the photos of the workshop. Using a magnifying glass, she examined the pictures, one by one, taking her time, minutes turning into hours.

Nothing caught her attention until she came to pictures of racks by the room's entrance. Open framing that ran all the way up to the ceiling covered an area, she judged, about twenty feet wide and ten feet deep. Vertical members were cross-hatched by horizontal members, spaced about four feet apart as they rose from floor to ceiling. The result was a set of stacked spaces for storing and drying lumber. The lumber itself was arranged in piles of varying sizes, boards separated by spacers to allow air circulation.

Eventually she began to concentrate not on the shelving and its contents, but on the hand-lettered label near each stack of wood. More to keep herself awake than anything else, she began reading aloud: "alder", "birch", "maple", "Douglas fir". Douglas fir? "DF"! She looked more closely and saw numbers beside the wood names. Could they be lot numbers? Of course, a fine woodworker would want to use woods that were milled at the same time. So,"DF.L6.8X10.7". Could it indicate Douglas fir in lot six, the next numbers signifying the dimensions of the lumber? *Maybe* she had something!

The fact that only one wood lot was listed—hidden, perhaps—in the middle of unrelated job orders could mean that Will had made a special reminder of that location.

She didn't consciously consider what she was doing when she grabbed her cell phone and punched the by-now familiar speed dial. By the second ring, she realized it was only just after six am, and too late to stop the call. Bill's voice answered, sleepy sounding but alert.

"Bebe, are you all right? Anything happen?"

She started to apologize and he broke in.

"Hey, none of that. Just tell me what you've got."

She fumbled through a garbled explanation.

"So you think Will might have hidden something in his workshop? In a pile of lumber?"

By now she felt worse than sheepish. Fully embarrassed.

"I'm so sorry to wake you with nothing more than a guess, and maybe a bad one. I got excited and just wanted to tell you right away."

"Hey, it's okay. I can always get more sleep. You should know by now that you can call any time."

She was registering pleasure in those words when she remembered something else.

"Remember that scrap of paper I found the day we first met?"

"Sure."

"Sara Winter saw it and said it reminded her of how Grant Tomson kept his daily calendar on his computer. Not much. But I thought you ought to know."

Bill was silent for a few seconds, thinking before responding.

"Not much by itself. But if we find out more, it could be a helpful part of a complete case. Don't lose it."

His tone changed again.

"Hey, but what I said about calling wasn't just about what you've found out. Hope you know that. I'd rather hear your voice than just think about it."

She could hardly recall the gruffness he used when they first met. She let out something that sounded to her like a giggle. Where did that come from?

"Careful, you could lose sleep pretty often. But I'll try not to abuse the invitation."

"No worry about that..."

He paused again.

"...I appreciate everything you do and say, and I mean that. We'll talk more later, but right now I should get up to Will's workshop. You should get some more sleep."

When she turned away from her desk and headed for the kitchen, it all felt more like a dream than reality. It was now only six-thirty. Curio stood by a cabinet, wagging and waiting for his morning treat. Luckily, History House was closed today for long-delayed electrical repairs. Her body would most likely resist going to sleep. Too much going on. Instead, she'd get showered and cleaned up. And wait for Bill's call.

Sara woke up early in the motel near Esterhill, resolving to search for a longer-term rental as soon as she could. The room came with free breakfast: day-old muffins, fruit, and coffee. She downed the coffee and a muffin and took a scrawny, hard apple with her as she drove to what, until a few hours ago, had been her home. Jeff's place is what she'd call it from now on.

Laura was waiting for her beside the big van by the barn. Several items were already loaded into the van's rear compartment.

Laura didn't stop moving as she reported.

"I checked that no one was in the barn before I began moving equipment. No sign of Jeff anywhere."

She added an uneasy smile.

Laura must have figured out that there was something wrong with Sara's marriage. Pretty soon the whole world would know. For the moment, all that was important was that Jeff was not around to be in the way.

"Thanks for starting early. Let's get the climbing ropes, pitons, and carabineers, and then we've got everything we need. As soon as I talk to Grant and clear up a few details, we'll move ahead with the installation. Ought to be able to get it up this week. You've got the moped in the back?"

Sara could hear Laura moving equipment around in the high-backed van.

"I'm mostly finished. From the sound of your voice when you called, I thought we were going to have to pack up the whole barn. We hardly need the big van if we're only installing a climbing wall. And, yes, the moped's in there."

Today's dawn brought a breakthrough in the funk that had been pulling Sara down. She didn't have to solve everything with Grant right away. The only urgency was to keep him interested in her part of his larger project. If she succeeded in that, they could look later at other matters, like her future with the new company. But if Grant were to drop the new Best Fit Adventures plan, everything else would be over.

Laura had helped her hone their ideas for BFA down to a primary pitch to families. Families, especially extended ones, often couldn't have real adventures together when kids were too small or grandparents too old. Those families might present a tremendous, untapped market.

The climbing wall would be their first completely designed offering. On it, experienced climbers could find real challenges in short but extremely difficult routes. Older people would get off the ground, just not so high. Children would discover progressive challenges, giving each child the chance to advance at his or her own speed and comfort level. There was nothing else like it out there in the adventure market.

If the wall worked, BFA would offer similar group experiences on the water, in snow, on horseback, even on mountain hikes, where different routes would take different amounts of time for varying age and skill groups. Then everyone would arrive at the same place for a picnic to be enjoyed together.

She had to make sure that the climbing wall appealed to Grant; then they could get their joint project back on track. She knew he was fundamentally a realist. Yes, she had made a mistake in discussing the bottling project with Jeff, and it was true that Grant's reaction to the blog post revealed a side of him that made her more cautious about tying her future entirely to him.

But why dwell on that? Grant's anger would surely pass, and his motivation could be regained. Concentrate on the moment! One project at a time. It would all work out. Everything now depended on making the climbing wall demonstration convincing. No, not just convincing—compelling! She was ready.

Laura wrapped up her work and left. Sara looked at her watch. Now she would drive the van up to Tomson Lake and decide whether it made sense to move some of the equipment right away to the escarpment on the lake property. She'd found the location with Google Maps and planned to install the demonstration equipment on that cliff. She could leave everything in the van until after a final check with Grant, and ride back here on the moped.

There was also an interesting question to answer: what was the purpose of the small structure she'd spotted on the computer image by the escarpment? She saw what might be a roof line in the middle of a tight group of trees. But the resolution up close was too unfocused for her to be sure. Perhaps whatever it was could be worked into her plans for the climbing adventure.

Her car was parked next to Jeff's Xterra. She had assumed that he was still asleep in the house when she arrived. No need to talk anyway, so she'd be off. She had the van door open when she heard Jeff call out from the back of the house. Wearing a T-shirt, gym shorts, and slippers, he held out a coffee mug in her direction.

"How about one for the road?"

God, she didn't need the inevitable conversation, but coffee was a strong pull. Without a reply, she closed the van door and followed Jeff into the house. They sipped hot Vienna Roast in silence until Jeff put down his cup and gave her a long stare before speaking.

"Thought you should know that the relations between Grant and Will were worse than strained. Violent, even. I think you should be careful with Grant."

"And you know this how?"

"From a man who helped Will build a cabin up by the lake. He watched them get into an actual fight."

"You've seen this cabin?"

"Not yet, but I intend to."

He pointed at a strange implement lying on the table. A metal rod, a short cross piece at one end and an oddly dented and cut blade on the other, could easily have been a specialized tool. Now she saw it could also be a key. Jeff followed her gaze.

"Yeah. That key opens the cabin, or should. I brought it back with me by mistake. I'll return it later. Doubt if anyone will need it before I do. But..."

Sara watched as Jeff's tired face pulled itself together into something like resolve.

"... before you go, I want to pass on more reasons why you should be careful about Grant Tomson. I've learned more about him. He..."

My God, she was trying to make a difficult situation easier on both of them but he kept boring in. Enough was enough.

"Don't!"

She glared and he looked back at her, first with surprise, then... sorrow? So, he felt bad. She felt a little of that too. But it didn't dim her intensity. Jeff dropped his gaze first, rose, and shuffled toward the stairs, mumbling words she barely caught.

"I'm going to take a shower. Help yourself to more coffee."

Sara waited until she heard water running in the pipes. She thought a minute, then picked up the cabin key and put it in her jacket pocket.

Two minutes later she was pushing the van toward Tomson Lake.

The rocket, heading to a new orbit.

Bill waited until just before eight am and called Tom Cisek's cell phone. Tom answered right away.

"What's up, Bill?"

Bill gave him what he had: Sanford Gordon's information about the will, Chavez's description of the Tomson twin's relationship, and Bebe's hunch about a possible hiding place at Will Tomson's workshop in Portal.

When he finished, he could almost hear the chief thinking, even when he finally spoke.

"If, in fact, there is a hiding place at the workshop, you think it will tell you where to look for what might be documents relating to Mrs. Tomson's will? And what you find might show how bad the blood was between the

Tomson boys? And that bad blood might be motive for murder? That's your theory?"

"Yeah."

"A couple more 'mights' and I could begin to think we're in Oz. I suppose you'll next want to go have a look?"

"I'd like to do it now."

Cisek thought some more.

"Okay. Here's the deal. Since the mother's will hasn't gone to probate and the Tomson case hasn't been closed, you can go have another look around the workshop on my say-so. We're responsible for the safety of unoccupied property in our jurisdiction. I'll call Greg and have him meet you there. He's still the investigating officer, so you follow his lead. Understood?"

"Sure. And I'll keep you informed . . . That is, Greg will."

"That's better. And one more thing. If this hiding spot turns out to be empty, or non-existent, this case is finished. I'm already mostly convinced that none of what we have adds up to foul play in Will's death. We have too much else to do to add a speculative. But, okay one last look."

After Bill left the Chief's office and drove away, his phone buzzed. He pulled over and heard Greg Takarchuk confirm a rendezvous at Will Tomson's workshop. Soon after that he left Swiftwater behind and drove through Portal. Farther up a gradually rising road, sunshine and a clear blue sky created a halo over budding trees. A long narrow lake along the road sparkled like a strobe light as it appeared and disappeared through the branches. He guessed the business at Will's place could be over pretty quickly. If so, he'd call Bebe and maybe she'd like to come back here for lunch or a walk. Just the thought of that put a smile on his face.

He was fitting a key into the padlock when he heard a vehicle approaching and Greg Takarchuk's car pulled in behind his. They conferred for a moment. Once inside, Greg wheeled over a set of steep steps with a platform at their top, while Bill checked the labels on the wood racks by the front of the workshop. He pointed at one.

"Here it is, Douglas fir, lot 6. We need to look at the seventh board down."

Greg planted the stairs, climbed up and counted out loud the number of boards.

"I'll need to clear out the top boards."

He handed down a half dozen and stopped.

"The next board seems just like the others."

Disappointment hit Bill like a body blow. He regrouped enough for a last try.

"Count up from the bottom."

Greg handed down two more boards.

"The next two boards won't come apart. This may be what you're looking for."

A small shot of optimism added energy as Bill moved the double boards to the long work table. They were stuck together. Greg found a thin chisel and got it between the ends of the boards. They separated slightly. Inserting other chisels along the length and prying alternately along both sides, they heard the characteristic groan of wood on wood as the boards popped apart. Will Tomson had carefully fashioned a dozen square recesses along both boards and inserted hardwood joiners. Once pounded together, the boards were not easily separated—just the way he designed them to be.

A neat oblong, the approximate size of half a safety deposit box, had been cut out of the center of each board. What could be a shallow box projected from the cut-out space in one of the boards.

He signaled Greg and the two of them gripped the ends of the board, rotated it, and gently flexed it until the insert moved partially out of the recessed space. They pulled on latex gloves and, each using a chisel as a pry, worked in small increments until the whole insert came out.

The insert was, in fact, a hardwood box with an outside depth of an inch and a half, leaving an interior space about three inches wide, a half-inch deep, and a foot long: ample space for three folded documents. One consisted of three pages and bore the letterhead of Sanford Gordon, the lawyer in Kansas City. The second was a long hand-written letter on blue stationary with the initials GT in gold. The third document was addressed to Sanford Gordon, Esq., and had been signed by Will Tomson.

Bill handed Greg the blue sheets and kept the rest.

"Have a look, then we'll..."

His cell phone chimed. He glanced at the caller ID and saw Jeff Winter's name. There was no urgent tag, so he punched the call to voice mail. He returned his full attention to the document in his hand.

It was easy to interpret the main content. The first page was a cover letter, signed by Gordon, referring to the next two pages as a codicil to a will and making it clear that Gordon was sending a sole copy to Will, with no similar copy going to his brother Grant. The codicil allowed for a revision to be made to Grace Tomson's will if Will wanted that change and communicated his desire to the lawyer. Gordon already had the proposed change on hand, but would not obey its instructions to alter Grace's will unless he had written confirmation from Will.

Bill's thoughts went immediately to a possible connection between the provisions of the codicil and a motive for murder. So what was in the codicil?

He read it quickly. It dealt only with the Tomson Lake property, beginning with a statement of Grace Tomson's wishes that the property be kept "as much as possible in its original state" with the "addition of buildings and other man-made alterations kept to an absolute minimum". Second, it specifically endorsed the annual continuation of the multi-tribal powwow and supported its expansion as "expiation for sins once committed against our aboriginal spiritual brothers and sisters".

Bill looked away for a moment. Those first provisions were pretty general. What more was there? He returned his attention to the codicil.

As a third provision, it gave Will Tomson the "full and final power to determine any present and/or future uses" to which the lake property might be put. Fourth, it directed her attorney Gordon to send a copy of the codicil to Will Tomson only, and to retain the codicil in unexecuted form "until and if" Will approved it. Finally, it directed "my legal counsel, in the event of Will Tomson's death, to make arrangements for the gifting of the lake property in its entirety to a tribal entity or to tribal entities as determined by representatives of the Indian tribes which have attended the annual Tomson Lake Powwow".

Bill guessed that the final provision was a legal thicket that could tie up ownership of the property for years to come. But the whole document was a clear display of maternal favoritism toward Will, a choice that Grant would likely interpret as an insult. Or worse.

Greg was patiently waiting for him to finish. Bill summarized as briefly as he could what the documents contained.

"Now how about that letter, there? What does it say?"

Greg grimaced.

"You know English wasn't my first language, and I missed a few words because of the handwriting. But I don't think that's the problem here. An old lady is dumping onto paper her feelings about her sons. She tells Will that he is the favored one and reminds him that his name is a shortening of "Will of God". She also says that Grant's birth mother had chosen the name "Ernest" for her baby, before she died, but Mrs. Tomson changed it to Grant because the baby really was "Granted by God" to her.

Greg looked again at the two blue sheets, one in each hand, nodded, and went on.

"The rest of the letter is all over the place, referring to events and other conversations that Will must have been expected to recognize. I *think* they add up to something like: Will is blessed and has stayed close to the true faith. Grant has strayed and become a disappointment. She even refers to him as "Ernest" toward the end. It's like she had cut Grant out of her life."

Bill absorbed the implications.

"I think we can conclude one thing for sure: Will knew the importance of these documents and figured that Grant would want to get his hands on them. Why else would he go to such great lengths to hide them?"

Greg handed back the blue stationary sheets.

"Agreed. And, if Grant knew about the existence of these documents, I bet he would have tried to find them. The lab can check for fingerprints. But I doubt they'll find any of Grant's. Even if he came here, it's clear he didn't find anything. Otherwise he would have destroyed these papers."

"That's in line with my thinking. But suppose he knew about the documents and couldn't find them? Only Will, Grace, and the lawyer knew. Grace wouldn't have told him, and that lawyer is tight-lipped. That just leaves Will. And if Will told everything, Grant would know that the documents were meaningless unless Will officially acted on them. So, failing to get the documents, Grant could still protect his interests by silencing Will."

"A lot of 'ifs' there."

"Yeah, I know. But now we have some evidence to support conjecture. We'll need more, but it's a start."

They stood silent for a while, Bill staring into the unfocused middle distance. He shook himself back to the moment, then placed all the documents back inside the box. The box and their gloves went into a large plastic bag, onto which Greg wrote with a magic marker their names, the location, and date.

He held the bag out and a quizzical look appeared.

"You want to take this to the chief?"

Bill had to give Greg credit. Technically he was the lead, but he was acknowledging Bill's longer experience with this case.

"Only if it's more convenient for you."

Greg nodded.

"Well, maybe, yeah. I'm going to Portal to meet a social worker following up on a domestic violence incident. A gun was involved, and I'm just making sure there isn't another."

Bill took the evidence bag.

"I'll take these items to the station. Guess that does it for me here. Thanks for the help. Now maybe the chief will have reason to take a closer look at Grant Tomson."

They locked up the workshop and Bill was heading for his car when his cell sounded. He was surprised to see Jeff's name on the screen again.

"What's up, Jeff?"

"Remember I promised to ask Will Tomson's neighbors about their opinions of him?"

"Sure. Matter of fact, I'm just leaving his workshop. You get anything useful?"

"I was up there yesterday afternoon. People wouldn't talk or say much. Except one guy, who told me Will had a strange, almost mean side. He also built a cabin to use as a second workshop near the Tomson Lake house. I got tired last evening and thought all that could wait until today."

Bill heard Jeff clear his throat

"There's something else, though. The reason I'm calling."

Bill imagined he could hear embarrassment and worry.

"Go on."

"I told you my wife has been working with Grant Tomson."

"I haven't forgotten that."

"Yesterday, after I finished the interviews, I thought I'd have a look at the cabin Will built. Even started up the trail that runs from the lake back to where it's located, but my leg got too tired to go on. I forgot to put the key back. Had a talk with my wife, Sara, this morning and mentioned the cabin. She headed for the lake and took the key with her. I'm going there now."

"All right, let me know if you find anything else of interest. Thanks for the heads-up. I gotta go."

"Hold on a sec."

Bill waited until Jeff came back on the line, sounding confused.

"Sara just texted me that she's left the lake, and not to worry. Says she'll give me back the key later. But I'm on my way there and am already in view of the house. I can see our van. She *hasn't* left. There's another car, too, a new-looking black sedan."

A black sedan. The favorite car of successful businessmen. Even if there were lots of those around, Grant Tomson might have one.

"Okay. I'm on my way. Ten minutes. Keep an eye on things and call again if you need to. We've just found some evidence that could point to Grant being more dangerous than we thought. So don't do anything. Just wait. Got that?"

Bill heard a low grunt on the other end.

"Nothing. Do you hear me?"

The line was dead.

Ten minutes gone and McHugh hadn't arrived like he promised. Already inching beyond the Tomson house at the lake, Jeff looked at his watch for the third time in the last minute. Waiting longer was intolerable.

If the black car was in fact Tomson's, he couldn't leave Sara alone with that man. The two of them weren't here at the main house, door locked, and no lights on. Best bet was that Sara had gone to the cabin. Why else would she have taken the key? But why the text?

One other possibility occurred. What if Sara didn't send the text and it was Grant Tomson that did? Sara could be in real trouble. He didn't know what McHugh had meant by saying that Tomson could be "more dangerous than we thought". It was safest to assume the worst.

Maybe McHugh was only minutes behind him, but those minutes could be crucial. In a hobbled jog he hurried toward the tree where he had found the key, and then up the trail that led from it. Intruding thoughts pushed him on. He and Sara had their problems. Circumstances had taken their toll, as well as had her actions—and his. Maybe he and Sara were done. There might be no hope of reversing the past, but he still loved her. So help him God and everything else, he did. Each stride became a desperate lunge forward.

Still sore from yesterday's jump down from the boulder, his hip screamed at him to stop and, when he didn't, ratcheted up the pain with each additional stride. And the term "stride" didn't even faintly describe a crabbed push-off from his bad leg, followed by the long step with which his good leg tried to compensate. His concentration was so focused on the constricted mechanics of his gait that he lost any sense of the distance he still had to travel.

He was surprised, then, when Sara's face appeared in a gap between the trees ahead of him. He stopped, then moved again, concentrating less on speed and more on silence. Dropping under the larger branches, he saw a cabin in a small clearing. Sara stood in front of the cabin, an angry welt reddening one side of her face. A tall lean man with dark hair blocked part of his view. The man was glaring in Jeff's direction. Everything was still for a long moment. Jeff could hear the wind rising.

He could also hear Grant Tomson clearly as he returned his attention to Sara.

"I'm disappointed that you've joined the stupid attempt to tie me to my brother's unfortunate death. If what you've told me constitutes all that can be assembled against me, it wouldn't make the top ten of my concerns. You could, however, be an irritant; and I would rather do away with you now than have to deal with you later. You're of no more use, so why should you be allowed to be a bother?"

He gestured toward the ground, where Jeff could make out parts of ropes and metal fittings. Tomson's voice rose in anger and Jeff couldn't miss the intent in the fragments that reached him: "... fall from the cliff ..." and "... no one finds you until it's too late ..."

Tomson took a step toward Sara and she lunged forward, her fingernails aimed at his eyes. As Tomson slipped to the side, she hooked an arm around his neck. That was the last thing Jeff saw as he struggled up and felt a staggering rage propel him forward.

Tomson was pushing Sara down to the ground. He had started to turn when Jeff mustered his remaining strength and plowed into Tomson's side.

The advantage of momentum lasted only until both of them smashed onto the rocky ground. Exhaustion had stripped Jeff of strength, and a sharp pain in his hip temporarily immobilized him. His opponent, stronger and in better shape, rolled away and straddled Jeff's back. Pain shot through his upper body as Tomson wrenched his arm upward. Somewhere within the pain, he made out the shouted words behind them.

"Police! Let him go! Stand up slowly and keep your hands in the air."

More pain, a quick tussle behind him, then finally the pressure on his arm let up and Tomson's weight was lifted from his back. Little by little he pulled himself into the present. The object to his left came into focus:

a boulder, gray, almost white, with irregular bands of dull orange and tiny shards that sparkled in the sun.

Jeff allowed himself the luxury of feeling peaceful, now that Sara was safe. He'd just close his eyes for a second, and...

※

Bebe tried to concentrate, but none of her old tricks—the ones she had learned to protect herself from panic in crowds or from the dizziness brought on by heights—could help her now. She didn't need to get away from a situation; she wanted to run toward it, be part of it.

The sound of fifth grade feet dashing around History House temporarily broke through her thoughts, but not for long. She had asked her volunteers to manage today's visitors completely. Leave them to it. What good would she be in her current state anyway?

She knew that, realistically, she couldn't be with Bill right now. His job and her condition wouldn't allow that. She had never been one to meddle in other people's lives. On the contrary, her own life had become an exercise in building and maintaining separation. But now something had happened to her that was different from anything she'd experienced since she was a child. She wanted a connection. She wanted to be pulled into another life.

But how could she, a woman of such limited experience, be sure even of that? The girl had done better than the woman when it came to the opposite sex. At twelve, she developed crushes just like other girls her age. Her problems, the phobias, came later. With puberty, crowds became murky shadows that turned into dark, threatening storms by the end of high school. She'd looked for boyfriends and found one: quiet, bookish and—she thought—dependable. With him, she lost her virginity at sixteen, only to have him announce a breakup immediately afterwards. That left her wondering: Was it me? Or some silent signals that he read within me? After a while she stopped looking for an answer.

In college, she became a loner by necessity, having her first full-blown panic attacks, being admitted to a hospital, being sent to therapists. Friends, now only female, became increasingly limited until finally there were just two who had stayed with her. Male relationships were out of the question; mere touch was like a mortal threat.

Then a decade and a half of "adjusting". She had been warned that it could take that long. By her late twenties, she had learned enough defensive techniques that daily life could achieve a kind of balance, as long as she kept things consistent, and, as much as possible, predictable. That required a stress-free environment: a safe community, a job that would involve a limited number of people at the same time, and living alone. She had found that and now... she could think of nothing else but risking it all. Because she cared about a man. Because he had insinuated himself into her thoughts and her heart.

Maybe her inexperienced heart was left over from an incomplete adolescence, yet she was becoming what she swore never to be: a giddy girl who goes for a joy ride and afterward swears there was no warning sign before the car went over the cliff.

Her finger itched over the call button. It would be her third try in an hour. She knew there were tasks that resisted interruption. There could be a simple explanation for Bill's lack of response: he and his cell phone were out of range, or in a blind spot. Her brain knew, but fear hung to her.

All right, she would give it five more minutes, then just one more try.

Sara was present and yet she wasn't. It felt as if she were floating above, observing her own figure sitting hunched on the steps leading up to the cabin door. That person by her? Jeff? Part of the weight on her shoulders was a heavy jacket, the rest from Jeff's arm, draped across it. What difference did it make? There might have been something to focus on before, but now it was gone. She was gone. She couldn't care. About anything.

Listlessly, she raised her head and looked across the small clearing. Grant was facing two policemen. They were both tall, but one was leaner, the other big-chested and broad-shouldered. Broad shoulders wore no jacket, and she remembered vaguely that he was the one who had covered her.

"Are you all right?"

That was Jeff, breaking the silence. Am I all right? Hell no, she would have yelled, if she had the energy. The big cop looked at them, detached himself from the other two, and walked over.

"Mrs. Winter, I'm Officer McHugh. How are you feeling? That's a mean looking welt on your face."

Eventually she'd have to say something.

"It just stings. My shoulder hurts more, but I don't think my arm is broken."

McHugh nodded.

"We'll try to get it looked at soon. Paramedics are on their way."

She felt a tiny flare of the anger.

"I'm okay."

"All right. Before we leave, can you give me a quick version of what happened here?"

Did she have the energy? Might as well try. Officer McHugh was holding a notebook. Jeff pulled his arm off her shoulder and struggled to stand. Before he was fully up, he barked at McHugh.

"I heard Tomson say that he was going to kill Sara and make it seem like an accident."

McHugh addressed Jeff calmly.

"Let's do this right. First I need to hear what Sara can tell me. Then you. Why don't you go sit on that log over there and give me a minute with her before I hear your side of the story?"

Sara saw Jeff look at her with anguish, then hobble several yards to a fallen tree and, with an assist from one arm, lower himself into a sitting position across the clearing from where Grant and the other officer stood silently. Grant had quickly assumed his usual public pose: the observant, slightly bored man in charge. She tried not to dwell on that image. It broadcast a negative power that was already shaking the fraction of self-control she was able to hold on to.

McHugh returned his attention to her.

"Okay, what happened?"

She struggled for words and even as she spoke them wondered if they held together any more than she did.

"I came up here to put on a demonstration. Didn't finish yet when Grant showed up."

"Where were you when he arrived?"

"Inside this cabin."

She nicked her head up and behind her toward the closed door.

"How did you enter the cabin?"

"With a key I got from my husband, Jeff."

McHugh quickly looked over at Jeff, then at her again.

"There may be further questions about that key, but we'll hold off until later. Go on, please."

"When I started to install the equipment, I saw I needed other tools. Thought there might be some in the cabin. Went in. Saw a big black motorcycle with something like a long striped scarf folded across the seat. The light wasn't good, but I remember thinking red and orange. Just then Grant came in and was really mad about my being in the cabin."

"Go on. What happened next?"

She could feel her words slowing down.

"We stood on either side of the motorcycle and talked. Yelled, is more like it."

"What was your main subject of dispute?"

"Grant didn't believe me ... Accused me of hiding something ... Next thing I remember, he was yelling about his brother and who owned the lake ... and I had no idea what he meant. He got madder and madder ... Said I'd ruined everything. He leaned across the cycle and slapped me hard. Really hard."

Sara involuntarily reached toward her left cheek, but stopped before she touched it.

"Okay, we'll go back later to details about the conversation. He hit you. What then?"

"Hauled me out of the cabin and threw me down the steps ... Knocked me down ... Jeff tackled Grant. The rest you know."

"Where is the key now?"

"Gave it to Grant in the cabin."

"Before or after he hit you?"

She had to think.

"After, I guess ... I was pretty dazed ... He might have taken the key when I was down."

"Any idea where the key might be now? The door's locked."

She felt her mind clearing enough so she was seeing images, not just their shadows.

"No. When he threw me down the stairs, I might have passed out for a while. I remember Grant coming toward me, and it wasn't from the direction of the cabin. The cabin steps were the first thing I saw when I could focus. He might still have the key, or he could have thrown it away."

"So, after he came to you again ... ?"

Her mind was slowing and so were her words.

"He hauled me up and walked me a few paces and started in again. He got angrier and said he would get rid of me. Something snapped in me. I truly believed he was going to kill me. After that I didn't think; I attacked. Good thing you arrived. I'd probably be dead by now."

With that admission, all her reserves were gone. She slumped forward on her knees.

"One more question. Did you text your husband that you were leaving Tomson Lake?"

How could he think that? The stupid question gave her momentary energy.

"No. When do you think I would have had time for that?"

"Someone texted Jeff. Could Grant Tomson have used your phone?"

That hadn't occurred to her. He energy disappeared and she heard her tired, almost slurred reply.

"Maybe I was out longer than I thought. That was the only time he could have used my phone."

McHugh reached out to touch her shoulder.

"That's it for now. I'll stay with you and Jeff until the paramedics arrive. You both would have trouble walking out of here."

Out of the corner of her eye, she saw McHugh signal Jeff that he could return.

She was too weak to say that she just wanted to be alone. All the events of the past weeks felt as if they were encasing her in a monstrous straightjacket, one that bound her mind as well as her body.

She looked across at Jeff and, in one corner of her consciousness, knew she needed to talk to him about everything that had happened. Just not now.

Not now.

Alone in Cisek's office, Bill had a minute before the chief came back. He called Bebe and started speaking immediately when she answered.

"Bebe, I saw you'd called several times and wanted to call back as soon as I could, just to let you know things were all right. I'm in Swiftwater briefing Tom Cisek about what's going on. He'll be right back, so I'll have to call again later to tell you more when we're done."

He had to hang up before she could respond. Just knowing she'd called somehow made his brain feel lighter, clearer. Or was it his heart? Later, later.

Right now he needed to concentrate on the upcoming conversation. After getting Sara and Jeff Winter squared away with the paramedics, he'd taken Greg Takarchuk away from where he stood with Grant Tomson so they could decide how to handle him from then on. The issue was whether they could reasonably hold Grant for further questioning. As he and Greg had talked, he saw Grant speaking on his cell phone. Bill had reviewed the information they had, admitting to himself that the grounds for holding Grant, much less indicting him, were weak. Minutes later he'd gotten through to Tom Cisek only to learn that Tom had already been contacted by a lawyer on Grant's behalf and, even considering what Bill had to say, decided there was not enough defensible evidence to hold Grant.

Now the chief entered the room, holding two cups of coffee. When each man had taken a sip, Tom, as usual, cut straight to the chase.

"From the top. Besides the highlights you've already given me, I want the details in sequence."

Bill handed over the documents from the workshop, then laid out a straight line right down the middle: what he and Greg had found at the workshop, then what happened around the cabin. He held off until the end the conversation he had had with Grant Tomson after the incident at the cabin.

"Tomson said several times that his obligation to cooperate with us extended only to 'the narrowest and strictest interpretation of our authority'. Then he jumped into a rambling speech about the limits of authority over free capitalism or something like that."

"That wouldn't leave room for much real information."

"Agreed. I gave him a little space to rant, so he couldn't claim he was muzzled. When he started in again, I cut him off. And you're right. I got the impression he was mostly using all that talk to get the upper hand and to avoid having to say much about the situation right there."

"So what was his version?"

"Pretty simple, really. He says that Sara Winter called him to arrange a demonstration, but he told her he didn't have time. She said she would probably install some equipment so it would be ready when he did have time to check it out. Tomson claims he and Winter had had what he called 'preliminary and inconclusive' conversations about a joint business venture, and that he didn't trust her completely. So he decided to pay a surprise visit to the lake property. Which he did, this morning early."

"So he says he's too busy, but has time for the surprise trip?"

"I confronted him with that. He responded that he's extremely busy and changed his mind only when he realized that Winter was a 'potential liability'—his words—that was better 'dealt with earlier than later'."

"Go on."

"Tomson said he got to the main house and found Winter's parked van. Since she wasn't in the house, he went toward the place where she had told him the equipment was to be installed. That spot was adjacent to a cabin that Will Tomson had built."

Bill checked his notes and organized his thoughts while he took a long swig of coffee.

"Anyway, Tomson said he was surprised to find the door of the cabin open. When he looked, Winter was inside. Tomson said he asked nicely why she was there and she got 'defensive and evasive'. She refused to say where she had found the key, which was a concern since he himself never had a key. From that point on, Tomson claims, Winter got 'increasingly irrational, vituperative and out of control' to the point where he had to—in his words—'slap her lightly to bring her back to reality'. When he suggested they leave the cabin, she at first refused, and then, Tomson says, voluntarily left, locked the door, turned, tripped and fell down the steps. When he tried to reason with her again, she attacked him and he had no choice but to subdue her 'as much for her sake as for mine'."

"What is the woman's—Winter's—version?"

"She said she needed other tools and thought she might find them in the cabin. I'll get a fuller statement from her after she's been checked at the hospital. But, so far, what she described is the opposite of Tomson's version. That Tomson was the irrational party, that he hit her and threw her down the stairs, and threatened her."

"Where's the key now?"

Bill nodded.

"I was going to get to that. Sara Winter says Tomson took it from her. He claims he never had the key. When I asked him, he gave me this lecture about how upstanding he was, and would not tolerate the insult of being searched without consulting counsel. For your information, I had not said anything about searching him. He could have had it in his pocket. We did a preliminary search of the area around the cabin and didn't find any key. We'll try again later or call in a locksmith."

"So at this point all you've got is not much more than he-said, she-said?"

"Pretty much, except there's two details. Jeff Winter, Sara Winter's husband, told me that Sara had some kind of relationship with Tomson that went beyond straight business. Also, Jeff arrived on the scene ahead of me and heard what he claims was Tomson threatening Sara's life. That would corroborate Sara's account, except Jeff admits he couldn't hear everything Tomson said. Tomson claims he was only offering an admonishment, warning Sara that she would put her own life in danger if she didn't calm down."

"We'll deal with that later. Anything else?"

"About what happened, no. There'll be more details in my report. Sara Winter's at the hospital for an examination. So's Jeff."

Bill waited. There was one more matter, but he wasn't the right one to bring it up. That was for the chief, if he wanted to. Silence reigned for maybe half a minute. Then the oak chair creaked as Tom settled forward.

"You still disagree with my decision about how to handle Tomson?"

"We ought to have held him until we conducted a more thorough investigation of the cabin and of his person."

Cisek stayed calm, though his words took a formal turn.

"We need more than we have to hold him, even on a temporary basis. He did no breaking and entering. The cabin is on his family's property. We have no proof that he assaulted or threatened Sara Winter, just hearsay. Besides, if she had more than a business relationship with Tomson, anything she says will be countered with accusations that she's just expressing the bitterness of a girlfriend who's been dumped. Jeff Winter's statement that he heard a threat would not likely hold up under cross. Sara has not indicated that she will bring a suit for assault; if she does, we'll consider the merits and get a formal statement from Tomson."

Cisek paused, shifted his gaze away, then back.

"Wish I had a mirror so you could see the look on your face."

Bill didn't need a mirror.

"Tomson is guilty of something. He's the type who uses money, status, and people to get what he wants."

The chief's posture relented a hair.

"You think I don't know that? He's arrogant and sticking it to us, sure he can do anything he pleases. I can't be the bloodhound here, the single-minded law enforcer who won't stop, even when there's no evidence to make the case in court."

"And that's me?"

Cisek sat up straighter, hands gripping the wooden armrests.

"You came to us with that reputation. Frankly, I've seen none of that since you arrived ... until maybe now."

They stared at each other until the chief spoke again.

"You fixin' to go it on your own?"

Bill thought hard on that.

"The answer is not in any way that will involve you or the department."

"I've heard that before."

"Trust me."

"That, too."

Bill waited. Maybe this was the time to quit, but he tried again.

"How's this. I'll tell you in detail before I do anything and you say yes or no. I don't plan on committing any huge infraction. And if anything comes down it will be on me, not on you or the department. I'll take whatever happens, regardless of the consequences."

Cisek relaxed, sat back, and raised a hand.

"Despite what you may be thinking, I don't give in to men like Grant Tomson just because they've got power. But I've also learned that you get farther with patience, procedures, and an occasional end run than by charging in when you're outgunned, Sundance. Who knows? You might catch on to that someday."

He paused, lightened up a bit.

"You know, I'm getting to like you, Officer McHugh, and you do a hellava good job. You just gotta give me enough slack to do the job I have to do. Even when I don't like doing it."

"Just so big money and west side suits who think they own everything, including us, don't get a free pass again, like they always do."

"Who says we're finished with Tomson? We're getting a warrant to search the cabin and its premises, see what we find. Then we'll talk to the man again."

Bill wanted to resist. He'd seen how these situations play out. Give a man like Tomson more time and he'll hire more guns. By now, he probably had his lawyers talking to the judges who would most likely be approached for a search warrant. Those judges would be reminded of the potential for a lot of political trouble, and the warrant, at best, would be delayed.

"You want me in on that?"

"You and Greg. Be ready to drop other assignments and head for the cabin as soon as we get the warrant. If Tomson is guilty of anything, I want to nail the bastard as much as you do."

Bill tried to match Cisek's attitude. But it was hard to rinse out all the disappointment.

Cisek drained his coffee and set the cup down.

"On the other hand, it sometimes helps to give events a nudge. You use your judgment about whether you still need to go ahead. Just don't forget the part about keeping me informed."

Sara couldn't stop sobbing. Sofa cushions weren't thick enough to damp the continuous shudder wracking her body. Jeff adjusted to the rhythm until it began to feel like his own torment.

She'd held it together until they reached their house, sitting silent and rigid as Greg Takarchuk drove back from the hospital in Esterhill. She'd been so stoic at the hospital that Jeff began to wonder if she was feeling anything. The doctors in the ER found no broken bones; they taped her shoulder so a torn muscle would heal more easily, and warned her that she may have suffered a mild concussion. She shouldn't take sleeping pills for two days, though pain killers were allowed.

Meanwhile, the surgeon who'd patched Jeff up after his previous injury left a family gathering long enough to check Jeff for further damage. He found nothing obvious but ordered a visit to the PT specialist on Monday.

When Jeff opened the front door of their home and stood aside for Sara to enter, she stumbled straight to the sofa and collapsed into a corner. One arm reached up the back of the sofa while her face burrowed deep into a pillow. Jeff waited by the open door, trying to figure what to do next, when a low sound, more animal-like than human, started somewhere deep inside Sara, then gradually rose in volume and became a full-throated yowl of grief. Since then, Sara hadn't shifted her position for what felt like an hour, but by his watch was closer to fifteen minutes.

He approached the couch and sat down carefully. She paid no attention. When he put a comforting hand on her good shoulder, she whirled back toward him, her eyes wide with unseeing agony. He removed his hand and she went back to her earlier position, only now the sobs were gone.

In time she turned again, faced forward, and raised her red-rimmed eyes toward the ceiling, staring, rarely blinking. She didn't look at Jeff, though he couldn't take his eyes off her. Despite his bewilderment and hurt at everything that had divided them over the last weeks, he couldn't help absorbing more of her anguish. It matched his own; and just as he had no idea how to heal himself, neither could he decipher what she might tolerate in this moment. He had to try to help. A feeling that transcended deceit and loss impelled him, though he couldn't give it a name.

"You need to eat."

No reaction.

"I'll fix what we got."

In the kitchen, he mixed a salad, cubed an already-cooked chicken breast, and warmed a can of tomato soup. Dividing everything equally, he placed plates and bowls on a tray and went back into the living room. As he walked, an idea occurred to him.

Sara hadn't moved. He spoke to her over the tray.

"I'm going out to the barn with food for both of us. I hope you'll join me."

No reaction.

"It's up to you."

In the viewing area of the barn, where twin sofas formed a "V" facing a large flat screen, he retrieved two retro TV tables. Sara and he had found those tables in an antique store and bought them on a lark. Much of their best planning for Cascade Adventures had occurred when they watched videos Sara had shot on hikes, wedding the images to new ideas as they munched food from the little tables. Among the video discs was a slide show Jeff had made out of several photo files.

During the early months of their marriage, Sara had relished her art photography, preferring black and white because of its ability to bring out contrasts. She especially focused on close-ups of rock formations and unusual plants, and would often marry them to images of antiquities, arm-less Greek torsos or ruined Roman colonnades. The result was a collection of unique images, by turns peaceful and jarring, but always thought-provoking. He especially treasured them as glimpses of the interior Sara that she rarely revealed in any other form. When she stopped creating those images, he began to lose some of her. Of course he didn't realize it at the time. Now he knew only too well.

He put the slide show on as a repeating loop, laid out the food on two tables, one in front of each of the couches, and began to eat. In time, he sensed more than saw Sara arrive and sit down. She joined him in the silent viewing and, he hoped, in eating. He didn't look to see.

The photo images, blooming, disappearing, reappearing again, were a hypnotic journey into perceptions that paralleled but never quite inter-sected the experiences they had recently lived through. Sometimes they soothed Jeff, sometimes saddened him. He had no idea whether they spoke to Sara at all.

Jeff finished eating. So, apparently, had Sara, though she hadn't taken much. They sat just three feet apart at the point where the angled sofas met, but the distance felt immense. A low-wattage table lamp cast a low ambient light. When Jeff looked at Sara, he could see her mouth; above that her face was in shadow. Maybe she felt his eyes on her. She began to talk, still facing the slowly-changing images.

"He's crazy. Maybe not certifiable, but crazy. I chose to get close to a crazy person. I trusted him. You warned me, and I didn't pay attention. Went to bed with him. I'm crazy."

Her voice had the brittle sound of rusted wire scraping across some-thing hard and unforgiving. Jeff stayed quiet.

Now bitterness joined in.

"In the cabin, he changed from one minute—one second—to the next. He looked so different all of a sudden. I hardly recognized him."

She shook her head.

"I can't remember much, but I do remember the look on his face. An alien stood there in front of me, with a body that felt twice as big, as if he could crush me if he got too close. His arms waved around and never stopped, like two propellers."

"Did he say anything?"

Sara ducked down and glanced his way before turning back. In that brief second he saw only her blank eyes. When she spoke again, it was as if his question hadn't registered.

"And his voice. It was like walking into a tornado. Words flew around. So fast I missed a lot of them. It was like anger under such high pressure that it escaped faster than he could put it into words. Everything was dis-connected, but under it all was one thing clear: He wanted to hurt every-one who had hurt him. His revenge had no bounds. He didn't just want to hurt in return, he wanted to eradicate. And that included me."

Jeff tried again.

"Who else was included?"

Again she looked his way, and this time appeared to recognize him. Her chin movement was almost a nod.

"I was an easy and unimportant target. The big ones in his sights were his mother and his brother, Will. It was like the two of them were balled up into one target. When Grant went off on them, his words got really jumbled. Will was favored, he was not. Will was blood, he was not. His mother judged, Will gloated and rubbed it in . . . "

She paused.

"You know—you may not believe this because it's still hard for me to—there were a couple of moments where I actually felt sorry for Grant the little boy."

After that, she sat up straighter. Jeff allowed himself the hope that maybe her experience hadn't damaged her as much as he'd feared. A moment later, he knew how misplaced, or at least premature, that hope was. As if the new oxygen was escaping her, she deflated to the hunched position over her knees. Jeff waited until she sat back again.

"Did Grant say anything about how Will died?"

He could see her effort in processing the question. Finally she spoke, her voice a bit more reflective and calmer than what he'd heard before.

"More is coming back, but I'm still not sure how to sort it out. Grant was unloading pure emotion. He did say something about the lake. I think he mentioned 'legacy' and 'inheritance', and as he said that he turned furious. Then he stopped, and said something like 'but they can't take that away from me now'. When he said that, he had his hand on the motorcycle and was kind of stroking it. That I do remember because it was so weird. Suddenly he got ugly and said something about my 'ruining it'. Then he hit me."

"You'll need to tell the police all you remember."

She made a movement that could have been a nod and was quiet after that. After several minutes she rose, walked to the disc player and turned off the images. The only remaining light came from the small lamp by the sofas. She sat down again, wordless, staring straight ahead.

Jeff had no idea what to do next. Did she want him to stay? His instinct warned him that even asking that question would be a mistake. He waited a few minutes, then stacked their dishes on the tray. She'd eaten about half of what he'd prepared.

"I'll clean up and fix the bed for you in the house. The pull-out here in the barn is fine for me."

Sara gave no indication that she had heard him. A half-hour later he returned, carrying sheets and a blanket. She glanced at him, rose, and, standing in front of him, put her hand on his shoulder. Her head was down the whole time. Then she lowered her hand and left.

Jeff stayed standing by the window that faced the house, waiting until he saw the lights go out. Then he found his blanket and stretched out on the sofa.

It was a long time before sleep found him.

FRIDAY, APRIL 23

Waking up, Bebe luxuriated in a new world. Bill was out there on the sofa. Her day would begin with him. And end...? That answer would come later. If not tonight, then very soon she would wake with him beside her. Her cautious mind warned her about taking anything for granted. But her heart smiled and told her brain firmly to shut up.

He had called after dinner, after he'd finished writing a report about what happened up at the lake. His voice had sounded shy when he asked if it was too late to come over. Shy? That broad-shouldered, imposing presence she'd once thought might be a threat? She'd had many glimpses now of a quiet and thoughtful side of Bill, and knew that his willingness to reveal that aspect of himself was a sign that he'd come to trust her, too. But shy? She wanted to respond with a laugh. Instead, she put her feelings into a simple, "Please come".

Minutes later, there he was. He stood right near her, expectant, not hiding at all how much he wanted to grab her. And yet he waited. She was the one who closed the inches between them, let her body touch, then melt into his. When she put her arms carefully around his neck, she felt his arms gradually encircle her waist. He knew. He gave her control so she could gradually lose it. There is a God, she'd thought; and she thought it again now, wondrously.

The rest of the evening had that same feel. Bill never brought up what happened at the lake, and she never asked. All of that could wait. Instead, she brought out old photo albums and showed him her childhood. There were plenty of pictures of that childhood time, but few of her in adolescence, and only a smattering after that. She remembered acutely, almost to the day, when she had wanted no more pictures, no record of a dark curtain descending.

But Bill was unfazed. For him, her disappearance behind the curtain was simply a part of her story. Not even a sad part. She began to feel really special, instead of just being someone defined by special needs. Because of that, she did none of her usual editing as she filled in the details he asked for: When did crowds begin to bother her; when did heights? In his soft voice she heard a native lilt, telling her that he, too, was bringing back thoughts of the past.

Gradually Bill added details about his own life—about a father who disappeared into drink, then simply disappeared. About feeling alien in his own land, and about a different but similar curtain, one that separated the richness of his own culture from a society that often despised its distinctiveness. About what it was like to enforce the laws of those who had broken their word so many times in the past. About leaving the Sheriff's office and coming to Swiftwater, in part because he wanted a smaller, rooted community.

As they talked, her hand lay across his. Gradually she felt his hand begin to hold hers, caressing without pressure. In fact, that gesture perfectly described what was going on between them. A little after midnight, they acknowledged that was as far as they ought to go for now.

Bill held her while he whispered.

"I'll be right here on the couch. Tomorrow we'll tell each other our dreams."

Now it was morning, and what a glorious one. The sky was overcast. She had never before realized that clouds could sparkle! Bebe rose and got herself ready. In the mirror she noticed faint lines in her face. Should she add makeup? No, she decided. Bill had accepted her as she was. What need was there for makeup? She did, however, take extra time to pick out the right dress to wear. Right? For so long, clothing had meant serviceable, with not much more than the weather in mind. Picking clothing with Bill in mind added an additional flash of brilliance to the already bright day.

He sat on the sofa, exactly where she had left him after midnight; but now a cup of coffee was on the table, his mussed hair from the night before now combed. A faint pink glow on his cheeks told her he had been up long enough to shave.

There was another difference. The body that had melted gently into hers just a few hours ago had assumed the shoulder-straight posture of duty, with a cell phone pressed tightly to one ear. Bill glanced at her quickly, allowing a small smile that didn't change the seriousness in his eyes. He listened, responding in terse monosyllables.

"I'll get there as soon as I can. Within the hour...agreed. I'll meet Greg up there."

Then he leaned forward, stood up, and terminated the call at the same time. He opened his arms and she walked into them. They hugged, but almost immediately he released her and stepped back. His eyes added regret to the seriousness of his words.

"Couldn't come at a worse time. I'm sorry. I've got to go to Tomson Lake. There's been a new development at Will Tomson's cabin..."

A fleeting intimate look asked her to understand how much he really didn't want to leave.

At the door, he turned back.

"Jeff Winter also called this morning and I'll take him along. I don't know how long I'll be up there, but I'll call and be back as soon as I can. You and I are just getting started."

He opened the door and hesitated, reaching into a jacket pocket.

"I almost forgot. We found the documents that someone was looking for at History House. All along we had been focusing on Will. Now I think your midnight visitor could have been Grant, instead. The documents were concealed in the lumber, exactly where you thought they would be. They could explain a lot; but given what just happened, we may never find out everything. I made copies and I'll show them to you later."

He left. Through the glass panel in the door, Bebe saw clouds moving in, increasing overcast beginning to dim the day. But her thoughts were behind the clouds, imagining sunshine, just like the warm light that glowed inside her.

In her dream, Sara's rope snapped free from its carabineer and she began a long free fall, with no view of the ground far below her. Desperate, she twisted in bed and then calmed slowly as she felt the texture of the sheet that covered her. But where was she? In the dark room there were no reference points; she began to panic again. Her hand found the familiar lathed pattern on the antique bedpost. Tactile memory told her where she was—back in the home she had once shared with Jeff. In the bed that her Italian grandfather had made, that became her parents' and in turn made its way to her.

Without turning on a light, she began mentally reforming the room around her. The high dresser from an antique store in Leavenworth that almost matched the family bedstead. The braided rugs that she and Jeff had made together. But even as she put individual elements in their familiar places, she realized that nothing belonged to her anymore. Nor did she belong with them. That final thought, she knew, really meant Jeff.

The only sensation she could identify was emptiness, a state of mind and body that was beyond alone. To be alone, you have to be real, and she was nothing. To herself, to no one.

She would pack a suitcase. Then she would leave. To where? No idea. All she knew was she had to get away. Pack, sleep, then act. She rose, turned on a light and pulled down a suitcase from the upper shelf of her closet. It was the smallest one. When she stood in front of the clothes rack, decisiveness abandoned her. Her brain refused to single out which clothes to take, and her arm felt too leaden to react to commands. She went back to bed, leaving the open suitcase on the floor.

She tried, but sleep refused to cooperate. The wind rose outside, and the vine maples closest to the house raked full-green limbs along the exterior walls. Ponderosa needles rubbed together like rough-grade sandpaper on wood. Creaking branches could have been a human moan, but the void inside her couldn't find a translation.

Morning finally came, and to her surprise, she realized she must have fallen asleep sometime in the wilderness of the night. She remembered being briefly awake again when she thought she heard noises in the kitchen below. But now, in full consciousness, light filled the space between half-drawn curtains and she could see low overcast outside. She lay still and heard no sounds in the house. Jeff must have left early.

He deserved more than she could give him. She had gone away for the sake of work, or so she'd told herself, but had given up much more than a place of residence. Somewhere in that time with Grant, she had lost hold of a part of herself.

With that realization, the walls of the bedroom started to move inward. Her breath came in gasps and she knew she had to get out. To stay was to suffocate.

What to wear? She didn't care. She grabbed whatever was at hand and went briefly into the hall bathroom, willing herself not to look in the mirror. She walked downstairs and out the door. Leave the rest behind, including the things at the rental apartment. Just coffee, then the road.

At the coffee shop, where she stopped for a triple shot espresso, Calla Bianchi was sitting at the table in the back, discretely nursing an infant. Calla looked her way and motioned toward an empty seat. No! No nosiness. No sympathy. Coffee to go, and that was it. She ordered, trying to look relaxed and aimless. Her eyes roved the room but could not help meeting Calla's steady gaze. Suddenly, her legs lost their ability to hold still.

Her knees shook. She had to sit down; and, with that hazy realization, she found herself stumbling toward the free chair by Calla's table.

She managed to sit down, the strength in one arm hardly enough to maintain a canted upright position. Blurrily she watched Calla place the baby in a bassinet at her side, rearrange her blouse and sweater, and whisper that she'd be right back. Sara tried to nod, but her head continued down until it rested on her outstretched arm.

Years later, it seemed, she felt Calla pulling her up. She tried to put weight on her feet, but vaguely realized a lot of it fell on Calla's shoulders. They passed a waitress who continued wiping something on the counter without looking up.

By the time they reached Calla's car, wetness at the corner of her eyes had turned without warning into wracking sobs.

"Let's sit . . . "

Calla's voice reached her as if from the depths of a dark cave.

" . . . Maria will sleep now, and we can talk as long as you want."

"What do you mean, a riding bushwhacker?"

Jeff was incredulous. He had been waiting by the gas station they'd agreed on, and hopped right into the police SUV. Bill barely waited for him to slam the door before they were moving again.

"Basically, that's all I know. The department got a warrant this morning, and Greg Takarchuk went back to the cabin with a locksmith. When they opened the door, they found the bushwhacker, not a motorcycle. Chief Cisek called me as soon as he got the news."

They sped in silence to the highway, then west to Big Toad Road, bypassing downtown Swiftwater. At a rotary, they joined the route to Portal and drove fast toward Coho Corner until they reached the turnoff to Tomson Lake. At the elevated curve before descending to the lake, Jeff could make out the Cascade Adventures van and a police car parked by the main house.

As they pulled in, Greg Takarchuk stepped out of the police car and strode toward them. Bill and Greg moved a few paces away and exchanged words. After no more than two minutes, Bill called over to Jeff.

"Greg and I are going to the cabin to have another look. Come along if you feel up to it."

Bill and Greg hurried off in the direction of the trail and had disappeared down it by the time Jeff entered the forest. He followed, feeling his awkward steps sink deeper the farther he went. The ground was damp, evergreens showering large drops down on him. There must have been a cloudburst a few hours earlier. Short of the cabin, he recognized the place where he had first spied Sara in heated exchange with Grant Tomson.

Rounding the last bend, he paid more attention to details than he'd been able to during his first trip here.

A man, probably the locksmith, perched on a log off to one side. The low-slung cabin sat back in the surrounding trees, its broad eaves almost touching the branches. A platform extended across its narrow front, with a ramp descending from the middle part of the platform, and three stairs on either side. At the top of the ramp, double doors were wide open, looking out at the cleared area of mountain grasses and wildflowers where Jeff stood. He thought he could make out the areas that got trampled down yesterday.

Inside the cabin, Jeff could hear Bill and Greg talking. He hobbled up the ramp and found them standing on either side of what looked like a large riding lawn mower, except that a horizontal implement with two rows of toothed blades, one above the other, extended from the front of the mower. Bill was talking.

"Yeah, it's a bushwhacker, mostly for tall grasses and small brush. About right for keeping that clearing from being swallowed back up by the forest. An older model, but it's been maintained."

It was maroon, and in dim light might come close to appearing black. But the shape was all wrong. Jeff reached out and touched the turning wheel.

"No way could anyone mistake that for a motorcycle."

Bill voice sounded almost gentle.

"Someone who was really agitated might have."

Jeff shook his head.

"If you're talking about Sara, I'd bet my life she's never made a mistake that big."

Bill shifted some, looked at the bushwhacker, and replied in a more definite tone.

"I guess I'd have to agree with you. But if there was a motorcycle here, a switch had to be made last night. And whoever made the switch also took the scarf that Sara said she saw. Any ideas, Greg, about how the switch could have been made? You know these mountains pretty well."

"It would be quite a job, but not impossible. There's a loose rock trail that starts off the main road a mile or two back towards Portal. Take it and you get to a trail that brings you to the top of this escarpment."

He pointed up behind him.

"Over to our left there's a way to get down, a steep path that's narrower than the trail up above. It would take two men to move this whacker and the cycle up or down it. Say an hour from their vehicle to the escarpment, a half hour more to tote one machine down, three quarters to get the other back up, and another hour back to the truck. So if they parked at midnight, say, they'd be back to their vehicle with the motorcycle by about three am, three-thirty max. Anyway, before first light.

Bill stepped back from the bushwhacker. His grim expression matched the way Jeff felt.

"Let's look around."

For the next half hour, Jeff sat by the locksmith, trading a few words but mostly sitting in silence and watching Bill and Greg walk around the clearing and up the trail to the escarpment above the cabin.

When they returned, Bill summed up their conclusions.

"Hard to tell, but there are some signs that someone might have dragged a large branch around the clearing and up the trail to cover up tire tracks and footprints. The rain this morning would probably make any firm conclusions impossible. Once you're up on the trail back toward Portal, the rocky surface leaves nothing to work with. I don't think a real forensic team would find much more. In any case, not enough to be conclusive. Let's lock up and get back to Swiftwater."

Jeff joined Bill on a slow walk back to the main house. They were well into the woods before Jeff interrupted Bill's concentration.

"Most probably Grant Tomson's doing. You think so, too?"

"Who else?"

Jeff didn't think the angry tone was directed at him. He waited, and Bill went on.

"From what I've heard, I never figured Tomson for a nice guy. But now he's proving to be one of those who think they can get anything they want, and no one can stop them. Trouble is, it looks like this time he's going to get away with it."

Bill stopped walking, took a deep breath, and faced Jeff.

"I think we're done. When Sara told us about the motorcycle in the cabin, I thought we might just be able with the rest of what we had to build a case against Grant in Will's death. But now, with the motorcycle missing, we've got nothing. There's no way left to punish, much less stop that fucking Tomson."

"Bill..."

"Watch it! If you're going to say something about doing the best we can or that the rich guys always have an extra advantage, drop it. I know all that bullshit. Right now I'm not in the mood."

"I have an idea."

"Yeah? About what?"

"Not how to nail Grant—but how to fix it so he doesn't win completely. Actually loses something."

Bill looked at him, signaling grudging interest, then turned his gaze upward as Jeff explained what he had in mind. When he finished, he looked up, too, waiting for Bill to respond. The cloud cover had broken apart in places, allowing flickering sunlight to reach them through the swaying trees.

Bill released a long breath, shifted his gaze downward, then directly at Jeff.

"I'm glad one of us thought of another way. And I can see some advantages in what you got in mind. For one, I'd only be involved in getting things started. The main work falls on you; but I guess you figured on that when you fronted the idea—a really interesting one, I admit."

Jeff had already looked at what he would have to do from as many angles as he could dream up. There were lots of ways that what he proposed might not work. But something had to be done.

Bill was speaking again.

"Bebe has a key part in your plan, and I have no problem talking to her about it. She might have objections. If she does, I'm not going to push her. I think you need to know that, going in."

Jeff understood what Bill meant. Or thought he did. In any case, his old strategy of laying low when the shrapnel started flying was out the window. Welcome to the line of fire.

"I wouldn't have it any other way."

Bebe rose to close the curtains as the evening light left the sky. While she moved from one window to another, she spoke over her shoulder.

"And you're telling me that the way out of all this is for me to lie?"

Bill maintained the same stoic expression he had donned when he broached the suggestion. His eyes gave nothing away while he waited. She was more nonplussed than angry, responding in the only way she knew how when she felt stress. Calm down, she told herself.

She sat beside him.

"Maybe I got it wrong. Try it again."

Bill shifted closer, looking at her across the top of her sofa. They had gone there immediately when he started to tell her about a long afternoon of meetings and calls dealing with the fallout of the new discovery at Will Tomson's cabin.

"Grant Tomson either walks away from his brother's death and keeps the lake property, using it however he wants ... "

His expression went from neutral to deeply serious.

" ... or we take a step that denies him something and maybe limits the harm he can cause in the future. I sure would like the second outcome better. But we may have to cut corners."

"And right now I'm a corner?"

She didn't mean to let anxiety creep in. But there it was, her knee-jerk reaction. If Bill heard that undertone, he didn't let on.

"I don't know what you mean. Using you to lie? I could never do that, and hope you know it's true. It's more like I'm enlisting you. To do one small thing. You say 'no' and that's it. No pressure and—you have to believe me—no change in the way I feel about you."

His eyes bored in, wanting confirmation, reassuring her. What fear she had left began to loosen its grip.

"What exactly do you want me to do?"

"Not much. In fact, after a certain point, doing nothing is your job. It goes this way: I'll borrow your keys and go to History House when it's closed. I'll visit the cabinets where you keep the archives, and somewhere on them I'll tape a blank envelope containing a copy of the documents Greg and I found in Will's shop—the documents I told you about. I imagine that you or one of your helpers occasionally cleans those storage cabinets in the archives?"

"Yes. Not regularly, but maybe once a year and it's always me."

"When was the last time?"

"Not sure. We don't keep a schedule, but usually in the early fall, after the busy season."

"But it wouldn't be unusual now?"

"I suppose not."

He smiled and laid a hand on her shoulder.

"Good. So this week, you'll clean the file cabinets and discover the documents. Once you find them, you simply add them to the files. Grant Tomson is the only family member you might inform about your find, but since he is not a recipient of the original letter, you decide not to. And, by the way, you get your keys back."

She couldn't react to that bit of humor right now.

"What if there's an investigation later?"

"First of all, the chances of one are about zero. Will's death is officially an accident. No one has any reason to investigate your archives. And if you are ever asked, you can describe accurately how you found the documents in the process of cleaning. No need to lie about that. Besides ... "

He moved his hand to cover hers.

" ... I'll go to jail before letting them shift any blame to you. I will simply deny we had this conversation."

Engaging in any subterfuge was against Bebe's code of ethics. But Bill was convinced of Grant Tomson's guilt, and everything she had seen left her convinced too that, even if Grant hadn't killed Will with his own hands, he was responsible for serious misdeeds. And she felt something new and different that influenced her decision: Bill was both willing to act and to protect her. How could she not join him?

"Is that all?"

"Just be prepared to act normally if a journalist comes calling and wants help on researching the Tomson family."

She was beginning to feel relaxed enough to smile.

"That's my job, helping people research questions."

"I know. But I guess I'm just saying that you should treat this reporter like any other visitor. Don't help or hinder him any more than usual."

She wagged a finger at him.

"So I do have a second task. Will there be a third and a fourth?"

"No. Promise. And, anyway, what I just suggested was more a heads-up than a task."

She dropped her fake touchiness, put her arm around his neck and whispered in his ear.

"Okay. I'm with you. Now, why don't you show me if that means anything? To you, not to a job to be done."

He rose and stood looking down at her as a shy smile grew into a hungry grin. She led him to the bedroom, as if that was what they had planned all along. They were careful with each other, but all hesitation was gone. After they climaxed, they lay side by side, hands clasped, looking at the ceiling and stealing glances at each other. She wanted to make sure that his smile matched hers. It did. When they were ready again, passion pushed any lingering inhibition into a lock box. What they did next was like throwing away the key.

They showered and dressed. While they did, Bebe covered up returning shyness with idle chatter. Bill seemed a little shy, too. She hadn't expected that. They stuck to what was obvious: the nice spring day, the signs that it would be a hot summer, whether there were more or fewer songbirds than last year at this time. Gradually Bebe realized that she liked the happy awkwardness of adjusting to something so gloriously new.

Out of nowhere, Bill returned to the almost-forgotten topic.

"You know, I look forward to the moment when Grant Tomson learns that the documents he wanted to destroy are still around and in the public domain."

"How long has that been on your mind? Was that what you were smiling about in the bedroom?"

Bill looked sheepish and unsure. Bebe realized he must not have heard the teasing in her voice. Being playful was new to him, too.

"No, no. Of course not! It was just a spontaneous thought. It would have taken a house fire to interfere with the way you made me feel in there."

She pretended to think about that, adding a big smile when she raised her head.

"Would it surprise you to know that I had the same thought about Grant Tomson?"

He smiled, too, and pulled her close.

After a few minutes they disengaged, and he spoke for both of them.

"Let's try to get the rest of this job done, so we can concentrate on what we want most."

APRIL 24, SATURDAY

Sara looked around the interior office room. Sunlit landscapes, framed by white drapes, substituted for windows. Blue and white checked fabric on two easy chairs with dark blue throw cushions. A shellacked knotty pine writing table in the corner. Everything designed to project folksy cheer and peacefulness. Way too obviously designed that way. She told herself she didn't feel like arguing with the room, yet here she was, doing it already.

She still didn't know why she had lost control so completely at the coffee shop. A lot must have come out in her angry, sad emotional dump in Calla's car. Afterward the resolve to flee lost all its conviction, but the leaden half-existence back at her home only felt heavier and more hopeless than before.

Calla hadn't offered any advice, hadn't said much at all, except at the end when she recommended a meeting with Connie Lark.

The door opened and a short plump woman entered. Above sparkling white tennis shoes, she wore a short-sleeved dress with a pale green and yellow floral print. She was probably in her mid-thirties. Vivid blue eyes looked out from under a casual shag of light brown hair. Her left hand held a notebook, her right extended forward. Sara took it and felt a firm clasp.

"You're Sara. Calla's description did you justice. I'm Dr. Lark or Connie. Call me whichever makes you comfortable. Why don't we start with you telling me why you're here."

Lark motioned to the two easy chairs, and they sat down.

Okay, let's see how she handles the truth.

"Because Calla thought it would be a good idea, Connie."

As the words came out of her mouth, Sara heard the challenge in them.

Lark lowered the clipboard firmly to one knee and smiled.

"If you really mean that, then you've done your duty and I've just gained an hour of free time. It's been nice to meet you. Or we can start over. Your choice."

Not what Sara had expected. Connie's youth, the flowery dress, and the folksy room hadn't prepared her for pushback. She took a moment, forced herself through her negative reaction, and started over.

"I've had problems with my marriage, and I guess it was getting to me more than I knew. Calla thought you might help me straighten things out. Now that I'm here, I think I'd like to try, Dr. Lark."

Lark returned a careful smile, her eyes making an assessment.

"Stick with Connie; it suits you more. Okay, let's use the rest of this hour to see if Calla was right. Why don't we begin with you describing the problems that have been bothering you?"

That wouldn't be too hard. One thing Sara did well was reduce facts to their essence and reorganize them in crisp summaries. She dropped easily into a practiced routine. Two sentences took care of her work history. Three more got her to Washington State and through the first three years of Cascade Adventures. Two laid out the effects of the recession on the business. She took a quick break and thought through how to phrase the final part.

"As our finances got tighter, my husband and I began to see our business in different terms. The fact that he got injured didn't help; but basically, I wanted to regroup and push forward. He resisted, and yet didn't come up with any ideas of his own. So I decided, on my own, to explore a venture with a successful businessman. Unfortunately, my new potential partner decided not to go through with our project. I'd put a lot of effort into it and when it couldn't advance, frustration piled on frustration and I guess that led to my breaking down. But now I feel better. I'm confident I'll find a different solution."

Connie looked at her quizzically.

"Very neatly done. Does your husband have a name, by the way?"

"Jeff. Jeffery Corson Winter III, actually. Why?"

"Perhaps later you can provide your own answer to that question. For now—and only if you want to—why don't you leave work aside and tell me about your background, your life."

Curiously, this was a welcome suggestion. It was a topic she didn't need to organize. She started with her Italian-Austrian immigrant parents and their move to Colorado. How they established a normal life in America, he as an accountant and she as an at-home painter and part-time art teacher. How everything had been almost idyllic until her older brother died in a freak climbing accident. How, after that, her mother stopped climbing, and she, Sara, joined her father on climbs of increasing technical difficulty.

How right after college she had married an athletic, driven young man she had dated throughout her senior year, and how the marriage had wound down quickly after it was clear that her husband's fascination for the go-go business world left no time for the two of them together. How she'd met Jeff in the middle of a political conspiracy in Washington DC, from which they had escaped first physically and then existentially by moving to Washington State. And, oh yes, she should probably add that she had majored in classics in college—don't ask why. And, as long as she was at it, she should mention her photography. She'd once been quite good at it, even won a few awards.

That ought to do it, she thought. But her mouth opened of its own volition and she heard words that emerged without passing through her conscious brain.

"Jeff and I couldn't have children, hard as we tried. But we both adjusted."

Now more words were spilling out. As she talked, she lost track of time. But Connie hadn't. When Sara looked up, she saw that the open page of the notebook was half-filled with writing, and that Connie was starting to stand.

"Time's up. I have only one thought to leave you with: your life may have left you with more than marriage issues. My guess is that you might want to talk further about that. Call for an appointment, if you think I'm someone you'd like to have in the same room while you're doing that. If not, I'll say again: it's been nice to meet you."

"You too, Connie."

As Sara walked from the muted room into a brighter hallway, and finally outside into full sunshine, it was as if her eyes had stopped working. Or were working differently, seeing not ambient illumination, but instead searching inside herself for what lived in hidden corners.

There was something else, too. Anger and sadness were still inside— and momentarily welled up just to prove it. Only now they had company. Farther in the background, as if not willing to reveal itself completely, she could make out the outlines of ... was it relief?

APRIL 25, SUNDAY

Aaron Elkhorn raised his coffee cup in a mock toast. From the neck up, he was his same groomed, suave self. From the neck down, a sweatshirt with a Washington State Cougar logo, jeans, and running shoes had replaced his business attire.

"You guys don't waste any time. But what else have I got to do on a Sunday evening?"

Bill raised his cup in return, glancing aside to see Jeff do the same.

"My guess is that there's plenty more to occupy you. So I'm glad you thought it was important enough to come, and that it was okay by you for Jeff to join us."

Elkhorn nodded at Jeff, then back at Bill, turning serious.

"I wrestled about coming or not, but decided, finally, that it's fish or cut bait time. I already figured out that the day would come when I would leave Tomson. You've just faced me with it earlier than I expected. Bottom line, I can't go on working for a man who's increasingly secretive and irrational. And whose interest in involving the Indian tribes is only skin deep, if that much."

He sat straighter.

"But enough of that. What's on the table?"

The question was as bare-bones as the little café they were sitting in, off the interstate in North Bend. Bill had chosen it because it was on the west side of the pass, closer to Elkhorn in Bellevue. At eight pm, only one of the other five tables was occupied. The owner, who also waited tables, was busy behind a four-stool counter. He would soon bring them the only remaining menu items: vegetable soup, salad, and chicken-fried steak.

Bill responded.

"As I said on the phone, Tomson thinks he has won and will begin immediately to implement his plans for the lake property. If you guys want to stop him, you've got to start right away."

Elkhorn's eyes and a slight movement of his head signaled for more.

"Documents that have surfaced reveal that Will Tomson had the power to cut Grant out of inheriting the lake property. Will died without exercising that power. In my mind, there's no question that Grant somehow caused Will's death so he could go ahead with his development plans.

There may be a way you can help counter those plans. In fact, without your help, there may be no way to stop them."

Elkhorn eyed him carefully.

"Hard to miss how you keep saying 'you', not 'us'. Does that mean you're out?"

"You and Jeff will have to work it out. Getting you together is as far as I can, and should, go. From now on, I'm just a policeman who tried to solve a case that looked like murder and couldn't. Jeff?"

Elkhorn had dressed down, but Jeff had gone the other way: a blazer, khakis, and an open-collar blue shirt.

"Okay by me. Good to meet you, Aaron. Heard about you. Bill told me that someday you might choose to do something different from working for Tomson. It wouldn't be smart talking to you if that weren't true. Frankly, I'm here because of this hunch on Bill's part. Why are you here?"

Elkhorn shot a glance at Bill.

"Bill got it right."

Jeff shifted his chair so he was directly facing Elkhorn.

"Okay. We think that it will take two things to make Tomson back off from the lake property. The first is if suspicions were made public that Grant might have caused his brother's death because Will had the power to return the property to tribal ownership. The second thing is if a tribe shows interest in laying claim to ownership of the property. I could be wrong, but I don't see the second thing happening on its own—at least not soon enough. Your involvement could help speed up an Indian offensive, if we can call it that. If we have only the revelation without the offensive, I think we're the proverbial snowball in a very warm place."

Elkhorn sat back, crossing his arms. He looked down for a long time, silent, alone in his own thoughts. Finally he raised his head, looking calm but determined.

"I'm intrigued by what you're proposing. I assume you're going to place something in the media. But you haven't told me enough. Like, how are you going to get this revelatory story written?"

Jeff shot back an answer.

"That will be my responsibility. You don't need to know how the sausage is made. And, apart from maybe sending out feelers, you don't have to do anything that potentially reveals your involvement until after you see the piece appear. It could be in print, or online. I'll let you know before it comes out, if I get advance notice."

"I can live with that. Now the rest?"

Jeff leaned closer to Elkhorn.

"I've been a legislative consultant in Olympia for the last two years, and have put together a personal catalogue of where legislators stand on a variety of issues. I know of two or three who have been particularly sympathetic to the Indian point of view. Incidentally, the Governor's in that category, too. They're all looking for tangible ways to express their sympathy, especially in ways that won't cost money for a state that's looking at a budget shortfall."

"Ah, political advantage at no cost. Always a good selling point."

"That, too."

Elkhorn's expression was caught in a no-man's land between doubt and decision. He pulled one elbow, then the other, behind his neck, stretching it with the opposite hand, buying time. When he was ready, he spoke again.

"You're absolutely right about Grant. He's planning counter moves right now, sure that he'll be ahead of everyone else. I'll stick around him as long as I can, see what I can find out. But he'll become suspicious eventually, and he'll know that I've left the reservation, so to speak—although, come to think of it, it's exactly the opposite."

He laughed lightly, then went back to being serious.

"Jeff, I'm not sure which legislators you intend to contact. Here are two suggestions."

He pulled out a pen, wrote on a paper napkin, and handed it to Jeff. Jeff nodded.

"Those are already two of my three."

Elkhorn took over again.

"It's good you mentioned the Governor. Her legislative assistant, Art Graves, should also be kept informed. The way I see it, your principal tasks would be to keep up pressure on the Department of Ecology to reject, or at least delay, Grant's request for a change in his water use permit at the lake. You can bet he's been following that request, and if he senses more resistance, he'll know there's something else in play. Therefore, you—we—need to get to work immediately on that 'something else'."

Bill didn't miss Elkhorn's change in pronouns. Jeff responded.

"Tell me what you think that new effort should be."

Elkhorn was speaking almost before Jeff finished.

"What would help us right now is a legislative resolution that affirms the right of an Indian tribe or tribes to reacquire ownership of Tomson

Lake. The case should be made as a way for the State of Washington to implement Cobell v. Salazar and to right a flawed original purchase by the Tomson family. Frankly, almost all purchases of Indian land were flawed, if you look at the original treaty provisions. I know a lawyer who's familiar with those issues, and she might be willing to help informally with the drafting."

Jeff smiled.

"Those are strategies I thought of, too. I'll plan to go to Olympia tomorrow to get started."

Bill thought they'd taken matters as far as they could for the time being. Further, in fact, than he had hoped. Besides, if they wanted Elkhorn's help, it would be best not to ask too much of him.

"Thanks, Aaron, for coming. Even more for what you're willing..."

Elkhorn was looking at his hands and broke in, as if he hadn't heard Bill.

"This could be a significant moment. My dream is that Indians can keep tribal customs and beliefs, but also become modern Americans. That means a different kind of politics, cooperative politics that unites tribes and ultimately is the best protection for Native American cultures. It has to start somewhere. Why not here and with Tomson Lake? Why not..."

Elkhorn stopped in mid-sentence. He looked embarrassed. Bill reached across and squeezed his shoulder.

"Tomson first, then the rest. I like the sound of that."

APRIL 26, MONDAY

Jeff had reached Olympia by nine, about the time morning work got started. The legislature was just gearing up for the late-night, and occasionally all-night, sessions that closed every legislative year. By eleven-thirty, he'd managed to see two of the three legislators that he and Elkhorn had discussed. Both were noncommittal in different ways. One leaned toward enthusiasm but needed more information. The other was harder to read, though he did not blow Jeff off. Later, at five, Jeff would meet with Art Graves, the Governor's assistant.

The day was already crowded, with no surprises until the big one: his phone rang just before noon and a cool female voice announced that Grant Tomson wanted to speak to him. The voice invited him for two pm and was coy about what they might discuss. Jeff had a pretty good idea about the agenda. But why not? He might gain something by seeing Grant Tomson up close. Even the wiliest people gave more away than they thought. It would be tight, up to Seattle and back to Olympia by five. Tight but doable.

Later in the afternoon he was shown into Tomson's office. He was standing away from his desk, wearing a sleek black suit and an open-neck shirt of light weight cocoa-colored silk. Jeff took a hand, felt a perfunctory clasp, then quick withdrawal.

"Thanks for coming on short notice. You've been busy in Olympia. I admire industry, except when it affects me adversely. Don't think I haven't noticed."

Tomson's smile almost looked sincere.

Jeff sat and glanced at the window view of South Lake Union. An amphibious Duck tourist vehicle was lumbering up a ramp, water pouring from exit holes in the hull. He shifted his gaze back to Tomson on the other side of the desk. Only a cantilevered lamp and a laptop occupied its surface.

"That's an interesting statement, but I have no idea what it means."

A fleeting expression of sour impatience crossed Tomson's smooth face.

"You can do better than that."

Just be quiet, wait him out. Tomson didn't take long. He leaned toward his computer and pressed a key. Maybe actual information came up on the screen, but Jeff's money was on theatrics. Tomson switched to stern.

"You've been discussing my lake property with people up at the capitol. There may be legal reasons why you could be enjoined from doing that, but for the moment I don't propose to follow that path. You surely know that any long-term success in large-scale development projects requires political support. I have that in spades. I have markers I can call in at any time."

Jeff knew a lot of what Tomson said was true. But the full truth about political relationships is that they are always subject to change. What was more important than Tomson's implied threats was whether the same situation would prevail after the public—and the politicians—learned about recent events over the mountains.

"How impressive. And you're warning me to cease and desist?"

"I'm describing reality, that's all. If you hear a threat there, it's something you have imagined."

"You've said what you said and I heard it. If that's why I'm here, then we're finished."

Jeff rose and so did Tomson, rounding the desk and motioning him to keep his seat. Jeff complied, wondering what more there could be. Tomson leaned back against the forward edge of his desk. Less than a foot of space separated their knees. Jeff had to crane upward to meet downward-pitched eyes. Tomson was close enough for Jeff to whiff what was undoubtedly an expensive cologne, astringent, almost acidic.

Tomson smiled again, adding an unwavering stare and a pause long enough to start feeling theatrical.

"Jeff, I'm afraid we may have gotten off on the wrong foot. I have a ... proposition that you might be interested in."

Jeff thought he knew what was coming. Why not hear the whole spiel? He kept his eyes neutral but added an encouraging nod. Tomson upped his warmth.

"I've looked into your background. You're an expert on national and state legislative processes. You've been successful on both coasts. You've run a business. I could use a honcho for getting the state to understand and support my projects. I know what you're now making as a consultant and I'll quadruple that, plus set up a bonus structure. What do you say, does that sound attractive? You could start right now."

This guy was good. But not so good that he could erase the calculating gleam in his eyes. Jeff had to admit that maybe earlier in his life he might have been tempted. Except, Tomson was not just another ambitious guy. He was capable of murder.

Besides, Jeff was also conscious that the pull from an opposite direction was getting stronger. He'd spent most of his life doing other peoples' bidding, following their dreams because he didn't have compelling ones of his own. The recent talk with Elkhorn had hinted at a chance to help shape a cause that he found both worthy and potentially satisfying. Much better than an unsatisfying assignment in the slipstream of someone whose goals he couldn't believe in.

The idea of using Tomson Lake as a means to bring greater strength and unity to the goals of Native Americans had touched something inside him. Maybe it was the realization of ideals that had been there all along but that he had never been willing to acknowledge. Or to work hard enough to achieve. Was he ready to take on a task bigger than anything he'd dared before?

Right now, Tomson was waiting for an answer.

"Not quite what I'm looking for. I think I'll stick to what I'm doing. But thanks for thinking of me. You made my day."

The sarcasm leaked out. An instantaneous change on Tomson's face cracked the shallow depth of his forced charm.

"I meet stupid all the time. You're now among my prime examples. I'll chalk you up as a temporary lapse of judgment. Your wife, incidentally, was another. She had her charms for a brief, and thoroughly forgettable, moment. You two deserve each other."

Jeff didn't respond, throwing ice on the instant surge of anger that boiled up inside. Tomson probably could see the clenched fists in his lap and the way his skin turned white around the knuckles. Hoping that his knees weren't shaking as well, he rose and turned toward the exit, jostling Tomson as he passed, putting a little shoulder into it.

Tomson regained his cold composure and called out.

"Don't bother to tell me if you change your mind. The offer is dead."

Jeff kept walking, concentrating on that old adage about revenge: best when served cold. It helped, though his head still felt like a hot air balloon.

He just beat the worst of the afternoon traffic and got to Olympia on time for his meeting with the Governor's assistant, Art Graves, who wanted details about what Jeff had in mind for Tomson Lake. Jeff stressed how the Governor could obtain political capital in the process of helping the tribes reacquire the land. It was hard to avoid mentioning Grant Tomson. But, for the most part, he made his case without bringing up that name.

Graves walked him to the door with a concluding remark.

"Just remember that the Governor wants a positive outcome. So don't come back for more help unless that's what you're delivering."

Jeff nodded. He'd already figured that out.

Then it was on to the last meeting of the day, prearranged at a well-known watering hole near SeaTac airport, on the way back from Olympia to the other side of the Cascades.

The Dozen Dimes was one of those bars so public that you could count on anonymity. The high-ceilinged, cavernous place had a high turnover. Travelers came and went, often after one or more of the double-sized drinks featured at a happy hour that started at three pm. The décor, modern in the 1970s and unchanged since then, provided dim lighting to which it took time to adjust, while the Dimes' high-backed leather booths shut off both sight and sound from even their closest neighbors.

Page Bentley was already in a booth, a large glass of dark liquid half empty. Page had suggested the Dimes for a six-forty-five meet when Jeff told him he had something to discuss that he'd rather not do on the phone. Luckily the traffic direction was to Jeff's advantage, and he got there almost on time. He wasn't fully seated before an impatient Page fired a question.

"So whacha got? Don't stretch it out. I got a reception in Olympia that starts at eight."

Bentley always fronted his hurry—part of his act. So what? That irritating façade also made him vulnerable to being used. Jeff had already used him once. It should be easier the second time.

"Thanks for meeting. I know you're a busy guy and I won't waste your time. You were a big help the last time we talked, and I need help again."

Bentley waved magnanimously, his grin a little sloppy.

"I don't forget."

"I know you've got more important things, but maybe you remember talking about Grant Tomson and water use allotments at his lake property?"

Bentley squared his shoulders.

"Of course I remember."

"Well, on the basis of what you told me and what Zerbe, the staffer you pointed me to, said, there was no down side to helping Tomson out. That's what I reported to my guy."

Jeff was taking a small chance that Bentley would not know that he had already been fired by Mac Champlin.

Bentley responded by raising his head. Jeff could imagine him actually sniffing.

"And now? Something's changed?"

"I've got rumors, that's all, that Tomson had bad relations with his brother, the one who died, and he could have been involved with the death. Nothing to say that's true, but also nothing to say it isn't. I can't put my guy out on a limb if a secret Tomson is hiding could cut it off. You know what I mean?"

"I do exactly. But I've heard nothing on that subject."

"And I didn't expect you would, even knowing you're one of the best informed guys in Olympia. I was hoping that, as a favor, you'd let me know right away if you do hear anything."

"Absolutely."

A subtle shift in Page's tone and expression told Jeff that the bait was on its way down the gullet. He'd bet that guy was already thinking about which stringer, freelancer, or blogger would be most likely to go after a story on Tomson—someone who would also know where in Swiftwater to start looking for information.

Jeff had done what he could. Now it was wait-and-see time.

ELEVEN DAYS LATER

MAY 8, SATURDAY

It was nice to hear Bill laugh. Bebe was getting used to the idea that beneath that strong, stoic presence lurked an infrequently unleashed sense of humor. She hoped that over time it would show itself more often.

They sat in her living room on a Friday evening, Bill in an accustomed place beside her on the couch, Curio stretched out at their feet. His coffee was cooling in a half-empty cup on the side table. He was there so often now, after work and on weekends, that she found herself thinking of her home as "ours". Not that they'd ever addressed where their relationship was taking them. It seemed enough to bask in comfort and companionship that had become so natural. No drama. She couldn't imagine Bill, or herself either, in a situation that required drama.

Bebe was retelling what happened, delighting in Bill's request for more detail.

"I wasn't surprised when the reporter called a week ago. But I still didn't know what he would be like, or exactly what I would do if he decided to pay a visit. On the phone, he said he was Ed Kearny, a freelancer interested in how History House got started. He might do a story on it and see if he could get it published. I invited him to come over."

"And he did."

"You know that much already. I got his call on a Friday afternoon and he was here Monday early—tall, almost a scarecrow. If I hadn't known he was a writer, I might have taken him for homeless or a drifter. He listed to one side and kept shifting his feet like he had trouble keeping his balance. I was a little uncomfortable with him until he began asking questions. Then I could sense a calm and logical mind, and I could concentrate on what he was saying. He was supposed to be looking into History House, but his questions told me he was more interested in the Tomson family. Mostly about Grant."

She stopped for a minute and smiled. She hadn't told him anything about the next part. How would he react?

"When he started asking what we had in the files, I wasn't exactly forthcoming. I made it seem as if I hadn't gotten very deep into the Tomson family. I pretended not to know a few things, and told him that my main

255

interest was in Swiftwater's history and that those family records could hold anything."

Immediately Bill's voice coarsened, became almost a growl. Bebe could imagine herself in an interrogation room.

"So you have a sly side, lady! You played him. I'm going to have to keep an eye on you!"

Then he laughed as a mischievous look came and went. She was buoyed to tell more.

"Well, he did get more excited. Not that he showed it exactly; if he'd been Curio, I would say he picked up a scent. Anyway, I took him to the files and generally pointed out where he should look. I didn't help him. I figured he would pay more attention to what he discovered himself."

"And you were sure right."

Bill pointed to a copy of the *Seattle Reader*. The cover trumpeted a teaser for the main story inside. It read "Bad Blood and Death in the Mountains: A Prominent Family's Legacy". Then he opened to page three, where the lead paragraph began: "Seattle real estate developer Grant Tomson is a man on the move, with big ambition and highly visible accomplishments. But hidden in the Cascades town of Swiftwater, information has come to light that may cast a long shadow over that reputation."

Bebe smiled.

"I didn't expect something that big. But I'm glad to have helped make it possible."

"Well. It is big. You bet it got attention."

They were quiet for a while, looking pointedly at the *Reader* article, but stealing glances at each other. Bebe broke the silence, using a tone of concern.

"Do you really think you have to keep an eye on me?"

He saw through her act.

"Only if you let me."

More silence. She broke it again.

"Pretty soon we'll be back to normal, I guess. Have to admit, though, that all the excitement was a refreshing change. Once I got over the fear of dealing with it."

"If by 'normal' you mean going back exactly to how things were, my vote says no. My vote says that this ... "

He gestured at her then around the room.

"…at very least stays the way it is now. But I wouldn't be against changes even to that."

"What do you mean, 'changes'?"

She thought she knew, but wanted to hear it from him.

"You know. I'm spending half my time here. Maybe we ought to think about upping that percentage."

"It's the percentage of time you're interested in, then?"

He smiled, moved in close and pulled her toward him, gently. Keeping the pressure light.

"I'm not asking for marriage, just a chance to see how far we want to go. Maybe that's a long way, maybe a short one. But you can't get even a small slice of good life without taking a chance. Right now I want more, not less."

"I'll never be a great asset to your social life."

That got a laugh.

"Anything's more than zero."

"You're not really comparing me to nothing, are you?"

He looked flustered and unsure.

"No, that's not…"

Her laugh got him out of the situation.

"I didn't think so."

To prove it, she was the one who moved closer, purposefully.

"You'll get at least this much. More if you want it."

He put his arms around her.

"Who knows, maybe you'll be too much for me. Or me for you. But you'll never be too little."

The familiar room, she realized, felt warmer. And in his embrace, it was not contracting; it was expanding.

A knock on the front door startled Sara in the kitchen. Some of her things were still in the rental apartment. But since the events at Tomson Lake, she'd come back to the old house. She and Jeff still slept separately and no final solution was in sight yet. Habit and inertia guided their uneasy days, he with his work and her with her counseling sessions.

She opened the door to a sunny backdrop of alders now in full green, complementing the evergreen Ponderosas. In front of them, on the porch,

Calla Bianchi stood cradling her infant in one arm, a colorful scarf covering all but the head of little Maria.

"It's nice of you to ask me over. We can't stay long."

Yesterday in the market, on impulse, Sara had invited Calla to drop by some time. But then she immediately forgot, and now was not the best opportunity. Her morning counseling session had drained her to the core. At other times in her life, Sara had pulled multiple all-nighters preparing materials for a corporate board meeting; she'd gone almost sleepless on a two-day climb up a rock face. But nothing compared to the weariness she felt now.

The sessions with Connie were supposed to help get her head straight. But it was not her head that ached. Her stomach occasionally did, and though her heart did not literally ache, what should she call the downward pressure of sadness that bored a hole between her breasts? Sadness about her brother's death, sadness about the sadness that invaded her mother after he died. And a different kind of sadness, growing heavier as her sessions progressed: about how she had treated Jeff.

She pulled herself together, making an effort to smile.

"Come on in. I'll put on the coffee."

Calla was an experienced observer, and Sara figured there was no use hiding her fatigue.

"Are you sure? We could come back another time."

"Any other time would be the same. I'm glad to see you and Maria."

Calla chose one of the two barrel chairs that faced each other by the stove. Sara fixed coffee in the kitchen while Calla called out commentary on the beautiful weather and the delightful ways in which Maria changed every day. When Sara returned with two mugs, she found Calla nursing the child, mother and daughter bathed in a glow of contentment, a condition so rare in her own life that it took her a moment to register what it was.

Calla glanced at her watch and switched her attention to Sara.

"Frankly, I'm surprised you're still here. I hope things with Jeff are working out, and not getting in the way of the other work you're doing."

By "other work", Sara now knew, Calla meant the counseling and what she was getting from it. Using the word "work" that way at first had sounded strange. Now she was beginning to understand why it was well chosen.

"It's been strange, but it's all right. I know it can't last this way."

"This way?"

"The couch in the barn is comfortable, or so Jeff says. He sleeps there. When he's around, we sometimes meet in the kitchen, but usually we're on different eating schedules. We don't talk, because I guess Jeff doesn't want to, or he's figured out I don't. Or can't. By all rights, he should have the house and I should be in the barn. When he realizes that, we'll have to start another kind of discussion."

"I take it he's not here now."

"No. He's working on something I can't tell you much about, having to do with Will Tomson's death and everything that happened at Tomson Lake."

She needed to get another matter off her chest.

"I haven't told you that I got … "

This was hard.

" … involved with Grant Tomson."

She checked Calla's face for a reaction. There wasn't even a twitch, just a nod to say the information got through.

"Anyway, a lot's happening behind the scenes and Jeff's somehow involved. He's also spending time in Olympia and visiting Indian tribes. I don't know what he's doing, only that he's gone a lot. Most of the time I have the house to myself. When I'm here alone, I think a lot more about this once being *our* house and that I'm just here temporarily."

She wasn't sure what more to say. Calla finished nursing little Maria, reached down to remove a clean diaper from the bag at her feet, and held Maria to her shoulder until she got a contented burp in return. Sara stood up when Calla rose, apparently getting ready to say goodbye. Instead, Calla held the baby out in her direction.

"Would you mind holding her for a moment while I visit your bathroom?"

Calla didn't wait for an answer, and Sara automatically accepted the blanketed bundle coming her way. Then Calla was gone, and she became conscious of the tiny weight in her arms, of the warm, milky breath on her cheek, and of the open, innocent eyes that calmly regarded her. A wave of feeling engulfed her, canceling fatigue, opening a shuttered barrier inside. She felt disoriented and sat down for fear of falling with the vulnerable life she had been asked to protect.

After that, she lost all sense of herself but was conscious of something replacing it, something emanating from the baby, something that found her. The good in the baby flowed into a gulf of need. She didn't want to give up that feeling. Not now. Not ever.

All she wanted to do was sit here, like this, for the rest of the day, maybe for the rest of her life. She felt her heartbeat begin to merge with the tiny throb close to her breast. She didn't realize she was crying until salty moisture reached her lips.

From the weight of a hand on her shoulder, she sensed Calla beside her and heard a voice from far away.

"It's all right. We have all the time in the world."

MAY 9. SUNDAY

Bill was first to arrive, then Jeff and, less than a minute later, Aaron Elkhorn.

Jeff led off right after Elkhorn sat down.

"You ready to move things along, Aaron?"

The three of them were meeting again in the little café on the other side of Snoqualmie Summit, seated in the same booth as before. One more time and it might be called a habit.

Elkhorn answered the way Bill had hoped he would.

"Sounds reasonable to me. I've got no more restrictions. Grant must have had suspicions about my loyalty. Last week he told me he didn't need my services any more. That's the sanitized version. So let's get down to business. What have you got, Jeff?"

Jeff, who had looked tired when he arrived, brightened up and produced a satisfied smile.

"Once the story on Tomson broke in the *Reader*, the NBC affiliate TV station mentioned it, and two days later, the *Times* published a condensed version in its business section. By that time, at least a dozen blogs picked up the story."

Jeff looked directly at Bill.

"The *Reader* story focused mainly on the Tomson family history and the apparent bad blood between twins who, as it turned out, were actually cousins. The bloggers ran with the intrigue angle speculating about whether Grant Tomson could have had a hand in his brother's death. Several of them played up Will's intent to see that Grant didn't get the lake property. Has there been anything fresh on the investigative front, Bill?"

Bill felt his face twist into a grimace.

"Wish there were. There are times you know someone's guilty and just can't prove it. Grant Tomson is dirty, I'm sure of it. But the fact is we have no physical evidence to tie him to any wrongdoing, including moving a motorcycle out of Will's cabin."

Jeff shook his head.

"Okay, I've got to get used to the idea that we'll never know. But, just to satisfy my curiosity, what's your best guess about what happened?"

263

Bill had asked himself the same question but never before put the answer into words.

"Probably something like this. Will got the letter from the lawyer about the codicil to his mother's will. He decided he would exercise his option and cut Grant out of ever using Tomson Lake to make money. He may or may not have cared about the Indians. Mainly he wanted to stick it to Grant. Trouble is, he was dumb or naïve enough to reveal his intentions before he sent the signed codicil to his mother's lawyer."

"And Grant?"

Bill shrugged.

"That's even harder to speculate about, but here goes. Grant likes to make money; and because of his success, he doesn't take kindly to criticism, much less to someone saying no. He wanted to make money off of Tomson Lake, because that's what businessmen do. But the lake meant more than just profit. It was his chance to get the better of an arrogant brother and a judgmental mother. He probably suspected that some time bomb existed. First he may have tried to search the family papers at History House, making it look as if Will had been there. Finding nothing, he may have started thinking about getting rid of Will. He could have ridden his motorcycle—one identical to Will's—along the side road pretending to be Will, in order to set the stage for the accident later. If he did that, then Will's death was premeditated murder.

"Or, another version, Will confronted Grant about the lake property. Grant lost his temper and hit Will on the head, probably with a length of wood. That's why there were wood particles in the head wound. Then Grant banged up Will's motorcycle in a convincing way and transported it and Will's body to the spot where he re-created the scene of an accident. Then it's clear why Charlie Temple heard nothing that night."

Jeff broke in.

"And afterward he cleaned up the place where the real killing occurred, and drove back over the pass to Seattle, so no one could prove that he hadn't been there all along."

"That would be my assessment."

Elkhorn's face said he was listening closely.

"You got any reactions, Aaron?"

"Yeah, I do, on two counts. First, it seems to me that your speculation should be kept under wraps. Putting myself in Tomson's place, I'd be curious, maybe worried, about how much evidence actually still exists for how Will died. If we keep silent, but move ahead decisively with rekindled Indian interest in the lake property, he might be inclined to be cautious. He wouldn't want to open a can of worms."

He paused, his brow bunched.

"Don't get me wrong. Tomson is tough and devious and also very good at covering up both those traits. He won't give up the lake property without a fight. The only question is how long and how dirty the fight will be."

Bill had already figured that out.

"No guarantee we'll win."

Elkhorn gave a tightlipped nod, but his expression was more determined than discouraged.

"Absolutely none. It's good to know that going in. We'll use momentum and apply pressure. Then build on what we get. *Maybe* enough to win."

Bill waited as Elkhorn shifted his attention to Jeff.

"From now on, it's political on two fronts. One is shaping up: a cooperative effort among several tribes to obtain the lake property. It's easy to sell the idea that Indians should reclaim land that was taken from them or foolishly sold. But the second front is about what to do with the land if they get it. Just raising that question will open up old tribal rivalries. It could pit leaders who have already gained power and resources—mainly from casinos—against other potential leaders who want to focus on education and tribal services."

Bill gave him the hand signal to go on, and Elkhorn did, still looking at Jeff.

"Luckily, Tomson Lake is too remote for a casino. But it could be a thriving business built around wilderness experiences. And Tomson's idea about a bottling plant is not out of the question. I think there's a chance that tribes could get together around those ideas. That could be the push for acquisition. But we need a pull, too. Jeff, you know what I mean by that. If legislators, with the Governor's encouragement, introduced a resolution advocating Indian acquisition of the lake property, the tribes might be encouraged to see benefit in cooperation."

Jeff replied immediately.

"I'm more than willing to help on that. There are little details, though, like how I would support myself."

Elkhorn relaxed as he sat back.

"That's already on my radar. It actually helps that I was point man on Tomson's Spirit of Diversity Foundation. All my time invested in that activity can still be put to good use. The SDF name belongs to Grant. But we can start something like it—and better—with the same goals and a different name, while keeping some of the same people. The contacts and the structure don't have to be reinvented. A few core donors who remain anonymous agree with me. I think I can come up with a way to use some of that money to hire you. Just keep working the Olympia angle, and keep thinking of money-making ventures for the lake property. Tasteful ones, environmentally acceptable ones. You know what I mean. The more there is potential for some profit, the more I can work on building tribal cooperation. There's got to be a better way, and maybe we can help discover it."

He looked around almost apologetically, and held his hands out, palms up. Then he smiled.

"I was practicing for what's ahead, as you can hear. Thanks for listening."

Jeff responded.

"Good to see the big picture, Governor Elkhorn..."

Elkhorn offered no denial and smiled. But he hadn't lost his focus.

"Bill, I need you, too. Whatever tribal contacts you already had, and whatever you added in the Tomson investigation, should be kept alive. It's important to know what the general population is thinking as we move forward. Roper, for instance, could be helpful and you, too, Bill, if you're willing."

"Sure, as long as it's quiet and no attribution. But..."

He was a policeman, and there was something more that they all needed to acknowledge.

"...we can't forget Grant Tomson. I've met others like him. He'll track us, plan, and, at some point, try to get even."

The mood around the table turned somber. Even so, Bill could still feel the strength of the commitment they'd made.

MAY 10, TUESDAY

Sara stood by the kitchen sink, looking thinner than Jeff had ever seen her. Her eyes were opaque behind the dark shadows around them, so deep-set that Jeff sensed, more than saw, the dejection behind them. It was even more apparent when she spoke.

"The only answer is for me to get out of here and start over somewhere else."

"Well, that's one answer. Not necessarily the only one."

She still had some impatience in reserve.

"Jeff, cool and reasonable is not the answer to everything. At least acknowledge that we've got to figure out how to split up all of this."

Her arm made a circle broad enough to include the whole property.

"If you have to leave, you've got that right. But hear me out."

She hesitated, then sagged into a nearby chair. He remained standing.

"Leaving's not the only possibility. I don't know much about these things, but I have read that if you're facing a big change, it's best not to add the stress of other changes. This therapy you're going through may help you in the long run, but it's pretty hard on you right now. Moving away, facing all the problems of starting over completely, may not be what the doctor ordered. I'm not asking you to let me in on all you're going through. I'm not asking that we try to go back to where we were. But I am asking you to consider staying long enough to get something like the Tomson Lake project started."

She looked up at him uncomprehendingly.

"That project's dead."

"Not quite dead—yet. You could help determine whether it lives."

He summarized what Aaron Elkhorn was planning to do.

A hint of interest appeared in her eyes, and then in her voice.

"But why me? You could manage the new adventure experience at the lake."

"Actually I couldn't. Probably never, and, for sure, not while building the political backup that Elkhorn needs. That's going to be a full-time job. Sure, we might be able to find another organizer for the lake project. But that would take time and energy. You would have no learning curve, and you are a proven commodity."

269

"A convenient item on the shelf, is that it?"

"Pardon the inept figure of speech. You know exactly what I mean. You're really good at what you do."

He heard an unaccustomed assertiveness in his voice. Not a tone he'd used often with her. She heard it, too.

"Is this a job offer?"

"Just a reminder that you are an officer of Cascade Adventures. Regardless of what has happened to us personally, we still have a business. The only question is whether you want to continue in it."

"Tell me more of what you have in mind."

He elaborated on the necessary level of cooperation with the Indian tribes and how, if Cascade Adventures was successful, it might, at some time in the future, have to bow out, selling its interest to them.

She thought that over.

"So we wouldn't be building a business of our own?"

"Maybe yes, maybe no. It depends on how we succeed in these initial stages. The Indians might want us to stay on. We could walk away with a profit to invest in something else. Or there might be no profit. Risk is always there."

He thought for a moment that he had painted a picture with a lot at the bottom and only a little at the top. But she surprised him.

"I guess I could give it a try. But I intend to keep up the therapy."

"Absolutely. You have my encouragement on that. There is one other thing, though, that we have to face squarely. Grant Tomson is not entirely out of the picture. He might do anything to stop us, from throwing up legal impediments to doing something violent. Elkhorn will be taking measures that we hope will convince Grant to leave the lake completely alone. But at this point we don't know. No matter what happens, you may run into Grant. Can you handle that?"

A new expression combined a hint of old combativeness with hesitancy.

"Honestly, it depends on what he does. But, yes, I think I can handle him . . ."

She looked directly at Jeff.

" . . . which is not to say that I might not need backup."

A tiny upward twitch of her lips hinted she had lightened up, or could still appreciate irony.

"You can count on that."

He waited, thinking hard. There never would be a better or worse time than right now.

"That leaves our relationship."

She pondered that, looking at the floor.

"Is your verb choice intentional? Leaving?"

"No, it's not about leaving. But it is about getting along. We'll be better off if we can get past argument for argument's sake. If we can't do that, we'll never get anything done."

A questioning look appeared, and he went on.

"How's this? When I'm here, I'll continue sleeping in the barn. That works for me. We share the kitchen as before. We'll set up regular times to talk business. If we want to talk about anything else, it's outside of business hours. We have to divide our attention and our emotions for the sake of what needs to be done."

She nodded, though there was no enthusiasm in her movement. He decided to add more, so his explanation would be complete.

"I have loved you Sara, as best I could. The love is still there, but it has changed. Just how, I don't know myself. I have no idea what will happen to us. I only hope we get to whatever destination we arrive at without doing each other any more damage. Am I hurt and betrayed by what you did? Absolutely. But I also see that I'm partly responsible. I let us drift into a situation where you assumed all the real responsibility for our business while I drifted—again—into work that took me away and gave me no real satisfaction. You're interested in the outdoors, and my main attention is to politics. If anything positive happens for us in the future—whether we are together or apart—it will be because we each find a way to follow those separate interests. Wherever we are, I will work at being more upfront with you about what I want and why."

She looked down.

"I know you've been understanding and tried to help. More than I would have been. Don't think I haven't noticed..."

Then she raised her eyes.

"... I'll try to meet you halfway. That's all I can deal with now."

He risked a smile.

"Not to turn a discussion into an argument: it can't be the old halfway, where you always had the final word because I was too lazy or scared to fight for it. Now I'll be more likely to fight, unless there's a chance that we can settle things without fighting."

"I've been thinking about adopting a child, with or without you. Not right away, but that's what I want."

Defiance framed that blurt out of the blue, and she started to leave. But there was something else there, as if she was asking a question as much as announcing a decision. Jeff resisted pointing out that he had encouraged that very idea, only to be batted down by her opposition.

"Sounds positive."

God, that's the kind of thing he used to say. She was already climbing the stairs when he called out to her.

"No. More than that. Whoever you take into your life will be very lucky."

She half-turned, stopped, and nodded. Then she continued upward.

He walked out toward the barn. The Cascades, still tipped with snow, rose in the distance, the foreground a surround of maturing new growth.

Time for summer, he thought. The new day shimmered. By midday, it might be brighter still. Or clouded over.

Possibilities beckoned and, for the first time in a long time, he wanted to shape their outcomes.

THANKS

Margaret Amory and Roger Page, for early reading and comments that helped me restructure basic elements of the story.

Vernon Bogar, Scott Ferguson, Josie Florine, Harry Grant and Brian Walsh, for indispensable advice on specific issues.

The City of Cle Elum, Roslyn and South Cle Elum, for just being there, providing a lovely setting and rich history.

Adam Finley, for constructively critical editorial assistance and for the pleasure of working with someone so quick in his understanding.

Celeste Bennett, for skillfully pointing the way to publication and for being an endless source of knowledge and advice.

And most of all, Karen Jensen Neff, for daily tolerance, encouragement and contribution, my first reader, critic and sounding board, my soulmate.

With all of this help, if errors remain, believe me, they are mine.

3/2/2014

CPSIA information can be obtained at www.ICGtesting.com
Printed in the USA
LVOW06s0430190714

395023LV00005B/190/P